I0684833

From Indigo Sea Press
Novels by Donna Small

A Ripple in the Water

Just Between Friends

Through Rose Colored Glasses

indigoseapress.com

A Ripple in the Water

By

Donna Small

Perseverance Books
Published by Indigo Sea Press
Winston-Salem

Perseverance Books
Indigo Sea Press
302 Ricks Drive
Winston-Salem, NC 27103

This book is a work of fiction. Names, characters, locations and events are either a product of the author's imagination, fictitious or used fictitiously. Any resemblance to any event, locale or person, living or dead, is purely coincidental.

Copyright 2013 by Donna Small

All rights reserved, including the right of reproduction in whole or part in any format.

First Perseverance Books edition published December, 2015
.

Perseverance Books, Moon Sailor and all production design are trademarks of Indigo Sea Press, used under license.

For information regarding bulk purchases of this book, digital purchase and special discounts, please contact the publisher at indigoseapress.com

Cover design by Tracy Beltran

Manufactured in the United States of America
ISBN 978-1-63066-261-5

This book is dedicated to all the smart, wonderful, strong, and independent women in my life.

First and foremost, my mother, Tia Koziak, who despite nearly disowning me when her name was not mentioned in my first book surely knows that she was the first independent woman I looked up to. Mom, you are the one who taught me I could do anything I set my mind to.

My sister, Karen. Though we are miles away from each other, you are always close to my heart.

Cindy, who became a member of my family more than twenty years ago and for whose friendship I will be eternally grateful.

Beth Anne, your biting wit and sparkling personality have sparked more ideas and snarky comments than I'll ever be able to use in my lifetime. I am thankful every day for our friendship.

Deb, there are no words to describe our friendship and how much it has meant to me over the years. I find myself unable to express how much you mean to me.

All of my wonderful and supportive friends who have laughed with me (and at me!). Anyone who knows me knows just how important that is.

And last but absolutely not least, my two precious girls, Emily and Abby. I love you more than you will ever know and I couldn't be more proud of you.

I would not be who I am without each and every one of you.

—Donna Small

Chapter 1

Katharine Penner noticed him almost immediately—you'd have to be dead not to. She had been sitting beside the pool, minding her own business and trying to read a magazine but once her eyes locked on the tall, gorgeous man on the other side of the pool, it was hopeless.

She blinked several times, certain she was delusional; no one was this good looking. Maybe he was a mirage of some sort. She smiled. Maybe she was losing her mind. She looked up again. Nope. He was most certainly standing there in the flesh, looking absolutely delicious . . . and completely *ripped.*

From where she sat, she could clearly see the well-defined form of his broad shoulders, his perfectly sculpted abdominals and the long, taut legs that held him upright. Her eyes were glued to him and she was powerless to look away. All coherent thoughts had simply vanished from her mind save one— the fact that she'd long forgotten what it was like to have this stirring inside of her. She bit her lower lip. There was something so…primal about her reaction to this man—whoever he was—that had become altogether unfamiliar to her.

She felt her cheeks flush with warmth as she realized she had been staring at him for much longer than was appropriate. Coming back to her senses, she furtively glanced around to see if anyone had noticed. She breathed a sigh of relief as she realized her ogling had gone unnoticed by the other parents who were seated around the perimeter of the pool. She was safe for the moment.

Of course, she knew it would only be a matter of seconds before her gaze was drawn back to this stranger.

What was the matter with her? This behavior was so unlike her. Normally she was for the most part oblivious to members of the opposite sex. Sure, she'd seen good looking men before. But she'd not reacted to any of them like this. She'd notice, but not really give them another thought. And they certainly wouldn't drive her to distraction and prevent her from reading some stupid magazine article! But for whatever reason, today she wasn't able to push this man from her mind. Once she'd noticed *him,* she wasn't able to focus on anything else and found her gaze being pulled back to the other side of the pool as though he was a ham sandwich and she hadn't seen food in a week.

Pretty soon, she thought, she was going to start salivating.

Kate quickly peaked over the top of her magazine and stole a look at him. She felt herself inhale sharply, almost as though she was seeing him for the first time instead of the mere seconds ago when she first laid eyes on him. There was no denying how extremely good looking he was. She shook her head and forced herself to look back down. Of course, after viewing this tall, blond stranger, she found her brain had turned to mush, save for the images of his lightly bronzed chest flashing through her mind each time she blinked. The image of this man in a tiny swimsuit that left little to the imagination swiftly squelched any hope she had of getting any reading done– not that she held any desire to do so, what with eye candy a mere hundred feet or so away from her.

Ever so slowly, Kate once again lifted her eyes and peered over the top of the page, trying to steal another glance at him. She felt her stomach turn a flip-flop as she once more took in his muscular form. Good Lord, he was gorgeous, she thought as she released a tiny sigh. She forced herself to look down, yet again, at her magazine and tried to comprehend at least a picture or two. That attempt, however, was just as futile as the others so she resigned herself to the fact that she was not going to get any reading done while that Greek god was standing anywhere in the vicinity of the pool.

She glanced around once again to make sure no one was watching her. Once assured the other parents were engrossed in their own books, conversations or simply watching their children swim, she resumed her inspection of the man who was garnering all her attention. Though she was seated in the shade, she put her sunglasses on in order to feel more confident that her inspection would be undetected by the others at the pool. She shifted her position slightly so she was facing him directly. Conveniently, there were children in the water between where she was seated and he was standing. She smiled, pleased with herself. If anyone were to glance her way, they would think she was simply watching the kids in the water.

At least, that's what she hoped.

Of course, at this point, she was so drawn to this man that a part of her didn't care if anyone saw her ogling. Surrendering to her internal desires, she tossed the magazine she'd been holding into her bag and resumed her inspection of the tall stranger.

Kate began to notice that he sparkled just a bit as he moved. She squinted, convinced that her eyes were playing tricks on her. She then realized that it was simply drops of water that glistened in the sunlight as he moved. She smiled, realizing she was in full fantasy mode. Sparkling? Really?

She continued to watch the water drip down his chest and abdomen. She couldn't help but notice they had a very smooth ride since there was not an ounce of fat on him. His arms were well-defined and his shoulders were broad and then narrowed into a slim waistline that held a clearly defined six pack. Kate allowed her gaze to drift lower and saw the shadow of blond hair that led a path down to beneath his swimsuit. His legs were long and lean and Kate thought if she were just a bit closer, she'd be able to see the outline of each muscle in his legs.

He was beautiful, she thought. Now where did that come from? Since when did she use the term beautiful to describe a man? But without even looking back, she knew once again, the word was completely appropriate. But who was he? She squinted again, this time trying to make out exactly who this man was. She'd been coming to this pool for three years now and hadn't ever seen him before. Of course she was normally watching her daughter, Hadley. But still, she would have noticed *him*. You'd have to be unconscious to not notice this god-like creature if he walked by in a swimsuit like the one he was wearing at the moment.

Good lord, he was sex on legs.

She silently chastised herself. What the hell was she doing? If she spent any more time looking at him—whoever he was—she was going to start to drool. She forced herself to tear her gaze away once more, determined to do something—anything—besides spend her morning staring at this stranger. She looked from side to side, making sure—for the last and final time!—that her ogling had not been noticed by anyone else at the pool. Once she felt assured she was in the clear, she reached over and grabbed her magazine once again.

She shifted her position, figuring if this stranger wasn't in her direct line of vision, she'd be able to settle in and concentrate on the magazine. She flipped through the first couple of pages, silently thankful they were filled with advertisements and required only a minimal amount of concentration. Despite this, she was still unable to focus on any of the pages in front of her. It seemed this man had scrambled her brain, leaving her unable to have a coherent thought. She frowned and looked down again at the magazine in front of her. She managed to flip through a few pages and found an article: "How to increase your sex drive in your 20's 30's and 40's." Okay, really? This was certainly one article she didn't need at the moment. Her sex drive was just fine, thank you very much. Not that she had any use for it, but still, it was fine.

Desperate by now to have anything that would distract her, Kate read the first paragraph but found that by the time she'd finished, she had no idea what it was she'd just read. Dammit! She thought, slapping the magazine down onto her thighs. What was *with* her today? Normally, she was able to relax a bit while her daughter was in the pool but today she wasn't about to concentrate on anything thanks to this photo-shopped demigod who was . . . poised to dive into the pool. Kate swallowed hard as she watched him pull his goggles down over his eyes and then leap into the pool, long legs trailing in the air behind him.

She sighed. Clearly, she wasn't going to do anything today but be distracted by this man so she figured she might as well give up on reading her magazine and watch Hadley practice. It couldn't hurt to actually learn something about the sport her daughter was so excited about. She re-positioned herself once again, and began to watch the sixty or so kids who were swimming laps. Of course, it didn't hurt that her delicious stranger was swimming with the team, she thought, smiling. None of the other parents needed to know she was trying desperately to determine who this stranger was.

She watched as he swam the length of the pool and then sprang up out of the water on the other end and tossed his head quickly to shake off some of the water. His hair formed short ringlets of waves over his head which caused Kate's fingers to tingle as she imagined what it would be like to run her hands through those locks. She noticed that a group of the kids had surrounded him and were laughing and horsing around. It seemed odd to her that not a single parent was the slightest bit concerned about this man splashing about with their children. As she looked around, it seemed that the other parents weren't even paying attention to the frolicking going on in the deep end of the pool.

"Huh," she muttered. "That's odd."

Turning her attention back to the water, she noticed him talking to one of the children that looked an awful lot like....

Kate sat upright, trying to make out exactly what was going on. She leaned forward to get a better look then felt her mouth drop open as her very own daughter climbed up onto this man's shoulders and dove off. Hadley laughed out loud as she sailed through the air and then came up a few feet away. Both Hadley and the stranger and were grinning from ear to ear.

What the . . . ? Her mouth formed the words but no sound came forth.

It was then that it dawned on her who this man might be. She'd gotten numerous emails over the winter detailing the resignation of last year's swim coach as well as emails regarding the search for a new coach. Kate figured this man was probably the coach they'd hired. She realized she was very behind on checking her emails since she had no idea if her guess was correct. She made a mental note to do a better job of keeping up to date on her mail.

Kate sat back against the chaise lounge, feeling somewhat confident that her assumption was correct. She felt even more certain of her assessment as she watched Hadley climb out of the pool with this . . . new coach? And then saw him demonstrate the arm movements for one of the swim strokes. He stood behind Hadley and moved her arms in the proper motion. Kate's jaw dropped open as she watched the coach (God, she hoped he was the coach) began to mimic the pelvic thrusting motion required for the butterfly. She felt her mouth go dry as she watched his hips sway back and forth in a motion that her daughter (thankfully!) would only associate with a swim stroke. Kate however, realized that not only was she sitting erect and immobile watching him, but other not-so-swim-related thoughts were entering her mind. This man *had* to be the new swim coach.

Surely, if he wasn't the swim coach, someone would have stepped in during the hip-thrusting display. Right?

Then again, she hadn't moved from her spot either.

One thing was certain, if this was the new swim coach, there would be very few absences to the daily practices this season since the moms of the kids on the swim team would certainly enjoy looking at this specimen—especially if he wore that tiny suit. The thought of the moms gathered around the pool watching their little darlings with attention they'd never displayed until this man's arrival made her chuckle. She knew that while the parents came to the practices, it was as much a social gathering for them as it was for the kids. Actually, there were some days that the swimming just got in the way.

Kate leaned back against her lounge chair suddenly realizing that having a child on the swim team meant she should watch practice. And if that meant she was forced to have this man enter her line of vision from time to time, then so be it. We all have our crosses to bear, she thought as a smile worked its way onto her lips. Hell, she might even learn something. She settled into her chair, preparing to watch the rest of the practice.

She'd only watched the kids swim a lap or two when she heard a familiar voice calling to her.

"Kate! Hey, Kate!"

She looked up to see Wendy Morgan waving enthusiastically at her from the three foot section of the pool. Once again, Kate was struck by how poised and elegant Wendy always looked. Though she was well into her forties, Kate thought she looked much closer to thirty five. Today, her straight blond hair hung down to just below her shoulder, though more often than not she would pull it up into a ponytail that only further accentuated her smooth, nearly wrinkle free skin.

Kate felt a small pang of guilt knowing she hadn't seen her in nearly a month. The end of the school year was so hectic that she barely had time to shower, let alone see friends. Between the end of grade testing and the final projects that Hadley had due, there was simply no time. Kate was glad summer had finally arrived. She would be able to spend some time with Wendy and the other swim team moms, since they'd all be here for the daily two-hour practices. With the kids in the water for that amount of time every day, there was really nothing else to do but chat with one another . . . or watch practice, Kate thought, a smile coming to her face.

The swim team was made up of about 60 kids, ranging in age

from four to eighteen. The families of these kids were all members of the Danbury Country Club pool and regularly clustered together while their children practiced. There were several coaches, each one focusing on a particular age group. In addition to the instruction the children received from the paid coaches, the older swimmers took some responsibility and gave pointers to the younger ones, which helped to cement the camaraderie among teammates.

This was Hadley's third summer with the swim team, the Dolphins, and it was Kate's third year of membership at the pool. The first year she felt a bit out of place and found it difficult to develop friendships with the other moms. She wasn't sure exactly what it was that prevented her from developing friendships that first year. Kate could only compare it to being the kid who arrived at a new school in the middle of the year. It seemed that the friendships had already been formed and Kate was just shy enough to accept that fact. She did her part, though, working at the swim meets, handing out water, filling out ribbons, and doing anything that was needed. Towards the end of that first season, Kate began to feel as though, to a certain extent, she fit in with everyone and even chastised herself for not making more of an effort.

Hadley's first year swimming was difficult, though for a different reason. She made friends with everyone in her age group and had even begun to hang around (and on) some of the older children. It was shocking at first, but Kate soon learned that the younger kids would jump, climb and crawl on any teenager on the swim team. It didn't matter if they were in the water or out, every older teen would end up carrying one or two kids with them wherever they went. Pretty soon it became normal, even to Kate. While Hadley excelled at the social aspect of the swim team, she had difficulty in the actual swimming portion. Irony at its best, Kate thought.

Last year, their second, had started out easier than the first. Hadley had a basic understanding of the strokes and seemed to get back into the rhythm of things quickly. And her friendships with the other swimmers picked up exactly where they'd left off. Even Kate found that the friendships she'd developed the year before were quickly re-established. Of course, last summer was difficult for reasons that had nothing to do with swimming. Last summer was when Hadley and she had their lives altered forever. During the middle of the season, Kate lost her husband and Hadley lost her father when he was killed in a car accident. It was then that Kate learned just how thankful she was to have these ladies as her friends. She knew that without them, particularly Wendy, she and Hadley might not have made it through that terrible time in their lives.

This year she and Hadley were looking forward to a new beginning. Hadley had been swimming all winter at an indoor pool so she wouldn't be completely out of practice when June rolled around once again. Kate had spent the school year passing through the many stages of grief and trying to help Hadley do the same. Though she still had bad days, Kate felt as though they'd passed a turning point and was now ready to reclaim a bit of her former life. The summer swim team would be one way of providing just that for both of them. Kate had feared that, since it was in the middle of last year's swim season that Hadley's father had died, she wouldn't want to participate this year. Thankfully, that had not been the case. Kate would have been even more worried about how losing her father would affect Hadley if she'd suddenly developed an aversion to a sport that she'd been so excited to be a part of.

Kate had survived the year since her husband's death and she knew she had Wendy to thank for it. It was Wendy who'd helped her get her life back on track and wade through the depression that enveloped her during the first few weeks after Todd's death. Now, she knew she'd be fine, but that was all she'd be—fine. Sure, she was doing all she was suppose to do—raising her daughter, running her interior design business—but those who knew her, really knew her, could tell that she was simply a muted version of the old Kate. Kate knew it, everyone knew it. The glint from her eyes that was so utterly Kate was now gone and she had no idea how to get it back.

Kate stood up and waved back to her friend, watching as she made her way around the edge of the pool. "Hey, Wendy! How are you?" She enveloped her friend in a bear hug. "It's so good to see you. Are the boys here?"

Wendy nodded. "They sure are. Let's see . . ." she said, shielding her eyes from the sun as she searched the deep end of the pool. Finally, she pointed. "There. See the caps with the stars on them? That's the twins. And Riley? He's . . ." She searched again. "Well, he's somewhere...." Her voice trailed off as she looked around for her son. After a moment, she shrugged, giving up her search.

Kate surveyed the pool trying to locate the twins amongst the group of thirty or so kids who were in the pool at the moment, swimming their warm up laps. She finally located the twins who were frantically swimming the length of the pool, each one splashing the other in an attempt at distraction—or drowning , she wasn't sure which. She kept looking into the choppy water but couldn't locate Riley, Wendy's oldest son.

She motioned to the chair beside her. "Sit down, would you? I haven't seen you in forever! We need to catch up."

"I know," Wendy replied, nodding.

She sat down gracefully, a trait that Wendy seemed to have in abundance. Kate couldn't help but notice, as she did every time she saw Wendy, how different they were. Wendy was a tall, thin woman who never seemed to be the slightest bit flustered, despite having three boys. She had long, blond hair and the palest blue eyes that when looked directly at you, made you feel as though you were the only person in the world. She was the most nurturing woman Kate knew and frequently Kate would find herself saying a prayer of thanks for having Wendy in her life.

"End of school…it's a nightmare! And I've got two that need to get through it!"

"How are the twins, anyway?" Kate asked.

Wendy beamed. "They're great. Just great."

Kate smiled back at her, knowing that Wendy meant every word of it. After having their son, Riley, Wendy and her husband, Bill, tried for years to have another child. They could conceive and did so many times, each one ending in a miscarriage. The doctor's couldn't seem to determine what was going wrong and, more importantly, what they could do to fix the problem. Depressed and frustrated, Wendy and Bill gave up hope of carrying a pregnancy but were unwilling to give up their dream of adding to their family. After their fourth miscarriage, they began the process of adoption. Of course they'd only begun the mountains of paperwork when Wendy found out she was pregnant. Despite this wonderful news, both Wendy and Bill felt they should continue with the adoption process, not because they feared yet another miscarriage but because they already felt a commitment to the child they hoped to adopt.

Months went by and Wendy's pregnancy continued without incident. Only a week or so before their due date, Wendy and Bill were informed that there was a good possibility a child would be placed with them. Ten days later Wendy delivered their son Tyler, only to find out they were in fact going to be the adoptive parents of a little boy born on the same day as Tyler. Baby Ben was welcomed home one week to the day after Tyler had been born. From that moment the two infants were inseparable.

Wendy handled everything in stride and somehow managed to care for what amounted to twins. Of course, Ben knew he was adopted but Wendy did not want to label him as her "adopted child," feeling as though he might be viewed as somehow less than his brothers. Without fail, each time the "twins" birthday was mentioned, inevitably someone would ask which of the two had been adopted. Wendy, always gracious, would smile broadly and reply that she simply couldn't remember. The look on the face of the person who asked the question never ceased to make Kate giggle. Without even a hint of irritation, Wendy had managed to put the individual in their place without even suggesting that their question might be considered rude.

"And Riley?" Kate asked. "How's he doing in school?"

"He just finished his junior year at Carolina. Dean's list!" Wendy was beaming with pride speaking of her eldest son's accomplishments.

Kate smiled back at her. "I still can't believe he's in college. It seems like just yesterday he was on the swim team. . . ."

"I know. It goes by so fast." She pointed a finger at Kate knowingly. "You just wait. Hadley will be in college before you know it."

"Ugh. Don't remind me. I still haven't adjusted to her being in elementary school."

"Kate! Wendy!" She looked up to see Angela Martin approaching, a huge grin on her face.

Angela had two boys who had been on the swim team for several years and she was somewhat of a fixture at the pool. Most days, Angela could be found sitting at one end of the pool with a stopwatch in her hand while her boys swam laps and tried to beat their best times and each other. As a result of this "training," her boys placed first in nearly every event they swam.

"Angela! How are you?" Kate stood to hug the woman that she had not seen since last year at the closing of the pool. Despite the length of time most went without seeing each other, the swim team families came together at the first practice as though it had been no more than a few days. Moms greeted each other with welcoming hugs while their children immediately began to plan the next sleepover. Of course, there were some families who lived near each other or had children in the same school so they were able to see each other during the school year. The rest just picked up right where they had left off the previous summer.

"Really good. We got here first thing this morning so the boys could get some laps in before practice. They're really excited for this year. Itching to have a little competition. I guess it's boring having your mom time you all the time." She shrugged and smiled.

"At least they have each other to promote a little competition," Kate said. "Unless someone sounds a buzzer, Hadley swims as though she's got all day."

"True," Angela replied. "But it's not exactly fair when your competition is three inches taller and two years older than you."

Kate chuckled. "No. I guess not..."

Angela's gaze softened. "So, how are you, Kate? You and Hadley . . ." She left her voice drift off as though she didn't want to mention that it was only the two of them now, as though the mention of it would make Kate realize that her husband was no longer alive.

Did people honestly think that she didn't think about his absence every moment of every day? She sort of understood their discomfort, though. No one ever wanted to think about your husband being ripped out of your life in an instant. If fact, most people were afraid to mention what had happened to her, as though it were contagious and the simple act of asking about would transfer the fearful disease of "death by car accident" to them. Wendy was one of the few that didn't shy away from the subject at all, asking how she was and what she needed frequently.

"We're fine," Kate replied and trying to communicate with her smile that it was okay to ask. "Thanks for asking."

Angela smiled but Kate sensed she was still uncomfortable with the subject matter. Sure enough, she turned to Wendy and smiled, ready to change the subject. "So, Ben and Tyler ready for the season?" She asked.

Wendy laughed out loud. "Are you kidding? Knowing their big brother is going to be coaching has made them so excited I can barely tear them away from the pool!" She turned to Kate. "Hadley must be excited as well knowing that Riley's going to be helping out."

Kate looked back at Wendy guiltily. "I have to admit. I've been a little lax on checking my email and didn't even know Riley was coaching this year. Telling her that he's coaching will only add to her enthusiasm."

"Ladies! Yoo hoo!"

The three women turned to see Brenda Williams approaching with a clipboard. The three of them shared a knowing look. Brenda headed up the volunteers each year for the swim team and spent the first several practices tracking down all the parents in order for them to sign up for their required volunteer assignments.

"I know you're all just waiting to sign up!" Her smile was contagious and all three women laughed out loud.

"Of course we are! We were just waiting for you to get over here with your little clipboard!" Angela replied, grinning.

"If I didn't know you so well, Angela, I might believe you," Brenda said, waggling her finger at her. She smiled and handed the clipboard to Kate. "Here you go. You know the drill. Just sign up for whatever you want."

Kate, Wendy, and Angela perused the clipboard and signed up for their duties for the several swim meets that were coming over the next few weeks. Kate signed up to be the team mom for Hadley's age group, figuring she'd know most of the girls since they were friendly with Hadley. Plus, it meant she'd be able to keep an eye on her daughter for the meets. Hadley had been known to wander off in search of frogs, butterflies and pretty much anything that was *outside* the boundaries of the pool. On a couple of occasions, she'd nearly missed her race.

Once she was done signing her name in the appropriate slots, she passed the clipboard to Angela. She looked up to find Brenda inspecting her with the same concerned look she'd seen on Angela's face earlier.

"You okay, Kate? You and Hadley? I mean, you're . . ."

Once again, the voice trailed off and the sentence was left open as though the person doing the speaking couldn't even bear to say what had happened to her. Kate had to stifle a sigh. While she was thankful to have all these people who were concerned about her and

Hadley, it was hard to continue the healing with all these concerned faces hovering around her. She knew they were just making sure she was doing well but it was unnerving nonetheless. What did they think she was going to do? Curl up in her bed and stay there for weeks at a time? She couldn't do that. She had a daughter to raise. Besides, she'd done that already. Just the thought of the time immediately after Todd died and how useless she became made her glance toward Wendy and think about all she'd done for Hadley when Kate found she couldn't.

She would be eternally grateful for this woman's friendship.

But Angela? She didn't have the heart to tell her and everyone else she'd be fine if they'd just stop asking how she was doing with a look of sadness and concern on their faces. But Kate knew she'd never be able to say anything even close to that. Instead she just smiled and nodded, and said she and Hadley were doing fine, just fine.

Brenda continued to inspect her and, for just a moment, Kate wondered what would happen if she were to break down into hysterics. The thought brought a smile to her face, which caused Brenda to smile uncomfortably and look away.

"Wow, Brenda," Angela said. "You are on the ball this year. Everything's just about done!"

Brenda, obviously thankful for the change of subject, looked at Angela and beamed. "I'd love to take all the credit but you know I really have nothing to do with it. It's all the parents who sign up! They make my job easy!"

"Now, come on. You've got to take a little credit," Angela said. "You're the one walking around with that clipboard, shoving it our faces the first chance you get! We all know if we didn't volunteer, you'd clock us with that thing." She nodded toward the clipboard, which was now held tightly in Brenda's hands.

"Well, I haven't had to do that yet, thankfully." Brenda replied, giggling. "I should go. I've got to hit up the Masterman's. They somehow escaped my radar last year and didn't volunteer for *anything.*"

The three women made the appropriate expressions of shock and horror, then watched as Brenda made her way across the pool deck.

Kate turned to Wendy again. "You said Riley's coaching this year?" She asked.

Wendy nodded. "Yeah, he's very excited about it. And I have to say how proud I am of him for doing this."

Kate looked at Wendy while she spoke. Out of the corner of her eye, she noticed Angela roll her eyes as Wendy went on about her son. Kate bit the inside of her cheek to prevent herself from laughing. Of course, Kate knew that Angela was just as bad as Wendy was at touting the merits of her children and never seemed to notice the glassy-eyed look of the person they were speaking to. Neither Angela nor Wendy had ever grasped the concept that the only person who truly cared about every minute detail of a child's life was their own mother.

Kate looked away from Angela quickly, trying to ensure Wendy hadn't noticed anything amiss. As she did so, she caught a glance of the man she'd been staring at earlier. She tried to follow along to what Wendy was saying but *dammit!* The man still hadn't put any clothes on and was, at the moment, traipsing around in nothing more than a tiny black bathing suit. She turned just bit so that the stranger in the tiny suit wouldn't be directly in her line of vision, then she tried to focus on Wendy.

"...could have gotten another internship but wanted to come home and help the twins..." Wendy continued.

Kate nodded, now only half listening to what Wendy was saying. She knew from experience Wendy could talk about any of her kids endlessly, especially Riley. She also knew if she nodded at appropriate intervals, Wendy wouldn't have any idea her thoughts were elsewhere. Kate stole another look at Angela and thought for certain she was paying close attention to Wendy. It wasn't until she noticed the color rise to her cheeks that Kate realized Angela had gotten a glimpse of the tall, gorgeous man who was . . . walking towards them with Hadley? She groaned softly. Of course it would be her daughter who latched onto this particular coach.

As Hadley and the coach made their way toward her, she noticed they were engrossed in a conversation together. Kate smiled thinking how seriously Hadley was taking this season's competition and she assumed the conversation was about some part of her stroke, time or dive. Both the coach and Hadley were moving their arms around, mimicking the movements of the butterfly stroke once again. That particular stroke was Hadley's weakest of the four and it was quite a source of frustration for her. Of course, if he spent much time mimicking the stroke out of the water as he'd done earlier, Kate felt certain all the moms would be asking for private lessons and swimming the butterfly before the end of the summer. If not for the health benefits of swimming, then most definitely for the physical benefits—that is, the physical benefits of watching the coach.

Hadley, being seven and completely obtuse to a man thrusting his hips, wouldn't have the same reaction her mother was having and hopefully, she'd grasp the concept quickly. She'd spent countless hours over the winter trying to force her body into the rhythm of the stroke, often times leaving the pool with fingers and toes wrinkled from so much time in the water. She was determined to learn it and got extremely frustrated when week after week, she couldn't quite master it. For a seven-year-old, she was quite mature when it came to her swimming and Kate hoped this new coach would be able to work with her on that particular stroke.

The two stopped at a table and Kate watched as he reached over and grabbed his sunglasses. He put them on and then grabbed his towel, wrapping it around his waistline leaving his abdominals exposed. Hadley looked over toward the table where Kate was standing with Wendy and Angela and pointed at them. He nodded, then together they began walking toward the three of them. As they approached, Kate got an odd feeling of déjà vu. She felt almost certain she'd met this man somewhere before but struggled to determine where that might have been. It seemed the answer was tucked away somewhere just out of her reach.

She frowned in frustration, then realized Wendy was still talking about Riley. Kate had been so distracted by this man who was with her daughter that she had no idea what she'd missed. She looked at Wendy and nodded, trying to show she was paying attention. She was very nearly back to giving Wendy her full attention when Hadley and the coach came close enough for her to realize exactly who he was and where she'd seen him before. She felt the color rise to her cheeks and her insides turn to water as this man leaned over and gave Wendy a hug.

Oh, God, she thought. *This cannot be happening to me.*

"Hey, mom," he said.

Kate wished a hole in the ground would suddenly appear beneath her feet, swallowing her whole. She found she was rooted to the spot and unable to move a muscle.

This man that she'd been ogling all morning was Wendy's son.

Chapter 2

Wendy's son.

How could she not have known who he was? She wracked her brain, trying to figure out why it was she didn't recognize him. Surely she'd seem him just last summer, right? Well, if she did, he certainly didn't look like *that*...

Once again, she prayed for the ground to open up and swallow her but since it didn't look like that was going to happen anytime soon, Kate just stood there and forced herself to smile. She knew she looked like an overdone Botox patient, given the plastic smile that had been apparently glued to her face, but it was the best she could do under the circumstances.

Wendy grinned and turned around to give her son a hug. "Everything go okay today?" Seeing his nod, Wendy turned to Kate. "Riley, you remember Kate, right?"

"Of course!" He said, smiling at her.

Kate forced herself to banish her earlier incestuous thoughts and respond to Riley without sounding like a complete idiot. Of course, she failed. "Riley! Gosh, I barely recognize you!"

Brilliant, she thought. She resisted the urge to smack her forehead with her hand. Where was a hole in the ground when you needed one?

He shrugged, seemingly embarrassed. "Well, it has been awhile since I've seen you."

Kate thought she detected a hint of color in his cheeks. Surely, he wasn't embarrassed, was he? She stood there for what seemed an eternity, trying to determine if she should apologize or not. Riley was staring back at her and Kate thought he was trying to figure out what to say next as well. After a few moments, he looked down at Hadley and spoke to her. "So, what do you think about working on that stroke a bit?

Hadley took a few steps closer to the table and reached for her towel, swinging around like a cape before wrapping it around herself. She shivered slightly and hopped a bit in order to get warm. "Mom, are we going to stay for a bit today?"

"No, honey. I've got to drop you off at Gram's house. She's going to watch you while I meet with a client. Remember I told you that this morning?"

"Awwwww, man!" She said, stomping her foot on the cement. "I really want to stay and work on my fly!"

"I wish you could, honey. But I've got to go to work for just a bit. If you like, I can bring you back later," Kate bargained.

Kate ran an interior design business out of her home and since it was a relatively young company, it was only her working there. While she normally loved the flexibility of being a one man show, there were times, like today, when having a co-worker around to cover for you would have been a very good thing. She would have loved to skip today's meeting and stay at the pool with Hadley. Of course, today's meeting was with Mrs. Wyndham, one of her most difficult clients. Kate cringed inwardly, thinking that "difficult" was probably too harsh of a term. Mrs. Wyndham knew what she wanted and that was that. The problem was that she wasn't very effective at communicating those wants. As a result, Kate was spending more and more of her time just guessing what the woman wanted, since she had no earthly idea. The kicker was, the elderly woman only wanted to have two chairs reupholstered and it was taking more time than most entire rooms normally took.

Hadley pouted as only a seven year old can do – hands clasped together under her chin, eyes wide, and her mouth turned upside down into an exaggerated frown with her bottom lip jutted out. Kate wondered if they were actually teaching this in school, she was so adept at it. "Pleeeeeeease?"

"Honey," Kate replied, annoyance creeping into her tone. Kate had never liked it when Hadley chose to argue with her in public, even if it was something as silly as staying at the pool. "I wish you could stay here but I've got to go to work."

"I'll stay with her," Riley interjected. "I can even bring her home after we're done here." He looked down at Hadley and grinned. "Besides, she could sure use the extra practice."

"Rileeee!" Hadley squealed. She reached up and poked him several times in his stomach, which made him clench those particular muscles, further outlining the tautness of his abdominal wall. Though she tried to look away, Kate found herself staring at his stomach as

17

he clenched his muscles each time Hadley poked him. She felt a flutter in her own stomach and forced herself to look at something else....anything else. She found it easiest to focus on her daughter and quickly moved to stop her from poking Riley anymore.

"Hadley!" She chastised. "Please stop that!"

Riley spoke up. "It's okay. I'm use to it." He lowered his voice and leaned in toward her. "Besides, I asked for it, right?"

He grinned and winked at her and Kate felt herself inhale sharply. What was the matter with her? She was acting like a high-schooler, for God's sakes! She quickly looked down at her daughter in an attempt to allow her thoughts to focus on anything other than the man in front of her who looked as though he'd been photo-shopped. She needed to get a grip and realize that despite how gorgeous he was and how (admittedly) attracted she was to him, he was her friend's son. Her *very dear* friend's son.

Hadley looked up at her once again and pleaded her case with her eyes. Kate knew she didn't have a leg to stand on, what with Riley offering not only to watch her, but to drive her home as well. She bit the side of her lower lip while she thought about it. "You sure you're okay with this?" She asked, looking at Riley.

Just then, Wendy chimed in. "No need to worry, Kate. He's great with the kids."

He nodded. "Besides, one kid's easy. Normally, I watch two at once. And they're a handful!"

"Now watch it," Wendy said. She was looking sternly at Riley, but smiling as well and Kate knew she was joking. Wendy shrugged her shoulders as she glanced at Kate. "He's right, you know. Tyler and Ben are a handful! But if it makes you feel any better, I'll be here for a bit."

"Oh no, It's not that. I mean, I don't worry about Hadley with him at all. I'm sure she'll be fine. I just don't want to inconvenience you," she said, looking at Riley. Truthfully, it wasn't that she was afraid something might happen; she knew Hadley would be safe. She worried more about inconveniencing someone she assumed had far more interesting things to be doing. Surely, someone who was what...eighteen? Nineteen? had something more exciting planned than taking care of a seven year old for the afternoon.

Riley smiled. "It's not an inconvenience. Besides, I offered, remember?"

A Ripple in the Water

Kate looked up and found herself staring into Riley's eyes. She couldn't help but notice the striking color – green with flecks of gold – and she once again found herself drawn to him in a way that there was only one explanation for. She was attracted to him on a physical level; it was undeniable. With Riley looking at her and her looking back at him, she began to lose her train of thought.

This was ridiculous. What was it about him that all of a sudden had her unable to think a coherent thought? God, she needed to get hold of herself. She shook her head slightly, trying to enable that thought to sink in. She was then able to focus her attention to her daughter and whether or not she could stay at the pool.

"All right. She can stay." She said, knowing that agreeing to let Hadley stay at the pool would enable her to leave all that much quicker. She didn't have the energy to argue with her daughter at the moment; she needed to leave this man who made her pulse race. Quickly.

Before the words were even out of her mouth, Hadley squealed in delight and began to jump around excitedly. "Thanks mom. You're the BEST!"

Kate rolled her eyes at Wendy, who chuckled in response.

She looked down at her daughter. "Hadley, best behavior! I'll see you at home later." Looking up at Riley, she said. "If you have any problems, call me – your mom knows my cell – and I'll come get her."

He nodded. "No worries. We'll be fine."

"Yay!!! Thanks mom!" Hadley jumped up and down and then threw her towel on to the ground and grabbed Riley's hand, tugging on it impatiently. "Come on, Riley. Let's go swim!"

He allowed himself to be dragged toward the water, smiling broadly. "I'll bring her home later, okay? Say, around two or three?"

"That would be great Riley. Thanks."

Wendy reached down and picked up Hadley's towel and flip-flops. "I'll put this over by our stuff so it doesn't get lost."

"Thanks, Wendy. I'll see you tomorrow, all right?"

"Bright and early!" She said, as she walked across the concrete deck toward the chair that held the pool supplies for three boys.

"I guess I should get back over there as well. You know, at least pretend I'm interested in watching the boys do yet another underwater handstand." Angela rolled her eyes and smiled.

19

Kate nodded in response. "I hear you. Hadley feels the need to show me every single one." She glanced down at her cell phone, checking the time. "I guess I should head out. Mrs. Wyndham will expect me to be punctual."

"Oh, God!" Angela said. "You didn't say your client was Mrs. Wyndham! I'm so sorry, Honey."

Kate laughed and turned to her friend but found she was staring at the far end of the pool. She followed her gaze and saw Riley being pulled by Hadley into the deepest part of the pool. They both watched as he allowed her to pull him in, making a large splash.

"Mmm...mmmm....She's going to have a great time with him," Angela said as she stared into the pool. "You know...maybe he could babysit me sometime..."

"Easy, Mrs. Robinson." Kate said, laughing. "He's barely legal!"

Angela leaned in toward Kate with a conspiratorial smile on her face. "I do believe he'll be twenty in July. That makes him legal in any court." She laughed as she walked away, leaving Kate to stare, mouth agape, at her retreating figure.

Kate smiled, shook her head, then walked out of the pool area toward her car, not even noticing that she was being watched by the same individual who, only moments before, had rendered her nearly speechless.

Chapter 3

Riley rose to the surface and shook the water from his head. He swam to the side of the pool effortlessly, his powerful arms slicing through the water easily. As he reached the side of the pool, he folded his arms on the warm concrete and rested his chin there. He glanced around the pool deck and found his gaze automatically searching out Kate's whereabouts.

It only took a moment before he found her. Once his eyes locked on her retreating form, he didn't want to look away. He watched as she opened the gate and then gracefully stepped through. He gave himself a few extra moments to admire her toned legs, which were exposed beneath tan cargo shorts. She wasn't a tall woman by any stretch of the imagination but more than half of her was legs, and that suited Riley just fine. He continued to watch as she sauntered down the stone walkway and across the parking lot toward her car, all the while unaware that Riley's eyes were watching her every move.

He had always found her attractive but then, most of his friends did as well. In fact, there were more than a few of them that had developed quite a crush on Kate. To them, she was nothing more than something unattainable, both because she was the elusive "older woman" and because she was married. At one time, he would have considered himself to be a part of that group as well but he figured out a long time ago his feelings were more than just some school-boy fantasy. Unlike his friends, Kate wasn't forgotten the moment another pretty face walked by. If anything, the moment she was out of his sight, he wanted her all that much more. And since he was away at college for nearly ten months of the year, it had become quite a distraction.

He turned back toward the water and focused on Hadley who was swimming back from the other end of the pool. She reached him and grabbed onto the side of the pool with one hand while moving her goggles to the top of her head with the other. She was breathing heavy from swimming the length of the pool, which made Riley smile. The first day of practice was always rough on the kids. Even though he knew Hadley had been swimming all winter, the summer team kicked it up a notch since there all the meets led up to finals and then the championship meet, which was held at the end of the season. While the winter teams did offer some sense of competition, it focused more on the social aspect of the sport and was more laid back. It was the summer season that ignited the desire for the ribbons that were given out to anyone placing in the top three of each event.

Riley let Hadley catch her breath for just a moment while he planned out some drills for her in his mind. He knew that she'd swim all day if he let her but since it was only the first day, he wanted to take it a bit easy on her. When he felt she'd rested enough, he nodded at her.

"You ready?" He asked. Seeing her nod and adjust her goggles back over her eyes, he called out the first drill. "Okay…50 free. I want to see quick legs, all right? Ready…go!"

Hadley pushed off the wall and kicked with a vengeance. Riley smiled knowing that Hadley would give her all her effort until she collapsed. He wished all the kids on the team had her determination.

As Hadley made her way toward the opposite side of the pool, Riley glanced at her form, making note of a few corrections she could make, then allowed his thoughts to return to Kate. His lips turned upward into a smile as he thought about her short, dark hair and how he'd love to run his fingers through it. He thought about the sprinkling of freckles that ran across the bridge of her nose and the three freckles that were located in the spot where her shoulder met the delicate incline of her neck – a spot he longed to kiss. He couldn't remember a time when he didn't have feelings for Kate. Of course, up until last year, she had been off limits. Then of course, the tragedy occurred and Kate found herself a widow and Hadley found herself without a father.

Riley thought back to the night he found out Kate's husband had been killed. He hated to admit it, but in the moment he found out, the tiniest, miniscule spark of hope lit within him. God, how he hated how selfish he was at that moment. He knew he was an absolute shit thinking of his own feelings while Kate was going through the most difficult time in her life. He couldn't help it, though. He'd thought of her for so long as something unreachable and impossible that the idea of it all changing made him excited before he could squelch the emotion. He still, with utter clarity remembered his mother calling him last summer to tell him about the accident. She had been practically hysterical. She went on and on about "that poor child" and how she would grow up without a father.

As a result of that phone call, he knew two things: His mother would be the leader in the "Let's Help Kate the Widow" campaign and his feelings for Kate had suddenly become something that was not going to be denied.

He had, of course, wanted to come home for a couple of days for the funeral but had gotten a much desired internship with a CPA firm in Charlotte. His mother had insisted it would look bad if he were to leave –even for a few days- in the middle of the summer. He certainly couldn't explain to his mother exactly why he'd wanted to come home so he'd just dropped the subject and continued on with his internship, though thoughts of Kate entered his mind more often than he cared to admit.

By the time his internship had ended, it was time to return to school with boring classes all day and endless hours of tedious homework each night. There simply wasn't time for him to come home. He knew his mother was taking care of Kate and Hadley and while that gave him a small amount of comfort, he also knew that it annoyed him just the tiniest bit. Even now, he rolled his eyes as he thought of it. He loved his mother, sure. But there were times when she was a bit much. Take this whole Kate situation. His mother didn't really know Kate all that well until the accident but she'd stepped in nonetheless, just like she always did. She thrived on things like that and took care of anyone who was the slightest bit injured, as though they were a baby bird that had fallen out of the nest. Wendy would do anything in her power to make sure anyone she was even remotely acquainted with survived heartbreak or any other event that might be traumatic, even if the possibility existed that she wasn't needed or wanted. He couldn't help think his mother liked the attention of being the person closest to someone who had suffered through some tragedy or another. In Lancaster, North Carolina, like most other small, closely-knit communities, there was a certain amount of notoriety in being the person who was able to give all the dirty details of how the victim was coping. While most were generally concerned with others, he'd learned that some just want to know all the gossip and his mother was more than willing to supply it.

So, Riley had been stuck at school for the summer while his mother helped Kate and Hadley get on with their lives. The feelings he'd kept hidden from Kate and everyone else were now able to be released and the rush of the emotions he felt were nearly impossible to reign in. For a time, he had been entirely consumed with the entire concept of what might be possible now that Kate's situation had changed. So consumed, in fact, that he worried his grades might suffer. They didn't, and for that he was thankful. He kept his grade point average up and found that as a result, was offered the same internship again this summer. He knew within moments he would turn it down, choosing instead to come home for the summer and see Kate. He did feel a little guilty about declining the internship that so many other students wanted but he really had no choice. He had to come home for the summer. He had to see *her*. He couldn't wait any longer.

So, with one brief phone call, he turned down the internship and instead, offered to coach the local swim team – the team he knew Hadley would be a part of.

Once his summer plans were in place, it seemed it couldn't arrive quickly enough. His excitement was palpable, though he did his best to hide it from his roommates. They had embraced college life with two arms and were mostly occupied with cute co-eds. As a result, they were oblivious to Riley's distraction. None of them – and his roommates were his closest friends – would understand his feelings for a woman from his hometown or his lack of desire to date any of the coeds that were constantly hanging around in their apartment as though it were a designer shoe store having a clearance sale.

Occasionally, though, one of his roommates would push the dating issue and even more occasionally, Riley would succumb to the pressure and take some girl to a movie or campus party. A part of him hoped that doing so would help him forget his feeling for Kate but it never did. The girls he dated were just that - girls. They were insecure and full of themselves at the same time. How was that even possible? How could these girls look down their noses at someone and then in the next moment, be upset because some guy called you five minutes later than he said he would? Riley shook his head. He was tired of the drama. Tired of double dating with another couple, only to have both girls leave to go to the bathroom at the same time. Tired of the stupid ones who called and hung up, not realizing that in this day and age, everyone had caller id. And he was tired of the giggling. It was maddening, and he was done.

Once he'd made that decision, it only seemed the natural progression to date women who were older. Of course, his roommates were all for this and would high-five him before each date, then poke each other in the stomach while giving each other knowing looks.

Riley, for whatever reason, found older women fascinating, making this method of dating somewhat easier than his earlier attempts. Older women were self-confident and didn't give a shit if you called or didn't call. They had lives of their own and while they were pleased if you called, they wouldn't give you the third degree if you didn't. They were comfortable with themselves and truly believed that if you didn't call, it was your loss.

If you didn't call, they would make other plans.

Older women had their own lives to lead and they certainly weren't going to sit around waiting for some guy. Riley smiled, thinking of the ladies he'd dated. They were all wonderful, confident, intelligent women but, truth be told, they weren't Kate. Despite dating these women, some of them he truly cared for, he was unable to rid himself of the ever present feelings he had for Kate.

It was Kate he wanted and there would be no substitute.

Hadley reached the side of the pool and once again, grabbed onto the side of the pool in order to rest. She smiled at him and pulled her goggles off her face, placing them on the top of her head.

"How was that?" She asked.

"Really good," he replied. "Your legs are moving much quicker now. This time, keep the legs moving like you just did, but keep your fingers together during the stroke." He took her tiny hand in his and held her fingers straight and closed together. "Like this. It's the small things like your fingers that are going to make the difference between first and second place."

Hadley listened intently and then nodded. "Got it," she said. She adjusted her goggles back over her eyes and looked toward the other end of the pool, seemingly reviewing her stroke in her mind. She pushed off and Riley watched as her hands came out of the water during each stroke. Sure enough, her fingers were pressed tightly together. He smiled, knowing she would listen to every piece of advice he gave her because she was always trying to improve.

He watched for a few more strokes, then found that his mind wandered -not surprisingly - back to Kate. He wasn't sure what he was going to do but he knew any steps he took toward her had to be tiny ones. He had no idea how Kate would respond and didn't want to risk her running in the opposite direction. To begin with, he wasn't even sure if she was ready to date again. How much time does one need to mourn after they lose their husband? Hadley seemed to be back to her old self but she was a kid...kids bounce back from nearly everything. He wasn't so certain Kate would bounce back as easily. He thought about that for a moment. He might have to ask his mother how things were going with Kate. Of course, she'd have all the information...and if she didn't? She'd whip up a casserole and deliver it to Kate's house with the intent of getting the aforementioned info. One the one hand, he was lucky his mother was now so close to Kate. On the other, he didn't like the fact that she was somewhat of a busy-body. Then again, if she were busy with her friends, she would have less time to get into his business, which was just how he liked it. His mother tended to be a bit overprotective when it came to him and his brothers but for God sakes! He was nearly twenty! It was time to cut the cord, so to speak. He didn't respond well to her hovering.

He realized that her hovering was one of the pitfalls of moving back home for three months. He knew his mother was going to treat him like he was five years old again. He shook his head. *What was I thinking?*

He smiled, answering his own question. He knew *exactly* what he had been thinking of...those three freckles, and everything else that belonged to the woman that had long ago stolen his heart.

And for a chance with her, he'd tolerate any amount of hovering his mother could dole out.

Wendy sat down on the end of her chair and watched the twins swim their laps. She noticed Hadley swimming beside Riley, who appeared to be giving her more instruction. She felt a pang in her chest as she looked at that beautiful child who lost her father last year. She shuddered, thinking of what she'd do if she ever lost Bill. He was her rock. She couldn't even imagine the pain Kate had gone through.

She remembered that night as though it were yesterday. She had just gotten the twins out of the tub and was attempting to dry them off, which was like trying to herd cats. She had managed to grab Ben and wrap a towel around him, holding him fast against her. She heard the phone ring and before she made a move to grab it, Tyler ran into the kitchen naked, dripping water the entire way and answered it. Their phones were constantly disappearing because the boys insisted on answering them when they rang. Once they had the phone, they would walk around talking and then drop the phone wherever they were when the call ended. The battery in the receiver would then die, often leaving Wendy with only one phone that worked.

When the caller asked for Wendy, he simply dropped the phone and ran back into her room and told her the phone was for her. Frustrated, she lifted up Ben; fearful he would escape and run naked and wet through the house, and carried him into the kitchen to grab the phone.

She recognized Brenda's voice almost immediately as she began to explain that Kate's husband had been killed in a car accident. In her shock, Wendy slumped against the counter, releasing her grasp on Ben and allowing him to slide down her body onto the floor to freedom. Almost immediately, he stripped himself of the towel and ran to find his brother. Together, they ran upstairs, relishing their nakedness, while Wendy figured out what she could do to help.

She called Bill, who was still on a job site and then called Riley, who, of course, offered to come home for a few days. She nixed that quickly, telling him how important it was for him to stay right where he was. After arguing about it for several moments, he finally agreed to her way of thinking.

After making some calls to a few of the other moms in their group of friends, Wendy decided she would be the one to organize the dinners and general checking up on Kate and Hadley. After the funeral, Wendy showed up at Kate's house ready to ensure that all of their needs were met. She had no idea what to expect; her only experience with loss were limited her miscarriages and while they were traumatic, they were different. Not less painful, mind you, just different. Wendy understood that the loss of your husband, your soul-mate, and the person you had chosen to spend the rest of your life with would rip your world apart.

Initially, her intent was to make sure that Kate and Hadley had food delivered by their friends at appropriate intervals so Kate wouldn't have to worry about cooking but when she showed up at her house two days after Todd was buried, she found a very distraught Kate in bed still wearing her clothes from the funeral. Hadley was curled up beside her mother and wouldn't budge from her side. The scene was heartbreaking but it was also just what Wendy needed to see in order to know how very much she was needed.

From then on, she was there daily. She managed to coax Kate out of her funeral clothes and into the shower. Hadley quickly followed suit and it seemed that once she realized her mother was being taken care of, she found she wanted to return to normal activities. Wendy would simply pick up Hadley on her way to the pool so that Hadley could have a couple hours of normalcy, then return after practice with all three kids to see to whatever needed to be done. After a few days, Kate was getting up and eating the food Wendy prepared for her but it took several weeks for Wendy to feel comfortable that the healing process had begun.

Now, nearly one year later, Kate seemed to be back to her former self, for the most part, that is. There was still something missing that Wendy couldn't quite seem to put her finger on, though she suspected it was that the loss of her husband had simply shut down something inside of Kate...something that could only be re-ignited by interest in someone of the opposite sex. Of course, Wendy wasn't completely obtuse. She knew it was difficult to find someone, particularly once you reached the age of having-already-been-married. But Wendy, being the constant problem-solver, knew just the way to fix this particular problem.

But first things first, she needed to give Kate a little push in the right direction. Not a push, really. More of a nudge. Wendy wanted Kate to move on with her life and to be honest; Wendy wanted to see her smile again. She missed the old Kate; the one that laughed all the time and made every day a little bit brighter. Wendy knew the only way to get the old Kate back was to make her feel alive again. And the best way to feel alive was to fall in love.

Wendy nodded her head. She was certain Kate needed just a little nudge in the right direction....and she knew that she was just the person to do the nudging.

Chapter 4

Kate slowly drove back to her house, unable to stop thinking about Angela's remarks. It wasn't that she was surprised at the comments – she assumed most women would find Riley attractive. No, what surprised her was the fact that Angela felt so comfortable talking about it while Kate had been mortified to even realize she found him attractive. Angela, it seemed, felt that someone with a body like that should be pointed out and identified, something Kate knew she'd never be comfortable doing. Any lingering attraction she had to Riley would be kept to herself. End of story.

She thought back to her earlier conversation with Riley and felt the color rise to her cheeks once again. How was it possible that she stared at him for the better part of an hour and didn't recognize him? She'd known Wendy and her family for nearly three years. Had Riley changed so much during the winter that he was unrecognizable to her? Apparently so, she thought wryly.

Kate pulled into her driveway just as her cell phone rang. She picked it up and glanced at the number, somewhat confused. She had some vague recollection of the number but wasn't entirely sure who it was. Not that it mattered. Since she ran a business out of her home, was a single parent, and most of her clients had her cell phone, screening her calls was a luxury she couldn't afford. She answered the phone regardless of whether or not she knew who was calling simply because the call might be a future client and bring more income into her business.

"Penner Interiors. Katharine speaking."

"Ms. Penner? This is Sylvie, Mrs. Wyndham's assistant?" Kate couldn't help but roll her eyes when she heard voice rise at the end of the sentence.

Sylvie had been working with her employer for nearly three years. Kate had only met the young woman a couple of times but had liked her immediately despite the fact that she still spoke as though every sentence was a question – clearly a mark of her youthfulness and insecurity. It was as though she needed assurance from whomever she spoke to that what she was saying was appropriate.

Sylvie was a tiny blond with boundless energy and it seemed to Kate at least, that she kept Mrs. Wyndham on her toes. Kate also suspected that Mrs. Wyndham, a woman in her late eighties, rather enjoyed having someone with Sylvie's energy around.

Normally, Kate's contact with Sylvie was limited to her visits to Mrs. Wyndham's home, a sprawling mansion in the well-to-do part of Lancaster. Today's call was out of the ordinary, which immediately made her wary.

"Hello Sylvie," she said, somewhat hesitantly.

"I'm calling to let you know that Mrs. Wyndham is going to have to postpone her meeting today. She isn't feeling too well."

"She's all right I hope?" Kate asked,

"Yes, ma'am. She's just feeling a bit under the weather. She was out a bit late last night," Sylvie whispered. Kate could hear Sylvie's smile through the phone and pictured her grinning from ear to ear.

She smiled in return. "I understand. Would you like to schedule another time now?"

"No, Ma'am. Mrs. Windham said she will call you in the next couple of days."

"All right. Thanks Sylvie."

"You're welcome, Ma'am."

At Kate ended the call, she realized that Sylvie had called her "ma'am" three times during their brief phone call. While she understood it was a sign of respect from someone with Sylvie's southern breeding, Kate realized she didn't like it at all. She also realized this was the first time she'd even thought about being 'older' than someone and she couldn't help but think her feelings had a little something to do with the events of this morning. Nothing like being attracted to someone much younger than you to put a spotlight on your own age, she thought.

Kate tossed her cell phone back in her purse and headed into the house. She realized that since her meeting had been cancelled, she now had some unexpected time on her hands. Hadley was at the pool with Riley until – what had he said? At least two o'clock. That meant she had at least three hours to get something done before he brought her home. She decided she would use this newly found time to review the emails that she was certain had been flooding her in-box since she last checked it. While she was pleased that business was picking up, a part of her wished that it could have waited until Hadley was back in school at the end of August. She knew she'd barely keep her head above water with her daughter around all summer. Add to that swim practices every day and swim meets once or twice a week and well...she'd be lucky to finish the projects she'd already committed to.

With Hadley gone, the house was oddly quiet. It was nice, she thought, having time to actually think without being interrupted. Thinking, though, almost immediately led to visions of Riley. She felt herself blush for the umpteenth time as she thought of him climbing out of the pool, his powerful thighs walking towards her, how his abs had fit so neatly into that tiny swimsuit and what they'd looked like when Hadley had been poking him.

Once again, she found herself shaking her head. What the *hell* was she thinking?! He was so young, for God sakes! Not even out of college. It was ludicrous for her to even spend another minute on the subject of Riley's abs...or any other part of his body. She needed to banish any of those thoughts and get to work.

In any event, it was probably just some weird fluke she'd even reacted that way when she saw him this morning. It was probably hormones or something...maybe she was going to get her period.

Almost the moment that reasoning entered her mind, Kate dismissed it. She didn't believe for even an instant it was hormones at all. She knew exactly what it was – good old-fashioned sexual chemistry. Well, maybe it wasn't good, exactly, but it was chemistry, of that she was absolutely certain.

There was a small part of her that was pleased to discover she could respond to someone in that way at all. Since Todd's death, she'd felt certain that the ability to have any feelings for a member of the opposite sex had been buried somewhere deep inside of her and until this morning, she hadn't been sure if she'd ever be able to unearth them again.

Clearly, it was possible, even for her. Her reaction to Riley this morning was completely natural. He was extremely good looking and her body responded as it would have with any other man she found attractive.

Of course, it hadn't. Not in the last year, anyway. Frowning, she tried to think of a time when she'd felt such an intense response as she'd felt this morning. Surely there was someone she'd responded to like that?

Wasn't there?

She thought back to when she and Todd had first met. She knew there hadn't been any sort of reaction like this morning, but then again, she'd known Todd for some time before they'd started dating. Maybe it didn't have the sort of spark you read about in romance novels but what they had was solid. It was something based on mutual respect and companionship.

She rolled her eyes. God, she sounded like someone with an arranged marriage! She shook her head. It didn't matter what their relationship was or was not based one. It was a good one...or had been a good one.

She walked over into the living room and looked at her wedding picture, which still rested on the mantle. She felt her chest tighten as she looked at the picture of her and Todd on their wedding day. They'd had numerous staged photos of that day but this one had not been scripted and as it turned out, was her favorite. The photographer had caught her and Todd immediately after the ceremony as they walked out of the church and stole a moment off to the side. Todd has whispered in her ear how much the tuxedo shoes were killing his feet and Kate had laughed and told him that her bra was digging into her ribcage. They'd grinned at each other, both extremely happy to be married, yet both in excruciating pain as a result of the outfits they'd put on. The snapshot had been taken right before they burst into a fit of giggles realizing how much they hated the entire wedding production. After looking at all the photos from that day, they'd both decided this particular one was their favorite and it was the one that hung on their wall. Looking at the photo now, she could still scarcely believe he was gone.

It was hard for Kate to believe that almost a year had passed since Todd had been killed. It seemed like only a few brief moments ago that she'd received the phone call that would alter her life in ways she could have never imagined.

On that day, Kate had been working in the tiny office of their home that she used for her interior design business. Hadley had been sitting on the floor coloring. Kate's cell phone rang and she'd answered it without even so much as looking away from the reams of fabric splayed out on the table in front of her. When a strange voice told her about the car accident on Route 85, she grabbed then six year old Hadley and drove frantically to the hospital, hoping and praying her husband would survive.

He did not.

As it turned out, Todd's accident was just one of those ordinary situations where someone wasn't paying attention to the road, either because they were changing the radio station or fumbling through their purse in search of something. In any event, no charges had been filed on the woman who'd caused the accident because it was just that – an accident. Her husband was gone, she and Hadley were on their own, and Kate was left with a hole inside of her she didn't think would ever heal.

Although Kate had managed to survive the day of her husband's death, it was the following days and weeks that she seemed to have trouble with. Each morning, she would open her eyes and in the few, brief moments before becoming fully awake, she would forget that he had been taken from them. Her arm, seemingly having a mind of its own, would reach across the bed in search of Todd. Once the moment passed and the knowledge of her reality seeped its way in, the wave of depression would wash over her and she'd find herself unable to move. She'd lay there crying into his pillow, searching for any lingering scent of her husband. Hadley would eventually wake and crawl into bed with her mother, curling up beside her. The two of them would lay there, day after day, surviving, but not living.

It was Wendy who had stepped in when it was clear Kate wasn't going to be able to function any time soon. For that, Kate would be eternally grateful. It was Wendy who practically took over Kate's home during the time immediately following Todd's accident. It was Wendy who organized all their friends to make sure that a meal was there each night; it was Wendy who took clothes to her own house to launder, knowing that Kate simply couldn't manage it. And it was Wendy that kept the house to a standard of cleanliness that Kate had never aspired to. Kate knew, without a doubt, she might not have survived the loss of her husband without the help from her friends, especially Wendy.

Oddly enough, Kate and Wendy hadn't been extremely close prior to Todd's death. Sure, they were acquaintances, friends even, but now they were much closer. Kate had often wondered why it had taken such a tragedy for the two of them to become so close. She'd even felt a pang of sadness that it had occurred that way. Why hadn't they become close prior to Todd's death? She wondered if perhaps their age difference had something to do with it (Wendy was forty-seven to Kate's thirty- two), though Kate couldn't recall ever thinking Wendy was all that much older than she was. Whatever the reason, Todd's death had changed all of that and Kate would be eternally grateful for the time Wendy spent taking care of both her and Hadley.

It had been a rough year for she and Hadley, more difficult than Kate could have ever imagined. It wasn't only that she'd lost someone she loved, it was that there was a piece missing in everything they did and each time they did something, that empty space reminded them of their loss. They came to realize that the healing process would be arduous and slow until they figured out how everything would work without Todd. Once he died, everything they did together now had to be taken care of by Kate alone. Kate was left to figure out when the gutters needed to be cleaned, when the lawn needed to be mowed, and a host of other things that she'd never even thought about before.

And if those things weren't enough for her to handle, she also needed to figure out how to handle the little things – going to the grocery store with Hadley instead of letting her stay at home with Todd; meals where there were two people instead of three; figuring out how to entertain Hadley while she attempted to clean the bathroom. These things – and dozens of other normally insignificant tasks – now needed to be re-configured and Kate had to determine how to get it all done without having a spouse to help. Each day brought about new reminders that Todd was gone and wasn't ever going to be back. Somehow, they managed to find their way through all of this and though they weren't yet whole again, they were well on their way to some semblance of normalcy.

It had taken some time, but she'd managed to get her life back in order. She'd begun with tiny things at first; making Hadley's breakfast, performing some mundane tasks around the house – really anything that would give her a sense of normalcy. Before long, she found she was able to return to work and once she'd gotten a few new clients, she focused her energies there, trying to keep her depression from taking complete control over her.

As the weeks turned into months, she found she spent more time feeling normal and less time feeling as though she were one part of something that was continuously searching for its missing piece. She soon realized she needed to get back to work, not only for her own sanity, but to provide a steady income. Kate finished the projects she'd taken on prior to Todd's death – the ones she'd left untouched since his death. Once she'd eased her way back to work by completing those few jobs, she took on a few new projects – ones that she could have done in her sleep - reupholstering a couch, replacing a rug, selecting a few paint colors. Little by little, her days began to be filled with work related tasks instead of endless periods of time where she could wallow in her own grief undisturbed. Once those first few jobs were completed, word spread that Penner Interiors was back in business. For not the first time, Kate was immensely thankful for the close-knit community she lived in. People in her small town were more than willing to hire her do some work, even if (as Kate frequently suspected) they didn't really need to have anything done. In any event, Penner Interiors kept her busy enough while Hadley was in school during the day and she found that slowly, she was becoming human again.

As her business grew, Kate found there wasn't much time left after working and taking care of Hadley, which was exactly how way she liked it. She wanted to be there for her daughter as much as possible – even more so since the death of Todd. It was up to her to be both mother and father to Hadley, and she was determined to do both of them well. She didn't want Hadley to ever feel as though she was missing anything because of the absence of her father.

Kate turned away from her wedding picture and walked back into the kitchen. She sat down at the small part of the kitchen that was a makeshift desk. She lifted the first piece of paper off of the pile she'd just made and looked at it. It was a credit card offer from nearly six months ago. She tossed it into the trash, somewhat frustrated with herself. She'd gotten so behind on things and now found that because the pile was so large, she was a bit hesitant to go through it, feeling a bit overwhelmed. She never seemed to have the time to get to this sort of thing. Luckily, most of her bills were paid automatically– Todd had set up their personal checking account so that most of them were automatically drafted. It was almost as if he knew something were going to happen to him and had begun preparing for it, knowing his wife wouldn't be able to function without him.

She was thankful for his forethought since she knew that if the auto-draft had not been set up, her power, telephone and even water might have been shut off God only knew how many times. Kate just didn't have it in her to deal with the everyday mundane things that made up life – not when her life had been ripped from her. Even the daily retrieval of the mail seemed to sap all of her energy. Sure, she'd walk to the mailbox every day and grab the mail, fully intending to go through it but somehow, it just ended up here, in the pile on the desk in the kitchen. Every time she laid something there, she'd make a mental note to review it later but unfortunately, "later" never came.

Well, it seemed "later" was here now. Hadley was with Riley and she had the house to herself.

Riley. She felt her insides flutter once again. Well, if anything was going to get her mind off of him, it was going through the pile of mail in front of her.

She forced Riley's image from her mind and reached for the envelope on the top of the pile.

Chapter 5

Kate had barely gotten through an inch of the pile when she heard a car pull into her driveway. She smiled, realizing she'd gotten a reprieve from the task in front of her. She tossed the mail she held in her hands back into the original pile, not caring that she'd barely made a dent in it, then got up and began walked towards the front door.

She was nearly there when it opened and Hadley came bounding in, dropping her bag and towel beside the front door and then ran into the kitchen to forage for a snack.

"Hey mom!" Hadley said, as she opened the door to the cupboard. Her hair was plastered to her head, more wet than dry and Kate knew that Hadley had probably been in the water until the moment before it was time for Riley to take her home.

"Hi Sweetheart. Where's Riley?" Kate glanced out the front door and saw Riley sauntering up the front walk.

"Right here." He said as he stepped onto the porch. Like Hadley's, his hair was still wet though instead of it being plastered to his head, waves of blond hair were slicked back from his forehead as though only moments before, his fingers had run through it. Kate felt a shiver run through her as she imagined her own fingers doing the same. She groaned inwardly as a shiver ran through her.

She stood off to the side of the front door, her body language inviting him in. He stepped in, giving her a wide grin and showed her what he was jangling off his index finger. Kate looked down at it, momentarily confused, then realized what it was and whose they were.

Riley walked into the kitchen and leaned against the counter, twirling Hadley's goggles around his finger. "Forget something?" He said, tossing them into the air.

Kate released a sigh of frustration. The location of Hadley's goggles had always been a source of aggravation for her. Hadley was forever leaving them at one place or another which resulted in Kate having to constantly replace them. She'd long felt that if it weren't to the detriment of the team, she would have stopped. Unfortunately, Hadley needed them to swim in the meets, which meant Kate was left to figure out another way to discipline her child in order to get her to remember her goggles.

Clearly, nothing was working yet.

Hadley leapt up and caught the goggles in mid-air. Riley held onto to them as well, causing them to stretch out between the two of them. He looked down at Hadley seriously. "Remember what we talked about at practice today? Your goggles are your only piece of equipment you need…"

"So keep them on your head," Hadley chimed in.

Kate couldn't help but smile. Maybe if Riley told Hadley to keep track of her goggles, she'd actually listen.

Hadley took her goggles from Riley's hand and placed them on her head, nodding to him with a serious expression on her face. He smiled.

"Of course, once you're home, you can put them in your pool bag."

She nodded, still serious. "Right!" She pulled the goggles off her head, placed them in her pool bag, then ran up the steps into her room.

Kate watched her daughter bound up the steps. Turning to Riley, she said, "You know, I think she might actually listen to you. I've been trying to get her to keep track of her goggles for three years now, with little to no success."

He grinned. "If there's one thing I've learned coaching kids, it's that they won't remember anything unless there's a rhyme or song or something to go along with it."

Kate nodded her agreement. She thought for a moment about her earlier conversation at the pool with Wendy. "You know, I'm embarrassed to admit I had no idea you were coaching."

Seeing Riley raise an eyebrow, she continued. "No, no," she said quickly. "It's not a bad thing. I was just surprised, I guess. I thought you'd be off with your college buddies or something. I didn't realize you were interested in coaching."

"I wasn't initially," he said, shrugging. "But I'm too old -"

Kate laughed out loud.

"What?" he asked, grinning.

"Old?" She said.

"Well, too old for competing anyway."

"Really? You can't compete once you're...what, eighteen?"

"Nineteen...almost twenty." Riley nearly slapped himself. God, he sounded like an *idiot*.

Kate frowned. "You didn't compete last year?"

"No." Seeing where she was headed, he continued. "Last year, I had an internship with this accounting firm so I didn't even come home for the summer."

"Oh, right." Kate calculated the time it had been since she'd last seen Riley, assuming that was the reason she hadn't recognized him initially. "So...no internship this summer?"

"Nope." Not wanting to offer any explanation, Riley left it at that.

Kate sensed that there was more to the story, but didn't want to press any further. After a moment's silence, she changed the topic. "Well, it's obvious Hadley is glad to have you coaching. And thanks for watching her, by the way."

"Not a problem. She's a great kid."

"I think so, but then, I'm biased." Kate looked over at Riley, who was leaning against the door frame of the kitchen, clearly relaxed, which pleased her more than it should have. Because he was right in front of her, she took the time to notice his height. She could now tell that he was at least six feet tall and would tower over her barely five foot-five frame.

Standing across from him, she mirrored his relaxed stance and leaned back against the counter. It occurred to her just then that she'd been having a normal conversation with Riley without any of the sexual tension she'd felt earlier. She was relieved, to say the least. Admittedly, she'd been a bit nervous knowing he was going to be bringing Hadley home. But things were blissfully normal and at the moment, she was just another mom having a conversation with the swim coach.

"So school's going well? I forget your major..."

"Finance. I've got one more year and then I need to figure out if I'm going to get my master's. Not sure yet what I want to do but the master's degree might give me more options."

Kate nodded, not having the slightest idea about anything even related to numbers. As someone who could barely balance her checking account, she had no idea why someone would go to school to learn more about them. What little she did know however, was that he had chosen a good, solid field. But then Riley had always had a good head on his shoulders.

"Do you want something to drink?" She said, walking toward the fridge. She saw her purse lying on the counter, which jolted her memory. "Oh! I almost forgot to pay you! Let me see how much cash I have…." She rifled through her purse, trying to locate her wallet.

Riley held his hands up in front of him. "No, no. I was glad to help you out. I don't want you to pay me."

Kate turned to look at him, her hand still inside of her purse. "I really feel I should pay you something."

He shook his head and shrugged. "I was planning on staying at the pool anyway."

She pulled her hand out of the depths of her purse and crossed her arms over her chest, looking at him closely. "Free babysitting? This is a great deal for me, you know."

He grinned. "We aim to please."

Kate reluctantly admitted she felt a stir within her when Riley grinned at her. As she stood there grinning back at him stupidly, she realized that not only was she finding it hard to look away but she also felt an urge to make him smile more often.

Just then, he looked away and pulled his phone out of his pocket. He stared at the phone, then texted something back. Kate felt a moment of awkwardness as he did so. Was she supposed to busy herself doing something else or was she supposed to stand there until he finished? Was texting like a phone call where he'd step out of the room if it was personal? She rolled her eyes, realizing she was being stupid. This was her house, for Christ sakes. If he wanted alone time, he could leave the kitchen.

As the feeling of self-righteousness started to seep in, Riley tucked the phone back into his pocket. The words were out of her mouth before she could stop them.

"Everything all right?" She asked, then immediately felt embarrassed for asking. It was really none of her business.

"Huh? Oh, yeah. My mom was texting me to see what time I'd be home." Riley rolled his eyes, causing Kate to smile.

Kate caught the eye roll and wasn't about to let it slide by. "What was that I just saw?" She asked, grinning.

A guilty expression came over him. "Sorry. I shouldn't have done that. It's just that being home is ...well, different after being on my own for the last couple of years."

"I take it you're not adjusting to being home?"

"No," he said, raking his hand through his still damp hair. "I'm not. But it's not that I don't like it. I mean, I love being around Tyler and Ben all the time, I just think my mom forgets that I've been on my own, you know? She can be kind of...well, she hovers."

Kate thought of the conversation she'd had earlier with Wendy and had to agree with Riley. Wendy was completely involved in every aspect of her boys' lives, bordering on obsession where Riley was concerned. It only made sense that since he was home, she'd keep tabs on him. But since Kate was a mother herself, she felt obligated to support her friend.

"I think all of us do that to a certain extent. We parent for such a long time that it's hard to let go. But you know what?" She looked at him and smiled. "You're only here for the summer. Before you know it, you'll have all your freedom back and be missing your mom."

Riley smiled, but Kate sensed something was a bit off with him. He didn't seem as excited as one might think. She pushed the thought from her mind and opened the door to the fridge. She stared at the nearly empty shelves, disappointed that there wasn't more to offer him. She spoke to him over her shoulder while moving some leftovers around in the hope that some drink options would suddenly appear.

"So, how's your dad doing? Is he still as busy as ever?"

"Yeah, his houses are still selling pretty quickly, which is surprising given this whole recession thing."

"Well, your dad's a great builder. I can certainly attest to that."

"Oh, right," Riley replied. "I forgot about that. This house was one of the first ones he built in this subdivision, wasn't it?"

Kate nodded. "It sure was." She located a soda in the vegetable drawer and pulled it out, wondering how it had ended up in there. "Is Diet Coke okay?"

"Sure," he replied. He motioned to the kitchen table with a nod of his head. "Okay if I sit?"

"Of course." Kate pulled out a glass for herself and filled it with water. She walked over to the table and sat down across from him. "Your dad worked a miracle for me on this house. I needed a room that could be used as my office but didn't want it to look too much like a bedroom." She nodded toward the back of the house. "We decided on that room and it's worked out great. Lots of windows, a door to the outside so clients can come to the house without seeing the mess I've got in here, and I can even shut the door and get some work done when Hadley's home."

Riley followed her gaze toward the back of the house. He opened up the soda and took a big gulp. Placing it down on the table, he paused for just a moment, then spoke. "You know," he began. "Anytime you need someone to watch Hadley, I'd be happy to."

"Well, thanks. But it's not all that often that I find myself needing to have a sitter. Normally my life is very boring, I'm afraid."

"Boring, I doubt that," he said, looking at her over the soda can as he took another sip.

Kate fingered the rim of her glass and smiled. "Sorry to disappoint you, but boring is exactly how I'd describe my life. I do most of my work here at home, which means I hardly get to see anyone other than my clients. I spend all my time on the computer, researching fabrics and designs. Now, occasionally," she widened her grin, "I'll head someplace exciting like Home Depot or Lowe's and *that* is where all the action happens."

He laughed out loud.

She grinned at him and then shook her head. "I wish it were exciting. Basically, all I'm doing there is matching paint colors or getting ideas for flooring."

He looked confused for a brief moment. "So, what do you do with Hadley when you have to run out like that?"

Kate's smile quickly left her face. "Well, that's the question of the day. Normally, she's in school but now I guess I'll have to drag her with me. She's going to *love* that." She sighed heavily, thinking about how she was going to juggle her child and her business while Hadley was home for the summer.

Riley was one step ahead of her. A solution had just presented itself to him and he knew he was a genius for coming up with it. Had he been alone, he would have reached over his shoulder and patted himself on the back.

"You know…" He began. Kate looked up as his voice trailed off. He was looking over her head, pretending to be deep in thought.

"What?" she asked.

"Well, I was just thinking. I'm going to the pool each morning for practice and I drive right past your neighborhood."

Kate knew where he was headed and began to shake her head. "I couldn't ask-"

He interrupted her, smiling. "You didn't ask. I offered. Well, I haven't yet," he joked. "Why don't I just pick her up each morning for swim practice? Then you'd have time to get some work done. You could come to the pool after practice to get her."

Kate sat at the table thinking of his offer; chewing the inside of her lip. She had to admit, it was tempting. She'd have time to herself to get her work done, run errands, and meet with clients without worrying about Hadley needing something. The thought of having her home quiet and all to herself was very tempting indeed. She hated to inconvenience Riley, though, so her first impulse was to decline his offer. "Oh, I don't know…."

"It's really no problem. You're right on my way and I have to be there anyway." He shrugged, trying to make himself appear nonchalant. In his mind, the bonus to this arrangement would be that he'd get to see Kate alone at her house each and every morning. Maybe he could get to her house early so they could chat or something…

Kate pondered the offer and knew she really had no reason that prevented her from accepting. If anything, it was the perfect solution. The more she thought about it, the more sense it made. She would be able to get some work done and Hadley would be where she wanted to be – at the pool. She'd be watched by Riley, the other coaches and the numerous other parents who were there. The more she thought about it, the better it sounded.

She looked up at him and grinned slightly. "I hate to say this but, it would really help me out. You're sure you wouldn't mind?'

"I offered, didn't I?" Riley's gaze held hers steady and Kate felt a tiny flutter in her belly. She smiled and quickly looked away.

"I guess I'd have to be foolish to pass on your offer, wouldn't I?"

"Yup," he said, grinning. He took another long drink of his soda and finished it, placing it down on the table. "So, I guess I'll see you tomorrow morning? Say, around 8:45?"

"That'd be great." Kate looked at him, thinking of how earlier he'd refused any payment. "You're going to let me pay you though, right? I mean, you are taking care of my child and helping me out immensely."

He shook his head. "I can't do that. All I'm doing is stopping at your place to pick her up. I've got to be at the pool anyway and Hadley can swim so it's not like I need to babysit. I'm just her…chauffer."

Once again, Riley looked directly at her and smiled. He leaned toward her and Kate found herself staring into the most beautiful green eyes she'd ever seen. She felt a mix of unease along with excitement and found she was unable to look away. She reached beneath her and gripped the chair she was sitting on, afraid she might topple over.

"Of course, I wouldn't turn down, say, a snack or a meal here and there." His smile widened and he laughed out loud. Kate found his laughter to be contagious and couldn't help but release a chuckle.

Once more, she felt a tingle in the pit of her belly and for just a moment, she thought it might not be the best of ideas to see him every day. Then she thought that it really wouldn't make much difference. She'd see him at the pool every day anyway. She quickly came to the conclusion that this would work…because it had to.

"Okay, Riley. You've got a deal. I'll feed you in exchange for a few hours of quiet time. I have to tell you, though. I think I'm getting the better end of this deal. I'm not a great cook by any stretch of the imagination."

He smiled again. He knew, of course, he was getting the better end of the deal.

Kate thought there was a glint of something in his eyes when he smiled at her and she felt it deep in the pit of her stomach. Okay, maybe even a bit lower….but she quickly pushed that thought from her mind.

"Don't worry. I'll eat anything." He picked up the now empty soda can and shook it, then walked over to the kitchen sink and placed it on the counter.

"I guess I should head on home." He paused for a moment, then turned back to look at her. "I'm glad I can help you out, Kate." Riley shoved his hands into the front pocket of his shorts and walked out of the house.

She had to admit that the thought of seeing Riley every morning made her feel all warm inside. She chewed on the inside of her lip, wondering (and not for the first time that day), why her body had chosen now – and Riley – to respond to when for so long she'd felt practically dead inside. She'd just have to figure out a way to deal with her insides performing back flips each time she saw him.

Once Riley left the house, she was able to think clearly and realized that Hadley had been up in her room since arriving home. Kate assumed she was occupied with some computer game of hers, given how quiet the house was. She decided to take this opportunity to get a bit of work done. She sat down at her desk and turned her computer on. She heard the sound of it coming to life and thought for probably the umpteenth time in the past two weeks that she was overdue for a new computer. She made a note to add that to her list of things to do. It seemed as though she never had time for even the simplest of tasks. But now, she might actually have time to get things accomplished. Just knowing that Riley would take Hadley to swim practice each day relieved some of the pressure she'd felt as swim season approached.

This is going to work out just fine, she thought.

Chapter 6

The next morning, Riley showed up as promised to pick up Hadley. Kate had failed to mention to Hadley that she would be picked up by Riley, fearing he would behave as an ordinary teenager and forget he'd ever made the offer. Of course, she'd never known him to forgetful or irresponsible but still, she wasn't going to risk the build up and subsequent let down if Riley was a no-show. She didn't even want to think about trying to deal with one of Hadley's meltdowns this early in the morning. But now that Riley was here, she knew it would be the highlight of Hadley's day, which made Kate smile.

She opened her front door and watched him unfold himself from the front seat of his corolla, a car that was clearly too small for him. He noticed her standing there and smiled at her as he began to walk toward the front door.

"Mornin'," he said. He stretched his arms over head and arched his back, releasing a yawn as he did so. Kate found that her gaze was immediately drawn to the wide expanse of taut stomach that was revealed between his swim shorts and his t-shirt. Immediately, she felt her pulse quicken so she ripped her gaze away, desperately trying to focus on anything else.

"Are you all right?" She asked, once she managed to find her voice. She couldn't help but wonder if he'd been out late the previous night, since he seemed barely functioning at the moment. Almost as soon as the thought entered her mind, a tiny twinge of jealousy ran through her.

"Yeah…just tired. I didn't get much sleep last night." He yawned once more and then grinned at her. "Sorry. Guess I'm more tired than I thought I was."

"Well, come on in. You want some coffee?"

"That'd be great, thanks." Riley strolled in to the kitchen and flopped into a chair at the table.

Kate poured him a cup of coffee and placed the steaming cup in front of him on the table. "Cream? Sugar?" She asked.

He lifted the cup up, took a sip and then shook his head. "Nope. Black." He moaned a bit and rubbed his face, trying to wake up. "Man! I cannot have another night like that. I'll never make it through the season if this keeps up."

"You know, you might want to keep the partying to the weekends," Kate joked. She cringed slightly, knowing that her statement was simply a means to figure out where he'd been the night before.

"I wish I had been at a party. Then I could have left." He took another sip of coffee. "This is great, by the way," he said, nodding toward the cup in his hand. She smiled her thanks. "Tyler, the poor little guy, was sick all night throwing up, and let me tell you, that kid is *loud*! I just hope he's better tonight so I can get some sleep!"

Kate felt a rush of what she foolishly knew was relief knowing Riley had been home all night instead of out partying. Of course, the relief she felt was immediately followed by concern for his younger brother, who she now knew had a horrible night. "How was he when you left this morning?"

Riley shrugged. "I'm not sure. He and my mom finally fell asleep sometime around six this morning so I didn't want to wake anyone to ask. I just sort of crept out of the house to go to practice." He looked at the clock above the sink. "Which reminds me... I should probably head out if I'm going to make it to practice on time. You think Hadley's ready?"

The two of them turned as they heard what sounded like a herd of elephants coming down the stairs, followed by a thud, which Kate knew was the sound of one seven year old girl making her way into the kitchen.

"Ready for what?" Hadley asked. "Riley, what are you doing here?" She looked from one to the other, waiting for a response.

"Riley is going to bring you to swimming practice today. I'm going to stay here and do some work and then I'll pick you up later. How does that sound?"

"Really?" She said, looking at Riley. "You're going to take me to practice?" Seeing him nod, Hadley squealed. "Yesss!!!"

"And you know what else?" Riley asked, leaning in to whisper in Hadley's ear.

"What?" She asked, her eyes opening wide.

"I'm going to pick you up *every day* for swim practice." He stood up and waited for her response. He knew that the younger kids thought it was the coolest thing in the world to have some sort of "in" with the coach and getting a ride to practice by a coach certainly qualified.

"Seriously?" She asked, looking from Riley to her mother, then back again, as though waiting for one of them to tell her it was all a joke. When Kate nodded, Hadley screamed. Both Riley and Kate covered their ears.

"All right, all right," Kate said, slowly removing her hands from her ears. "I get it. You're excited. Now go get your goggles." She looked at Riley and raised an eyebrow. "Geez, you'd think she won the lottery."

"Well," he said, grinning. "Who says she hasn't? Riding with me every day? Come on, that *is* pretty cool."

Kate crossed her arms across her chest and grinned. "Of course," she replied. "What was I thinking?"

"You know…" he said, stepping closer to Kate.

"Yes?" She said, doing her best to ignore her quickening pulse.

"I think I might have a bone to pick with you."

She raised her eyebrows. "Oh, really? What sort of bone, may I ask?"

He nodded toward Hadley. "She had no idea I was coming to get her."

"Er, no," she said. "She didn't."

"You," he continued, poking her gently in the shoulder. "Didn't tell her I was going to pick her up because you thought I might not show up. Am I right?"

Kate cringed, knowing it was the truth but also wondering how he was so goddamn intuitive. "Okay." She lifted her hands up in mock surrender. "You caught me. But you can't really blame me."

Riley raised his eyebrows and grinned, waiting for Kate to continue. He couldn't wait to hear this one.

Seeing his expression, she smiled and continued pleading her case. "Who knew you were going to be so responsible? I mean, it's not like the youth of today has responsibility as their leading trait."

"Touché," Riley said, as he leaned in closer, touching the tip of her nose with his finger. "Teenagers. We're not the most reliable group, are we?"

"No. You're not," she replied.

He leaned in just a bit closer. "That may be the case, but you can't really count me in that group. I'll be twenty in just a few short weeks."

"Okay," she said. "I'll give you this one."

"And I'll take it," he said, laughing.

Kate could only stand there and smile. She had to admit, it felt pretty darn good to kid around with someone, making jokes and poking fun at one another. She hadn't done that in a very long time.

"Ready!" Hadley appeared in front of them with her Hello Kitty towel slung around her neck and her goggles held tightly in her hand. She looked up at Riley with the most serious expression Kate had ever seen on her daughter. "I promise," she said, lifting up her goggles. "I won't lose them."

Kate's heart melted a tiny bit while she watched Hadley make what was surely a solemn vow in her seven year old mind. She looked up at Riley and caught his eye. She nodded slightly, hoping that he understood how thankful she was for his friendship to her and Hadley. He nodded back and her and smiled warmly and Kate felt certain he knew what she was trying to convey.

As they walked toward the door, Hadley bounded out in front of them, giving Kate the opportunity she didn't realize she needed until it was right in front of her. "Riley?"

He stopped and looked at her. "Yeah?"

"I didn't mean to offend you." Seeing his confused expression, Kate made an attempt to explain. "You know, about not telling Hadley?"

"Don't worry about it." He paused for a moment, as though pondering where exactly she stood in the situation. "But, I'll tell you what...." He grinned, then moved closer to her until his face was mere inches from hers. "You can make it up to me."

He winked at her, then walked out the front door, leaving Kate watching him, mouth agape. *Did he just wink at her?* Within seconds, he was bounding toward his car and climbing into the front seat. Hadley waived at her enthusiastically and Kate could see she was bouncing up and down excitedly within the confines of the seat belt. She watched as Riley slowly backed the car out of the driveway, then lift his hand to wave at her. Out of sheer habit, she slowly lifted her hand to wave back. Once the car had backed out of the driveway and headed toward the pool, Kate brought her arm back to its resting place beside her hip.

Then she closed her mouth.

Chapter 7

Kate managed to get a couple hours worth of work completed, "completed" being a matter of opinion. What she'd actually done was sit in her office rifling through fabric for two hours. As hard as she tried to focus, she found it nearly impossible. Her mind kept wandering back to her earlier exchange with Riley. She'd be comparing one fabric to another, and before she knew it, an image of him would be there in front of her...Riley seated at her kitchen table taking a sip of coffee... standing so close to her and looking down at her with those piercing green eyes... reaching out to touch her nose. And without fail, every time his image came to mind, she felt that familiar flutter from deep within her belly.

It was futile. She wasn't going to get any work done this morning. Might as well head to the pool, she thought. She had no pressing deadlines at the moment so a wasted day wasn't the end of the world. Tomorrow, she'd have her head back in the game, so to speak, and she'd at least go through the pile of mail that still sat, unopened, in the kitchen. *Sure you will,* she thought, chastising herself.

She changed into her swimsuit, grabbed a few snacks for the cooler and headed to the pool. She arrived to find Riley in the water with Hadley standing on the deck above him getting ready to practice her dive. After she steadied herself, she dove into the water and came up breathless about twenty feet away. Kate smiled and walked over toward the side of the pool where she'd come up out of the water.

"Hey honey. How was practice?"

"Good. Can we stay a bit longer?" She removed her goggles from her eyes and placed them on top of her head, squinting in the sunlight as she looked at her mother. "Riley's going to help me work on my streamline."

"I have no idea what that is but it sounds important," Kate replied, nodding. "You probably should stay. Did you re-apply sunscreen?"

Hadley bobbed her head up and down. "All right. I'll be sitting over there if you need me. " Kate pointed to an empty chair beneath an umbrella on the other side of the pool.

"Okay!" Hadley said. She pulled her goggles back over her eyes and dove back under water. Kate chuckled, realizing her daughter couldn't care less where her mother was sitting. That is, of course, until she was hungry. Then she would zone in on her mother's location and forage for snacks in the pool bag before immediately returning to the water.

She walked over to the empty table, tossed her bags down, then pulled a towel out. Once she spread out the towel on her chair, she sat down and reached for her magazine. She'd only opened the first page when she noticed Wendy walking towards her. Kate smiled, then stood up to greet her friend, opening her arms to embrace her. She motioned to the empty chair beside her, inviting Wendy to join her.

Wendy sat down and then looked Kate up and down as though inspecting her for damage. "You really look good, Kate."

Kate heard both the complement as well as the underlying question which was; *Are you really all right? Are you really healing?* "Thanks," she replied, waiting for Wendy to dive right in.

She reached across the table, took Kate's hand and gently squeezed it. "So, how are you, really? I mean, I know you look fabulous and all, but are you okay?"

Though she had expected it, it took her a moment to get her bearings and respond. She smiled back at Wendy and patted her hand, which was still tightly holding onto her own. "I'm doing really well. Business is picking up and thanks to your son, I'm actually able to get some work done while Hadley's at practice."

"Oh, right...right! I nearly forgot about that." Wendy looked over at her son and beamed at him. "He's such a good kid. I'm really proud of him. "

"You should be. It really is a big help to me. I'm able to get in a couple of hours working each morning and I don't have to worry about Hadley. He's really great with her. "

"Well, he's had a lot of training. I've been leaving him with the twins for years now."

"You know," Kate said, smiling. "I was shocked when I saw Riley this year. I almost didn't recognize him." She thought about *exactly* how she hadn't recognized him and felt the color rise to her cheeks.

Wendy sighed, lost in nostalgia and completely oblivious to Kate's discomfort. "I know, scary isn't it? He's grown so much over the past few years. He's definitely not a baby anymore. Where has the time gone?"

"Ugh. Let's not go there. Hadley's seven and I find myself looking at her wondering where the time has gone. Before I know it, she'll be off to college and I'll be all by myself."

"Oh, come on. You don't really think that, do you?" Wendy turned to look at her, her eyebrows coming together as she frowned.

"I don't know," Kate replied. She thought about the endless hours she spent in front of her computer and her weekends filled with mommy duties. "How would I meet someone? On—line dating? I don't think so." When Kate said "on-line dating" she looked as though it left a bitter taste in her mouth. "Plus, I've got a lot of baggage when you think about it."

Wendy made a funny sound that told Kate she was being ridiculous and waved her hand around as though wiping away the words that had just been spoken. "Oh, come on. Who doesn't have baggage these days? Besides, you're one of the most wonderful people I know. You're attractive and smart. You're a great mom and you're completely normal. You could have a moving van full of baggage and you'd still be a great catch for someone."

"Normal? I don't know about that," Kate joked.

Wendy looked at her seriously. "Of course you are. You're one hundred percent normal. And you're great. Any man would be lucky to have you."

"Thanks, Wendy. I really appreciate you saying that."

She reached over and patted Kate's hand again. "Well, it's the truth." She paused for a moment. "Out of curiosity, what is it you find so….horrible about on-line dating?

"Oh, I don't know if I think it's horrible…."

Wendy gave her a pointed look, causing Kate to giggle. "Is it that obvious?"

"I may know you better than just about anyone but even a blind man could see the look on your face when you uttered the words 'on-line dating.' You're positively disgusted by the concept. Now why is that?"

Kate sighed heavily. "I just don't think I'm ready. Besides, it just seems a little too…desperate, you know?"

"Don't be ridiculous." Wendy nodded toward the opposite side of the pool. "Sharon met her husband on line and they've been married now for, what? Two years? Did you think she was desperate?"

"No! Of course not! It's just.…"

"Just what? " Wendy raised her eyebrows and smiled knowingly. "It's fine for everyone else but not for you?"

Kate nodded and smiled back at her. "Exactly."

"Well, you need to get over that." Wendy's hand had been resting of top of Kate's and she squeezed, conveying her concern. "You're not ready and that's okay. But when you are ready? You'll meet someone. That's all there is to it. Any man would be lucky to have you and Hadley is his life. And I, for one, am looking forward to seeing you happy again."

Kate smiled tenderly at her friend. "Thanks, Wendy. That means a lot. You're probably right. When the time is right, it will happen."

"Of course I'm right!" Wendy said, laughing. She looked down at her watch and gasped. "Is that the time? Shoot. I've got to go. I left the Tyler with Bill's mother so I could take Ben to practice. Poor kid was up all night vomiting.

"I heard." Seeing Wendy's confused look, Kate continued. "Riley mentioned it to me this morning."

"Oh," Wendy smiled. "I'll bet that poor kid didn't sleep at all last night. When Tyler is sick, it's like he wants everyone to know it. I don't think I've ever heard anyone vomit as loud as him."

"That's hilarious, yet gross at the same time," Kate replied, grinning.

"You think that's gross, try cleaning up after him."

"Ewww…thanks for the visual."

"Anytime." Wendy stood up and yelled to Ben, who was swimming in the three foot section of the pool with his full snorkel regalia, right down to bright orange flippers. It took several tries of Wendy calling his name when he came up out of the water and finally, he heard her, though Kate felt certain he'd heard his name called the first time. She had a child of her own who would do the same, after all. Ben finally climbed out of the pool, walking awkwardly with the flippers still attached to his feet, and made his was over to his mother. Wendy wrapped a towel around his shoulders and handed him his flip-flops. "Come on." She said. "We've got to get your brother."

"Can we come back later?" He whined.

"I don't know, sweetheart. We'll have to see if Tyler's up for it." Turning to Kate, she said, "I'll see you tomorrow, all right?"

"You bet."

"And Kate? Will you at least think about what we talked about?"

Kate smiled, knowing she'd do pretty much anything for this woman – even consider on-line dating. She looked at Wendy and nodded.

After Wendy left, she returned to her magazine. She had only glanced at a page or so when a shadow fell over her. Looking up, she saw Riley standing in front of her.

"Hey, Riley." She placed her magazine on the table, motioning for him to sit down in the spot his mother had vacated only moments ago. She thought of how he'd not gotten any sleep the night before and found herself scanning him for signs of fatigue. She told herself it was motherly instinct as opposed to simply an excuse to inspect his physique. She couldn't help but notice he was still wearing the tiny suit she'd first spotted him in. Didn't he have a pair of board shorts or something?! Seeing him half naked like this was so damn distracting! "How are you? Feeling any better?"

"Still tired, but I'm okay. What about you? You get any work done?"

Kate felt the color rise to her cheeks thinking of how she's pretty much wasted the morning thinking about him. "Umm…yeah. I did. Thanks again for taking Hadley to practice. Was she okay for you?"

"Of course!"

"Great. I'd hate to think you made this offer and then she starts misbehaving."

He laughed. "No chance of that. She may be under the impression that I'll make her swim extra laps if she misbehaves."

"And I'm completely fine with that, just so you know." She smiled at him.

"Did Hadley tell you I wanted to work with her for a bit today?"

Kate laughed. "She mentioned it to me the minute I saw her."

"So you're okay with it? She's really coming along on her fly and I want to work with her while it's fresh in her mind. I can bring her home after."

Kate thought about heading home to start on that dreadful pile of unopened mail and though she didn't relish the thought of spending time going through it, the opposite – that of letting it sit there for another six months, seemed much worse. She knew she was being given the gift of more time, she also knew she needed to take it. "I'm sure she'd love that. Actually," Kate sighed. "I have a pile of paperwork that I've been putting off forever and I really need to go through it. You sure you don't mind driving her home?

"Not at all." He smiled. "I might even be persuaded to stay for lunch…" His voice trailed off as he waited for the invitation.

Kate laughed. "Of course! I'll have sandwiches ready. How's that?

"Sounds great. We should be there around one or so. I'll only work with her for a couple of hours. I don't want to wear her out too much."

"If you managed to wear out my kid, I'd owe you big time." Kate thought of Hadley's boundless energy and the fact that she'd given up naps more than four years ago.

Riley leaned forward conspiratorially and grinned. "Now that sounds like a challenge."

Once again, Kate was rendered speechless by his close proximity to her. "I, uh..,"

He sat there and grinned at her and Kate had the thought that he seemed a bit pleased with her discomfort. She avoided his gaze, trying to think of something to say. Riley chuckled, the stood up. "I'll see you later, Kate."

She watched, once again rendered speechless, as he walked over to the deep end of the pool where Hadley was floating on a bright orange noodle. He jumped in near her, causing a large splash. She squealed in delight and then splashed him as his head came up out of the water. Hearing her daughter's laughter, Kate couldn't help but chuckle.

By the time Hadley and Riley got home that afternoon, Kate had managed to put a solid dent in the pile of unopened mail. She ended up throwing most of it away, which made her wonder why she'd kept all of it to begin with. Of course, she knew it was just as Todd would have done, and keeping some of his habits, despite how insignificant they might be, made her feel as though a part of him was still around. Often times she felt she was stuck in the middle of the present and the past. She wanted to keep certain things exactly the way they were when he was around but she also knew in her heart she needed to make her own way…without him.

She heard the low rumble of a car pulling into the driveway so she organized the remaining mail into a neat pile, then got up to make the sandwiches she'd promised.

Hadley bounded into the house with Riley close behind her, and tossed her towel, flip-flops, and goggles on the steps as she ran upstairs. Kate sighed as she looked at the mess on the stairs. "You know, I just don't understand why she can't bring those things upstairs. I mean, she's going up there anyway!" Kate sighed as she smiled at Riley.

He laughed. "I used to do that same thing. It drove my mother crazy. Cleaning up after myself didn't even occur to me until I had a place of my own. I guess since there was no one there to clean up after me, I realized I had to do it myself."

"You have your own place? I thought you were living with your mom and dad."

"Just for the summer. When I head back to school, I'll go back to my apartment."

"So you come home to work each summer?"

"Well, so far on this year. Last summer I had an internship in Charlotte."

Suddenly, it occurred to Kate why she hadn't recognized Riley initially. It had been nearly two years since she'd seen him last.

"That's right! You worked with that accounting firm." She recalled Wendy telling everyone about Riley's summer employment the previous summer. How could she have forgotten? Of course, last summer was a complete and total blur, given all she and Hadley had gone through. She frowned as a flash of pain ripped through her. She pushed those thought from her mind and directed her attention back to the conversation. "I knew I hadn't seen you in a while. I must have forgotten you weren't around last year."

"Gee thanks!" he said, doing his best to look offended.

"No, no. I just mean- I'm a bit embarrassed to say this I mean, I sound like my mother, but when I saw you at the pool this year, I thought you had grown so much! I hardly recognized you!" Of course, she recalled just how much she didn't recognize him – every last inch of him.

She looked at the pained expression on his face and cringed. "See, I told you I'd sound like my mother."

He laughed. "That's okay. I'll forgive you. It has been a long time." Riley paused for a moment. "I'm actually glad I didn't do the internship. I really wanted to come home this summer."

"Yeah?" She replied. "Big plans for the summer?"

"You could say that," he mumbled.

Luckily, Kate was distracted by Hadley, or rather, her absence and didn't hear his mumbling. Riley watched as her brows came together in concentration.

"Hmmm...I wonder where Hadley is." She stepped over to the stairs and called for her. "Hadley? Do you want some lunch?" She stood at the bottom of the stairs waiting for a response. When after several moments Hadley didn't appear, she turned to Riley, eyebrows still furled together. "I'm just going to run up to her room and check on her."

She walked slowly up the stairs and opened the door to Hadley's room. What she found there made her smile. Hadley was curled into the fetal position on her bed sound asleep and still wearing her team swimsuit. Her hair, still damp from the pool, was flattened to her head. Kate covered her daughter with the comforter that was hanging off the side of the bed and then backed out of the room

She walked into the kitchen and smiled at Riley, the earlier tension forgotten. "Well, Hadley's out cold. I guess you wore her out! "

He laughed. "And you said it couldn't be done...."

Kate chuckled somewhat uncomfortably, remembering what she'd said earlier. She looked around the kitchen, once again feeling a bit self-conscious around Riley. She felt it best to keep occupied in order to avoid those moments of silence where she was forced to look into those green eyes. It was unnerving. Even if she had a coherent thought, it vanished the moment he looked at her. "Well, I guess we should eat, right? No sense waking her up. She'll eat when she's hungry."

Kate busied herself putting out sandwiches and an assortment of chips and pickles. She handed Riley a diet coke and got one for herself. They sat down at the table and began to eat their lunch. For several moments, no one spoke. Kate watched as Riley practically inhaled his sandwich. He noticed that she wasn't eating yet, but was instead focused on watching him eat. It was then that he noticed his plate was nearly empty and hers, still full. A sheepish look crossed his face, which made Kate giggle.

"This is really good," he said, wiping the mustard from the corner of his mouth.

"I guess so," she said, tossing a pointed look at his nearly empty plate.

He grinned, then took another large bite of his sandwich. Kate nibbled on hers and watched as he looked around the kitchen, studying the pictures on the wall.

"It's really weird being here." He said, still looking at the picture of Kate and Todd hanging on the wall.

Kate sat still, unsure of where he was going. Things were weird here? Was Todd's absence so obvious to everyone? Even someone who'd only been to the house on a few occasions? She felt like such a failure. If Riley could see how different things were here, what was Hadley feeling? Insecurity took over and panic began to seep in around the edges.

"Weird how? Depressing? Empty?" She looked across the table at Riley with such a look of concern on her face that he felt immediately remorseful for saying anything. He knew immediately she didn't understand what he meant.

"Kate," he said, looking at her strangely. "I meant that it's a different feeling for me to be here now. Not that the house has any sort of bad feelings."

"Oh," she said softy, feeling somewhat embarrassed.

"And I meant it in a good way."

Kate sighed in relief. "Okay, good. Because I'd be worried, you know? If you felt weird, then I'd be convinced Hadley would feel different and then that would lead to me worrying more about her and…"

"Hey," he said, placing his hand on hers. "Of course Hadley's going to be okay. She's got you for a mother."

She looked up at him, somewhat startled at his statement that seemed somehow laced with intimacy. Kate mumbled a soft thank you and self-consciously began to pick at the food on her plate.

"When I said I felt different being here, what I meant was," he smiled gently at her, as though trying to guess how she might respond to what he was about to say. He took a deep breath before continuing, knowing that he was about to cross a line and once he did, there'd be no going back. He felt his stomach lurch inside of him.

Kate heard Riley's deep breath and looked up into his eyes. She felt the warmth of his hand and realized how it might look of Hadley her to enter the room. For just a moment, she thought about removing her hand but found she couldn't pull herself away from the warmth of his touch.

"It's like…" He stopped, once again hesitating before making the leap. "I feel comfortable here…with you." Riley gave Kate a pointed look, one that he hoped communicated all that he was feeling.

"I'm glad you're comfortable here," she replied, offering him a shy smile.

His brows came together in frustration and he raked his free hand through his hair. Kate felt her insides to a tiny flip flop and once again found herself wondering what it would feel like to run her own hands through his hair. She quickly banished the thought from her mind and tried to focus on what Riley was telling her. She looked down once again at his hand, which still covered hers, and felt a tiny flutter in her belly, which although pleasant, felt incredibly wrong somehow. Flutters in her belly as a result of anything Riley said or did, however unavoidable, was not something she needed to be feeling.

"I'm not saying this right." He looked back at her and flashed a tight smile that told Kate just how uncomfortable he was. "What I mean is….I like being here…with you."

Riley's words hung in the air. He gently squeezed Kate's hand and ran his thumb over her knuckles, waiting for her to respond. He watched as Kate glanced down at their hands, still wrapped together. He could tell she was still unsure exactly what he meant by his statement and watched as she processed what he'd said. He saw the exact moment she understood what he was telling her and watched as she lifted her head to meet his gaze.

His eyes met hers and he made the slightest nod with his head.

Kate's eyes widened. "Oh," she whispered. "*Oh…*"

Chapter 8

Kate was dumbstruck as she looked at Riley. He had feelings for her? What was he thinking? Clearly, he wasn't thinking at all.

Ever so slowly, she pulled her hand away from his and placed it in her lap. Riley watched her pull her hand away and then lifted his eyes to meet his. She saw the hurt there and she felt a pang of sadness deep within her but it needed to be done. She couldn't sit there in the middle of her kitchen and let him hold her hand. What if Hadley were to walk in? What would she tell her daughter?

Kate had absolutely no idea what to say in response to Riley. Of course she was attracted to him, but that was beside the point. She thought back to the first day she'd laid eyes on him – before she knew who he was - and felt the familiar rush of pure sexual attraction. She felt the color rise to her cheeks but then a moment later, common sense kicked in.

"Riley," she said, in a tone she hoped was free of any sexual tension. "I'm very flattered…"

"Don't say anything just yet. Please? Can you just sort of mull it over for awhile?"

Kate looked up at him once again – an absolute mistake on her part, what with her inability to have a coherent thought when doing so. Riley was looking at her with such intensity, Kate's eyes widened. If she had no idea how he felt before, she was well aware of it now. Raw emotion was all over his face and she found she was powerless to do anything to stop it. She felt something stir deep within her and found herself wavering within seconds. "O…okay." She said. "I'll think about what you said."

As soon as the words were out of her mouth, she regretted them. What exactly was she going to consider? Riley's feeling for her? What was there to consider? Her own feelings? Now that was just ridiculous. What she felt for Riley was nothing more than sexual attraction. It wasn't as though she had any real feelings for him.

Or did she?

Immediately, a wave of guilt washed over her. What the hell was she doing? Her husband had only been gone for a year. She wasn't ready for this. She looked up at Riley, ready to break her word to him and tell him that was he was suggesting was impossible, but when she looked up and saw him smiling at her tenderly, all doubt vanished from her mind. All she saw in front of her was someone she was immensely attracted to and was absolutely wonderful and loving with her child. How could that be wrong?

She frowned. There was no way she was going to even try to justify this to herself. Anything between her and Riley was Out. Of. The. Question. He was off limits. Period. She wasn't going to get involved in anything and she needed to tell him. Right now. Screw what she'd just said. She needed to put an end to this immediately. Kate looked up at him and opened her mouth, then stopped when she saw the smirk on his face.

"What?" She asked.

"Kate," he said, leaning toward her. "You're like an open book. I can practically read your thoughts. But don't think about it right now. Please?" He looked at her so earnestly, she once again waivered and released a tiny sigh.

"It's just…Oh hell. I don't even know."

"Neither do I. Which is why I just want you to think about it for a little while. Please?"

Kate smiled softly. "Riley, believe me, you don't have to ask me to think about what you just said. I'm afraid that's all I'm going to be doing."

He grinned. "That's a good thing, right?"

"I have no idea," she replied. "It's just so out of nowhere that you've sort of shocked me with this.

"Yeah...sorry about that. I guess I've just gotten sort of used to it and didn't realize it would be such a shock to you."

"What do you mean 'you've gotten used to this'?" She fixed a level gaze on him, then raised an eyebrow. "Are you saying what I think you're saying?"

Riley felt the color drain from his face. He hadn't meant to tell her *everything* today. His plan was to feel her out – see if she might feel the same about him. If thing went well, at some time in the not so distant future, he might possibly consider telling her he'd always felt like this but now his mouth had gotten away from him. The cat was out of the bag, so to speak.

"I...ummm...." God, he was mortified. Color rose to his cheeks as he struggled to come up with something – anything to say.

Kate felt her jaw fall open. "I don't even know what to say." She looked across the table and saw Riley literally squirming in his seat. He shifted position several times, trying to hide his glowing red face from her. She felt a pang of sympathy for him and knew she needed to at least make and attempt to ease his discomfort.

"Hey," she said softly. He looked up in the general direction of her face, still unwilling to meet her eyes. She smiled tenderly at him. "It's all right. I'm actually quite flattered."

The words seemed to calm him somewhat and he finally managed to look her in the eye. "You are?"

She chuckled. "Of course I am. Have you looked in the mirror lately?"

Once again, color rose to his cheeks. This time, however, he managed to keep his eyes locked with Kate's and he laughed with her. She reached over and patted his hand with her own.

"You might as well tell me everything. This is great for my ego."

"Okay, but you promise you won't laugh?"

Kate allowed a grin to work its way onto her face, her earlier concerns forgotten – at least for the moment. "I'll do my best," she said.

He took a deep breath, then grinned. "When I was, I don't know, sixteen or seventeen? I had the biggest crush on you."

Kate's mouth fell wide open, then she closed it as the mentally did the calculation in her head. "Wait a minute. That was three years ago. Riley..."

"Hey, don't look so surprised. Just about all my friends thought you were pretty hot."

Kate felt the warmth rise to her cheeks. "Oh my God, Riley. You can't be serious! I'm old! I'm a mother for God's sake! Any hotness I had – if I ever had any - is long gone."

"You are not old! What are you, like thirty or something?

"As a matter of fact, I'm thirty two."

He laughed and waived his hand. "Ewww... Thirty two! Oh. My God! Where's your walker?"

"Veeery funny, Riley." Kate said, smiling. "But the fact that you *can* joke about my age should tell you something." She stood up and carried her plate to the sink, a half-eaten sandwich still remaining.

Riley turned himself around in his chair to watch her walk to the sink. "You don't seriously think of yourself as old, do you?"

She turned back toward him and leaned against the counter, crossing her arms across her chest. "I guess 'old' isn't the right word. Maybe older? But there are days I do feel old. Days that I'm running around with Hadley, work is getting piled up…you know, the typical boring stuff my days are filled with."

He nodded, then tilted his head to the side. "I'm sure it's got to be hard ever since…" Riley seemed to stumble over his words. "…well, since Todd died. I'm sorry about that, by the way."

She smiled gently. "Thanks. There are days it is hard but then there are days when it gets just a little bit easier and I know things are going to be okay."

Riley knew exactly what she meant and nodded. "I know what you mean. It's like, you're just about at your breaking point and then something goes your way and you think, 'I can do this.'"

She nodded, looking at him. It was odd, she thought, that he could understand how she felt. "Yeah…that's right."

Riley turned back toward the table abruptly, their brief moment of sharing seeming to have passed. He took a large bite of his sandwich and chewed for a moment, as though deep in thought. "You know, I've always wondered…how did Hadley get her name? I've never heard it before."

Kate paused for a moment before speaking. The story of Hadley's birth wasn't something that she spoke about often. Despite it being the most wonderful day of her life, it was also marred by sadness.

She paused as she thought about that day and all the long days leading up to her birth. For some odd reason, she wanted to tell him about it – she felt *compelled* to tell him. It was as though she knew she could share these parts of her life with him. Kate looked up at Riley as though pondering the question. Riley, of course, felt as though she were trying to determine whether or not she should share any aspect of her life with him. He said a silent prayer that she'd choose to share even the tiniest bit of herself with him.

When at last Kate spoke, Riley felt some measure of relief. If she felt comfortable enough to share something so personal, maybe it was some indication that there might be something else there. And maybe, just maybe, as she opened up to him, she'd grow to have feelings for him. It was a tiny possibility, but he'd take it.

"Hadley was my maiden name. When I was pregnant, my father passed away. I wanted to do something to remember him. When she was born and we saw that she was a girl, we thought that his last name – my maiden name would work for her."

He nodded. "It does work. And I'm sorry about your dad."

Kate shrugged, almost as though trying to shake off the pain any mention of her father's death had always carried. Instead of opening up about the pain she felt then and now, she replied with the customary response. "It was a long time ago, but thanks." She looked off in the distance, thinking about her father, something she rarely did. It was just too painful. She'd often thought that her father's death was even more painful than the death of her husband. She could never understand why. Maybe it was because she'd known Todd a shorter time? But that didn't make any sense – she and Todd had created life together, they were planning the rest of their lives together. She was devastated when Todd died, Riley's mother was perhaps the person who knew that best. But when her father died? Well, it was like a part of her died right along with him. She'd managed to find her way after Todd's death. She had to. She needed to care for Hadley. But when her father died? It was almost the reverse. The person who had always taken care of her was now gone. There was a certain finality to that she just couldn't seem to get over.

She looked back at Riley, who was watching her with an expression of concern. When her eyes met his, he smiled gently, as though telling her he was there for her; that he understood what she was feeling. She smiled back at him, realizing that he did understand her, and that realization made her feel a bit unsettled. How could Riley, at his age, have any idea of the pain she'd gone through? It made no sense – *no sense at all* – but despite just getting to know each other on this new level, she already felt an odd sort of connection to him. Maybe it was because she was so close to his mother. Maybe it was because she had known him for so long. Whatever the reason, she felt comfortable sharing things with him that she normally kept bottled up inside of her, which once again, caused a wave of panic to run through her. She'd never been one to share her feelings with anyone. Todd was the person who she opened up to the most and even he was frequently annoyed at how little she shared. So why now did she want to talk about her feeling? Whatever the reason, for the first time, she felt as though she might actually enjoy sharing her thoughts with another.

Kate pushed herself off the counter and slowly walked back to the table, sitting down in the chair across from him. She took a deep breath and began. "You know, my dad was sick for such a long time. He had lung cancer."

Seeing his eyebrows raise, she continued. "Never smoked a day in his life. Freaky, I know. He was diagnosed when I was in college and fought it for a long time – nearly five years. I met Todd in college and we dated for awhile. Once we graduated, we got married and then had Hadley as soon as we could. My dad always wanted to be a grandfather. He'd talk to me for hours about places he wanted to take his grandkids. When I told him I was pregnant, he cried he was so happy. He cried Riley." Kate looked down as she felt his hand cover hers. This time, in addition to feeling warm and comforting, there was a familiarity there, which both thrilled and terrified her.

"He was pretty sick by that time and I think we all knew he might not make it until she was born. By the time I was halfway through the pregnancy, he was admitted to the hospital. Once that happened, we knew it was only a matter of time. It was odd though…"

"What's that?" Riley asked. He looked down at their hands clasped together and gently squeezed.

"Well, dad was always so strong. He was…larger than life but the minute he was admitted to the hospital, something changed. I think he knew he was losing the battle and he just sort of gave up. Once I saw that happen, I told him we were going to name our child Hadley. I was doing anything I could to get him to hang on. God, I wish he could have met her."

"He never met Hadley?" Riley asked softly.

Kate's eyes met his and she shook her head. "No," she replied. "He died sixteen days before she was born."

"God, Kate. I'm so sorry. I had no idea."

"What about your mom? Is she around?"

Kate shook her head. "My parents divorced when I was little. My mom was always sort of a free spirit so once they separated, she moved to Nevada. She's still there doing all sorts of things – nothing long term or serious. She's one of those people who works to live, you know? As opposed to living to work. I talk to her occasionally but we were never really close."

Now that her story was out there and she'd bared her soul, Kate felt oddly uncomfortable. She sat up in the chair and looked around the kitchen almost as though she was wondering how she'd gotten there. After a moment, she looked at Riley and frowned. It was only a slight furrow of her brow, but Riley noticed it nonetheless. It somehow seemed to indicate she'd shared enough of herself and that tiny window was now closed and sealed off.

Riley noticed the change in her and felt a pang of sorrow as he realized she'd opened herself up to him, much as he'd hoped she would, but had closed herself off almost immediately.

"I'm so sorry," she said. "I don't know what is with me. I didn't mean to bore you with all of that."

Riley shook his head. "You didn't bore me. I'm glad you told me about it. Thanks."

She nodded. Riley noticed she was still sitting stiffly in her chair, a stark contrast from the warm and fluid woman from only moments ago. "I take it you don't normally have people over and tell them the sordid details of your life?"

"No. Not ever." She grinned, somewhat embarrassed.

He looked at her seriously. "Well, I'm glad you feel you can talk to me."

It was then that Kate noticed that he was still holding her hand. Ever so gently, she removed it from his grasp and placed it in her lap. Riley allowed her to take her hand back but she noticed he watched her with a vacant expression on her face. No question about why, no concern, just absently noticing that she'd removed her hand.

She looked at the clock and noticed it was nearly three. "Oh my God! Look at what time it is!" She grinned at Riley. "Hadley never naps; especially not for two hours! What did you do to her?"

He raised one eyebrow. "All part of the plan to get you alone," he said, chuckling.

Kate raised one eyebrow. "Riley," she said, her tone indicating her reluctance to banter with him. When her eyes found his, she felt a flutter inside of her. She quickly squelched the feeling. This was her friend's son – her much *younger* son. She needed to keep reminding herself of that, despite how green his eyes were and how sun-kissed his skin was….Geez!!! What was with her?

Just then, she heard a noise from above her head that sounded remarkably like a seven year olds feet hitting the floor. They both looked up at the noise. Kate thought she'd have to give Hadley extra dessert after dinner tonight for having impeccable timing. Then again, if she thought about it, if Hadley hadn't fallen asleep, she wouldn't be in the middle of this mess to begin with.

"Sounds like Hadley's awake. Maybe she'll eat something."

Riley stood up and brought his plate to the counter. "I guess I should probably head home. I'm surprised my mom hasn't started texting me worry messages yet. I'll be back in the morning for practice, though. All right?"

Kate walked with him to the door. "Thanks again for taking Hadley. I really appreciate it."

Riley looked down into her eyes. "Kate, you don't have to thank me. I want to do it. Anything that helps you..." he shrugged, his voice tapering off.

He shifted his weight awkwardly and then ran a hand through his hear, mussing it up. "Look, I know you're kind of freaked out about what I said earlier."

"Freaked out? I'm not freaked out." She cleared her throat, realizing her voice had come out an octave too high.

He smiled. "Okay, maybe you were thrown for a loop?" Seeing her nod, he continued. "I just want you to...think about what I said? Would you do that for me?"

Kate knew what her response was going to be. She was going to be firm and tell him right then and there that anything between the two of them was completely and utterly impossible. She was going to tell him that he needed to find a nice girl his own age. Someone he had more in common with. She was going to tell him the impossibility of what he was suggesting. The whole idea of Riley and her dating or whatever it was he was hoping for was absolutely ludicrous.

She looked up at him, standing there in her foyer, with such as look of intensity and sincerity in his eyes that before she knew what was happening, she nodded. Almost as soon as she felt the movement of her head, she saw Riley's face explode into a huge grin. He turned around, opened the front door, and was out the door before Kate could tell him that her stupid head nod was all a mistake, that she had a twitchy neck, or some sort of spasm....

She closed the door behind him and slumped against it. How the hell did that just happen?

"Mom?"

Startled, she turned around to find Hadley rumpled and sleepy, her hair mussed up and frozen into odd shapes from falling asleep on it while it was still wet. She stretched slowly and yawned, opening her mouth to speak while she did so. Luckily, Kate had years of experience listening to her daughter speak while yawning, eating, coughing, and any number of activities. As a result, she was fluent in language of Seven-year-old-just-woken-up and understood her daughter perfectly.

"Why are you leaning against the door like that?"

"I was...umm....just making sure the door was solid." She stood up and pounded a fist on the door for show and then turned to face Hadley. "Yup. Solid. We're safe. Hey! You want some lunch? You must be starved!"

Hadley looked at her mother oddly, then shrugged her shoulders as though to indicate she couldn't care less about her mother's craziness. She turned around and headed for the kitchen. "Can I have a sandwich?" She asked, looking back over her shoulder at her mother.

"Sure," Kate replied, thankful to have a seven year old with the attention span of a seven year old.

As she made Hadley's sandwich, it suddenly occurred to her that she knew *exactly* how she was going to handle the situation with Riley. It was something she did quite well, actually, and it was something that had gotten her out of many confrontations throughout her life.

Avoid.

Chapter 9

Riley heard the door close softly behind him and felt the smile leave his face. Although Kate had agreed to think about what he'd said, he knew she'd been pressured into saying she would. He saw the expression on her face when he told her how he felt and it was exactly the opposite of what he'd hoped. He had been foolish to think…what? That she'd secretly harbored feelings for him as well? He rolled his eyes. For someone who was pretty intelligent, he had been pretty stupid back there.

He slowly walked to the car, careful to keep his back to the front door, lest she see the dumbfounded expression on his face. Of course, after what he'd seen on her face during the past hour, he felt foolish for even thinking she'd be looking outside at him.

It killed him to admit it, even to himself, but Kate wasn't exactly excited or even happy to find out how Riley felt. What she was – and he had to give himself a minute to allow the thought to sink in – was terrified. He's seen the look of sheer terror cross her face the moment she realized what he was telling her. It could have been worse, he thought. She could have gotten angry and thrown him out of the house, but she didn't. She didn't do that at all. Actually, she sat with him and talked with him well after he told her how he felt. Now that he thought about it, maybe the afternoon wasn't a total waste after all. She opened up with him, telling him the story of Hadley's birth and about her parents, so that was something. Admittedly, it wasn't what he'd hoped for, but surely it was a step in the right direction. Wasn't it?

Besides, what had he expected? That this woman would leap into his arms the moment he told her how he felt? That she'd tell him how long she'd been waiting for him to say just that? Geez, she was probably still mourning the death of her husband and here he was trying to convince her to date him.

Now that he thought about the whole afternoon, he realized his timing couldn't have been worse. Just the idea of mentioning his feelings to her now seemed completely ridiculous. Her reaction being anything even close to what he'd fantasized about was so far off the mark that he had to laugh at how absurd his initial thoughts had been. Though admittedly, if her reaction had been of more of the leaping-into-his-arms scenario, he wouldn't have minded at all. Not one bit. But terror? Well, he hadn't anticipated that.

God, he was such an idiot.

Riley climbed into his car and backed out of Kate's driveway, stealing another look at the front door. What had gone wrong in there? He felt certain there was a measure of attraction on her part. And he wasn't one of those guys who believed every member of the opposite sex was attracted to him. He was normally pretty in-tune to knowing when someone was and wasn't interested in him. And with Kate, he felt certain…well, sort of. Did he misread that right along with misreading when the right time was to spill his guts?

Shit. He had no freakin' idea.

Riley drove out of the neighborhood, unsure of where he was headed. He just needed to drive. He banged his hand against the steering wheel in an uncharacteristic moment of anger. What the hell was the matter with him? He was going to handle this situation very carefully and what did he do instead? He barges right in there and tells her how he feels. Not only that, but he tells her he's had a crush on her for three years! Why in the world did he feel the need to tell her that?!?!

The whole situation in her kitchen played over and over in his mind. He thought back the moment right before he told her how he felt and still felt certain she was attracted to him. So was it the timing of his announcement? Was it the fact that it was in her kitchen? Not the most romantic of spots, he knew, but still. It couldn't have been his timing. If anything, that was perfect! Just the two of them…alone in the kitchen…Hadley asleep upstairs…the only thing missing was the soft music playing in the background!

He kept wavering back and forth, doubting his actions. He reviewed the look of fear in her eyes but then thought of all the stuff she'd shared with him. Intimate stuff. Why would she do that? She must trust him in order to share those things with him. And, he thought as a smile came to his face, she trusted him with her daughter. That was something, wasn't it?

So, if she trusted him with her daughter and felt comfortable enough with him to share intimate details of her personal life, what was holding her back? He just didn't understand her. He, for the moment, was going to assume she *did* find him attractive. So, what then? They were both single. What was the problem?

He rolled his eyes. He didn't have a clue. He'd never understand women. But then, does anyone?

So, what was he suppose to do now? Just sit and wait? See if she changed her mind? He shook his head. No. That just wouldn't do. He'd waited for too long to sit around for this opportunity to present itself. Kate was worth all the effort he could give.

Then a though occurred to him. Could she be at all worried about their age difference? He'd dated older women in the past and it hadn't really been an issue. Of course, he wasn't dating those other women with a future in mind. He was really just dating them to pass the time. With Kate, he was serious. Dead serious. Maybe for her the issue of their age difference was a big deal? She did say she thought of herself as 'older.'

He didn't get it. Who cared how old they were? Well, maybe she did. And he was just going to have to change her mind and convince her that it didn't matter. It didn't matter at all.

He pressed on the gas pedal and felt the car surge forward. He now knew where he was headed. Riley made a left and drove toward the pool.

He needed to swim some laps...lots of them. Maybe pure exhaustion would rid his mind of Kate. He rolled his eyes, knowing no amount of exhaustion, or anything else for that matter, would erase thoughts of Kate from his mind.

Kate went over and over the conversation she had with Riley. It seemed she couldn't stop thinking about it. Regardless, she knew anything he was suggesting was completely out of the question.

She was going to rely on the fact that Riley was young and would soon forget what he'd said to her. He was going to forget all about his feelings for her and until that happened; Kate was going to stay just out of his reach. Sure, it might prove to be difficult what with him picking up her daughter each morning, but she could handle that. She would make sure Hadley was ready each morning so that she could shuffle her quickly out the door as Riley pulled in. Timing would be everything. As soon as she saw his car pull into the driveway, she'd usher Hadley out the door, give a cheery wave, then close the front door and get to work.

Of course, she realized she was using her daughter as a shield and frankly, she was okay with that. She wasn't the slightest bit opposed to using her daughter this way, particularly since Hadley was going to prevent her from having a very uncomfortable conversation.

Kate had it all worked out. Or so she thought.

Initially, the days went just as Kate had planned. When Riley arrived each morning, Kate made sure that Hadley was dressed and ready to leave for practice. She was pleasant to him, lest he think he'd done something to offend her. She would usher Hadley out the front door before Riley even got out of the car and wave cheerily from the porch. As they backed out of the driveway, she would simply turn and go back into the house and get to work.

Each day when she arrived at the pool after practice, Kate would arrive with her cell phone glued to her ear, either legitimately on a call with a client or just pretending to be, in case Riley was hanging around waiting for her to enter the area. Once there, Kate would be sure to sit with Brenda, Angela or some of the other moms and work her way into the conversation so she was unable to leave. She knew Riley wouldn't dream of pulling her away from those women just to have a private conversation with her.

Kate did everything she could to avoid being exposed and vulnerable so Riley wouldn't have the opportunity to corner her. The end of practice was proving to be somewhat more of a challenge. Kate was polite and pleasant, waving to Riley if he caught her eye but swiftly turning her attention to something or someone else. Ideally, she wanted to snatch Hadley immediately after practice and head for home before running into Riley but that was proving to be more and more difficult with each passing day. Because Riley stayed at the pool nearly every day after practice, Hadley wanted to do the same. Of course, this left Kate with the impossible task of figuring out a way to get Hadley away from Riley in order to tell her it was time to go home. Since Hadley was never far from Riley and Kate didn't want to be far from other people, she found she had to catch Hadley's eye or wait for her to come to where she sat and forage for snacks.

Hadley, showing a streak of brilliance in her desperation to stay at the pool with Riley, simply began to simply get snacks from other kids' bags instead of coming to see her mother. It seems she knew her mother would snatch her up the minute she got close, thereby having to leave.

Kate felt certain she could continue like this all summer long.

And she couldn't have been more wrong.

Chapter 10

Riley continued to show up at Kate's house each morning to pick up Hadley. With each passing day, he got more and more frustrated. He knew *exactly* what she was doing and unless he did something bold and crazy, she was going to continue to avoid him all summer. He couldn't let that happen. He needed to talk to her.

After about a week, he'd had enough. He'd tried to speak to her at the pool several times but each time he looked for her, she was either engrossed in a conversation with someone or had her damn cell phone glued to her ear. After each day's practice, he hoped she'd stay for awhile with Hadley but most days, before he'd even cleaned up all the swim team equipment, they were gone.

His impatience was wearing thin. Desperate times called for desperate measures. And today? Well, he was pretty desperate.

He pulled into Kate's driveway to find Hadley sitting on the front porch next to her mother. Hadley was bouncing up and down on the concrete, clearly excited to head to the pool. God that kid loved to swim.

Just as he was pulling in, he saw Kate stand up and give Hadley a hug and then nudge her toward his car. *Oh no,* he thought.

He put the car in park and then got out of car, striding purposefully toward the front porch.

"Riley!"

"Hey kiddo," he replied, tugging on the goggles that were dangling around her neck. "You ready to go?"

She nodded.

"Why don't you climb in?" He said, nodding his head toward the car. "I'll be right there. I just want to talk to your mom." He looked at Kate as he said this and noticed the color drain from her face. Her eyes opened in surprise at being caught like this and Riley had to suppress a grin. He watched as Hadley climbed into the backseat of his Corolla. Once she closed the door and was out of earshot, he turned to Kate.

"I know what you're doing, Kate," he said. His lips worked their way into a tiny smile. "You're avoiding me. Why is that?"

Kate looked over his shoulder, down at the ground, and then at the planter on the front porch in order to stall. "Avoiding you? I'm not avoiding you. I see you every day, Riley."

"Yes. You do see me. And I see you. But you don't talk to me, and you haven't talked to me in over a week."

"We're talking now."

"And we're going to talk more…later."

"Excuse me?" Kate said, clearly surprised at the haughtiness she heard.

"I said, we're going to talk later." His voice softened. "Kate, I need to talk to you, all right? Please?"

Finally, Kate looked at him and saw the pleading look in his eyes. Her resolve weakened and she nodded. "Hadley's got a play date over at Sarah Wellington's house later. Why don't you come over later this afternoon? We can talk then."

Riley nodded, then turned toward his car. When his back was turned, he smiled; pleased with himself and knowing he was one step closer to Kate. He got in the car, waved to her, then headed to practice.

Two hours later, Kate showed up at practice without a cell phone glued to her ear, knowing it no longer served any purpose. Riley was going to swing by later and they were going to have the conversation that she'd managed to avoid for the better part of a week. There was really no sense in playing the "too busy to talk" card now. Her ruse had failed. She waived to Riley and then caught Hadley's eye and motioned to her wrist, telling her that it was time to go. Hadley made a pouty face, then reluctantly swam over to the ladder and climbed out of the pool.

Kate wrapped her in a towel, said a few goodbyes then loaded Hadley and all her stuff in the car. As they drove home, Hadley chatted incessantly about the day's practice. Kate's mind was elsewhere; specifically it was focused on the fact that Riley was coming to her home later in the day. Still, she managed to nod and occasionally "mmm-hmmm" as Hadley spoke.

When they arrived home, Kate stopped the car and rolled down the passenger side window, allowing Hadley to grab the mail. Hadley put what Kate felt certain were mostly bills in her lap and then they

A Ripple in the Water

pulled into the driveway. As Kate pushed the button to open the garage door, Hadley leapt out of the car and ran into the house to get changed. "What time can I go to Sarah's?" She yelled over her shoulder, barely slowing down to hear her mother's response.

"Three o'clock." Kate replied, rifling through the mail as she slowly walked into the house. "I want you to eat something before we go. Hadley? Hadley!" She stood at the bottom of the stairs waiting for a response.

"I heard you! Geez!" Hadley's voice was muffled and Kate immediately knew her daughter was buried in her closet, trying to find just the right outfit to wear. She sighed, realizing with dismay that appearance was already important to her seven year old and wondered what she would be like at sixteen!

She walked into the kitchen and placed her pocketbook on the counter. She took Hadley's wet towel and hung it on the back porch to dry, then came back in to grab a soda for herself. She opened the can and took a long sip, then surveyed the fridge, trying to determine what she could make for lunch.

Though Hadley was frequently being invited over to friends' houses, it was Sarah that Kate was particularly fond of, for purely selfish reasons. Sarah's mother, Bethany, was perhaps Kate's closest friend. Unlike her friendship with Wendy, which had developed as a result of her personal tragedy, Kate and Bethany had been friends for years now, a friendship that was based on common interests and of course, having girls that were the same age. That factor alone was enough to seal their friendship forever.

As Sarah and Hadley became friends, both Kate and Bethany had encouraged play dates over the years, which only further cemented their friendship. When one of them dropped off a child, coffee or wine (depending on the time of day) would be ready or opened as the case may be, and the children would disappear into their respective homes and the moms would sit in the kitchen and have "girl-time." Kate was more than happy to have Sarah over to her house or bring Hadley over to Bethany's because it meant she got to spend some time with her closest friend. Today, Kate would drop off Hadley, rush home and try to get some cleaning done, then return later for pick-up and a glass of two or wine. Of course, thrown into the mix of all that would be a visit from Riley and the talk that she'd successfully avoided for more than a week, which, most likely meant that her visit with Bethany would require the consumption of two (Or possibly more) glasses of wine. Kate desperately needed to talk to Bethany – she just wasn't sure she could actually get the words to come out of her mouth.

Hadley came roaring into the kitchen. "What time is it?"

Kate looked at the clock above the sink. "It's two o'clock. Why don't we make some lunch and then I'll bring you to Sarah's, all right?"

"Fine," Hadley said, sitting down at the table with such force that Kate knew instantly she was impatient and annoyed.

"Look, you're not going over there for an hour. You gotta eat, right?"

Hadley sighed heavily, not wanting to see the logic in her mother's statement. "I guess."

Kate chuckled and patted her daughter on the head. "I'll make you a sandwich."

"Okaaaay," Hadley said, resigning herself to the fact that her mother wouldn't drive her to her play date until she ate something.

Kate worked silently making Hadley's lunch. When she placed it in front of her, she practically inhaled it. She smiled, knowing how much exercise swimming was. Their grocery bill practically doubled during swim season since Hadley ate pretty much non-stop. Once lunch was cleaned up, Hadley gathered the items she wanted to bring to Sarah's house – a board game, a Barbie doll, her DSI and some plastic jewels – and loaded them in one of Kate's old pocketbooks, which Hadley now used as her own. Kate had to chuckle at the assortment of items she was bringing to her friend's house. She had no idea what in the world Hadley and Sarah were going to do with those particular items but she figured they'd come up with something creative.

She drove the short trip to Sarah's house, spoke to Bethany for a moment and made the promise to return later for pick-up and girl time. She then headed home, anxious to begin to clean Hadley's room. Once she started though, she found that she desperately needed to give the room a much more thorough cleaning. She grabbed some of the cleaning wipes from the bathroom and began to wipe every surface in the room. Once that was completed, Kate noticed Hadley's hand prints on the door and the mirror, so she wiped off the door, then grabbed some Windex to clean off the mirror. From that point, it was a slippery slope and before Kate knew it, she was on her knees cleaning the baseboards of Hadley's room with the Lysol wipes, which, she thought, was one of the greatest inventions ever. She used them for practically everything finding they managed to take handprints, dirt, and dried food off nearly every surface. Once she felt she'd wiped off every surface in Hadley's room, she stood up and surveyed the room, feeling pleased she'd found the time to clean at least one room in the house thoroughly. Without thinking, she took the wipe in her hand and rubbed it across her forehead, trying to rid her face of the sweat she'd worked up while cleaning. Almost the instant it touched her forehead, she realized what she had done. She walked into the bathroom to wash her face, unsure of what effect Lysol would have on her pores. Just as she'd splashed the water on to her face, she heard the doorbell ring.

"Crap," she said, reaching for a towel. She rubbed her face as she walked downstairs and toward the front door. She felt a sense of trepidation knowing who was on the other side of the door and what they he wanted to talk about.

She sighed softly, then pulled open the door.

Chapter 11

Riley walked in to the house and Kate closed the door softly behind him. He headed into the living room and sat down heavily on the couch. He leaned back as though waiting for her to speak.

Kate sat down across from him and took a deep breath. "Riley, look-"

"Are you embarrassed by me or something?"

She sat up, startled by the question. "Embarassed by you? Why would you think that?"

"Look, I know what you've been doing for the past week. You've done a great job of avoiding me. It's like you don't want to be seen with me."

"That is absolutely not the case." She sighed heavily. "I just wanted to give you the space to think about that you said and maybe...I don't know, forget about it?

"Why would I want to forget about what I said to you?" He looked at her completely aghast at what she'd suggested.

"Riley, I'm sure what you said was in passing and maybe you feel something for me but I'm sure it will pass."

He turned his body so that he was facing her, one knee bent up on the couch. "Kate, what I'm feeling is not going to pass. Of that I am certain."

"Riley," she smiled gently. "I'm flattered. Really I am. But what you're suggesting is completely out of the question."

"Why? Why is it out of the question?"

"You don't think there's something a little....oh, I don't know, out of the ordinary with that I think you're suggesting?"

"How is two people being attracted to each other out of the ordinary." He paused and looked at her, tilting his head to one side. "You do find me attractive, don't you?"

Kate had to smile at him. She wished when she was his age she had the self-confidence to ask someone of the opposite sex *that* question. "Of course you're attractive Riley. Someone would have to be dead to not be attracted to you…"

"But…" he prompted.

"But, there's more to what you're suggesting than just being attracted to someone. There's common interests, having something to talk about. What could you and I possibly have to talk about?"

"I don't know," he huffed. "But at least give us the chance to find out."

She looked at him sternly. "Riley, it's more than that and you know it."

He sat still on the couch and stared at Kate.

"You're going to make me come right out and say it, aren't you?" She sighed.

He nodded, his eyes never leaving hers.

"Riley, you are nineteen years old. I'm thirty-two."

"And?" He looked so thoroughly confused, Kate had to suppress a smile at just how young and naïve he was.

"And I'm sure there are lots of people who'd take issue with you and I…er…spending time together. It's just not right."

"Why, exactly? Because of our ages? Who cares about our ages? Who cares what other people think?"

"Look, I know you think it's silly but it's reality. Maybe not your reality, but mine. People look at me differently because of my age and more importantly, because I have a child."

He nodded. "Look, people date people who are much older or younger than them all the time. Why should we be any different?"

Kate sat and stared at him, trying to figure out the best way to communicate societal rules and the double standard that existed.

"Ohhhh….I get it. It's because you're the older woman, right? Well, why should that matter?"

"Look, I don't expect you to understand. If a man dates someone younger, there are high-fives all around. If a woman does it, she's labeled a cougar. I don't like it anymore than you do but those are the rules and I for one am following them."

"Are you attracted to me?" He asked.

"What?" Kate felt a hint of color begin to slide up her neck.

"Are you attracted to me? If you can tell me you're not, I'll leave and never bring this up again."

"Riley, I…" Color now crept across her cheeks as the thought about exactly how very attracted she was to him. She tore her gaze from his and looked down into her lap.

"So, there is something there," he said, leaning forward and grinning like the Cheshire Cat.

"Just because there may or may not be something there doesn't mean we have to act on it," she chastised.

"Kate," he sighed heavily. "I can't not act on this. If you only knew what I was feeling, you'd understand."

Her gaze met his and what she saw nearly took her breath away. He was looking at her with such intensity that she knew this was no ordinary crush.

"Oh my god," she said.

He smiled. "I know, Kate. Believe me, I know." He reached up and took a stray lock of her hair and gently tucked it behind her hear. "So you see, there's no way I can stay away from you."

Kate had no idea how to respond. Her insides had turned to water and she was immensely thankful for the couch beneath her. She recalled the first day of swim practice - the first day she'd spotted Riley - and felt her stomach turn a flip-flop. This man who she couldn't take her eyes off of, who had driven her to distraction was seated here on her couch and telling her he had feelings for her that couldn't be ignored? There was a part of her that wanted to hurl herself into his arms but the more logical, realistic part of her kept vocalizing the fact that he was so much younger than she was and...

Oh, God, Wendy's son.

Riley sat beside her staring at her as though waiting for a response. Of course, she had none. She needed some time to let it all sink in. How was one supposed to respond to something like this? Where was a handbook when you needed it?

A sound emanated from between them, breaking her train of thought. She looked at Riley with a confused look on her face.

His face turned bright pink and he chuckled. "Sorry," he said, rubbing his stomach. "That was me."

"Why didn't you say anything?" She said reproachfully.

"I had more important things on my mind," he replied, grinning wickedly.

"Riley," she scolded, then jumped up and walked into the kitchen, thrilled to have the distraction. She opened the fridge and peered inside. "Let me make you something to eat. Let's see... I've got some leftover pizza, I can scramble some eggs, or I can make a cheese quesadilla. I'm afraid that's about it. Like I said, I'm not much of a cook."

Riley sensed their conversation had taken a detour. Though he wasn't happy about it, he was starving. Once that was taken care of, he'd steer the conversation back to what Kate had so deftly averted.

"Leftover pizza would be great."

"Okay, pizza it is, then." Kate took the plate of leftovers from the fridge and arranged them on a plate, put them in the microwave and pressed the reheat button. She stood in front of the microwave and watched the plate spin around within. Out of the corner of her eye, she watched as Riley stood up and walked over to the wall where she had hung several family pictures. He stopped in front of one of the pictures and leaned in for a closer look. The picture he had chosen to inspect was one of the last ones of Kate's family together. It had been taken about a month before Todd had been killed.

Riley looked at the picture for a few moments and then spoke. "Todd was a great guy. I really liked him."

"I did too."

She stepped toward the picture and leaned in to get a closer look. She felt the memory of the day the picture was taken and felt a wave of sadness roll over her. It was odd, she thought, that this picture hung in her home every day but it was only occasionally that looking at it would cause her to feel such raw sadness. She sighed softly, lifting her hand to touch the picture of her husband. "This was a great day. We spent the entire day together. I'm glad I have that memory of us."

The microwave beeped, signaling the food was ready and summarily changing the mood, for which Kate was glad. While she spent much time remembering her husband and their times together, she felt a bit of discomfort sharing something so intimate with Riley, particularly given their recent conversations. It felt almost to Kate as though she were cheating on her husband somehow.

She walked away from the pictures and retrieved the plate from inside the microwave and then placed it down in front of Riley, who had resumed his spot at the table. "Diet coke okay?"

"Sure." He picked up one slice of pizza and consumed in three bites. She laughed out loud watching him inhale the pizza.

"Slow down, slow down! You would think your mother doesn't feed you!"

"Sorry." He looked almost embarrassed. "I guess I was hungrier than I thought."

"I'm sure it's no different than Hadley. During swim season, it seems I can barely keep food in the house. You're all just burning everything off the moment you eat it."

Riley grinned, barely able to contain the mouthful of pizza he held in his mouth. He chewed then swallowed before speaking. "My mom always used to complain about how much I ate during swim season. I think she spends just as much time at the grocery store as she does at the pool."

The mention of Wendy combined with the memories from the photo on the wall made Kate feel thankful for all the help she was receiving and had received from both Wendy and Riley. It further made her realize that she was making the right decision where Riley was concerned. It just seemed wrong somehow to become involved with her friend's son.

"She is a great mother, and a great friend. I'll never forget how much she did for me when Todd was killed. She pretty much kept me functioning." She looked into the distance remembering all the time Wendy spent at her house after Todd's death.

Riley spoke softly and broke her out of her walk down memory lane. "God, I can't even imagine how awful it was for you and Hadley."

"It was just such a shock. You never expect to get that call. It's always someone else, never you." She paused, looking down into her lap. "You know...I honestly don't know where I'd be right now if it weren't for Wendy. She was the one that made me see that I had to go on...for Hadley. She was tough on me but she got me through it." She looked up at Riley and smiled. "Your mom is a very special person."

He nodded. "I know. I'm lucky to have her."

"Yes, you are." Kate reached over and patted his hand, then got up to busy herself, afraid of showing Riley the tears that were forming.

Riley turned in his seat, watching her as she walked across the kitchen. "And Hadley's lucky to have you."

Something in Riley's tone made Kate stop in her tracks. She slowly turned and looked at him. "Thanks," she whispered softly.

"I mean it. That kid loves you; that's for sure. She talks about

A Ripple in the Water

you non-stop the whole way to the pool and I mean *non-stop!*" He grinned, then slowly the smile faded as he continued. "Don't get me wrong...I'm sure she misses her dad but honestly? I think she'll be okay because she has you. It's like...." Riley's brow furrowed together and Kate watched as he struggled to find the right words. Finally, he looked up. "...you're able to fill the void her dad left. Does that make any sense? "

Kate felt certain she was standing in front of Riley, mouth agape. How was it that he was able to so exactly pinpoint her greatest fear and tell her something that would ease that fear? How could someone without children understand that your greatest fear as a parent was that you would somehow not be enough for them? That you would mess things up? In Kate's situation, her fear was sharper than most simply because of the absence of Hadley's father. Not only did she have the worries that nearly every parent had, she had the additional fear that somehow she wouldn't be enough for her daughter and that she'd grow up somehow lacking...in what exactly? Emotion? Support? Oh Hell, she had no idea; she just knew there were days that worry consumed her. What was shocking to her was that although she'd never vocalized her thoughts to Riley, or anyone for that matter, he had just come out with it, figuratively hitting the nail on the head.

She stared at him for just a moment as she realized that he understood her...at least this part of her. Surely that was something, wasn't it? Kate suddenly realized that if she were to tell him her fears, he would understand.

But how was it possible he was so perceptive? It was unsettling, for sure. And it was making her question herself. She shook her head. Yesterday, she's telling him about one of the most difficult times in her life and today it's as if he's reading the manual to her soul! How could some *kid* do that so easily?

But maybe that was just it. Maybe he wasn't 'just some kid' and maybe - just maybe - Kate needed to stop thinking of him like that. Maybe she needed to start thinking of him as something else. But what was she telling herself, exactly? Surely she wasn't saying she should think of him as her friend, or more than that, as Riley hoped. She felt a quiver in her belly just thinking about *that* possibility. She couldn't go there...or could she?

It was just as she allowed herself to ponder Riley's suggestion

85

and all of its implications that she felt a small part of herself release within her, giving her permission to do exactly what she'd initially decided against. She knew she needed to squelch that part of her before it took over. After all, she was fully on the fence now and if the wind blew in the right direction, she was going to fall off and land in the arms of Riley Morgan.

"It makes perfect sense, Riley. I'm actually shocked at how much sense you make not having kids of your own. It's like you know what's going on inside of my head." She sighed heavily. "Sometimes, though…I wonder if it's enough for her. Will she be okay with only one parent? Will she be okay without her father? God, most days, I'm a complete mess! There are days I don't know how I'll make it."

Riley stood up and slowly walked toward her. He reached for her hand and clasped it in his. "I don't think you're a mess at all."

Kate felt the warmth of skin on skin and though she knew exactly what it was, she was still compelled to look down and see that it was his hand holding hers. It was nearly twice the size of hers and she noticed how small and insignificant her own hand looked inside of his.

Her eyes trailed upward and she found herself staring into gorgeous green eyes, which were looking at her with the intensity he'd shown her earlier. There was no question, no hesitation, and in an instant, she knew exactly what he was feeling. She knew there would be no talking now. The talking would come later.

Riley was going to kiss her.

And she was going to let him.

"Riley, I…."

Her words caught in her throat and she found she couldn't speak. Riley lifted up her hand and gently opened it. He pressed her palm to his lips and gently kissed. She felt the warmth of his lips there and felt certain her knees were going to give out. He took her hand and placed it on the side of his face. The movement felt so natural that despite the fear welling inside of her, she left her hand there, moving her thumb back and forth over his lips. He kissed the tip of her thumb as it grazed his lips. Her eyes were locked on his and she found she was unable to look away.

He leaned closer to her, wrapping his arms around her waist to pull her closer to him. As his lips met hers, she was thankful for those strong arms since she'd lost all feeling in her legs. Without those arms, she was certain she would have fallen to the floor in a puddle. Desperate to pull him closer to her, she wrapped her hands around his neck and wound her fingers in his hair. Riley groaned and pulled her closer. She felt a moan escape her throat.

Somewhere in the back of her mind, there was a tiny voice telling her how wrong this was. She tried to ignore it and relish the feeling of her body pressed against his. But the voice persisted. It became stronger and stronger until she could no longer ignore it. She pulled away from Riley and held him at arm's length. "Wait," she said. She was out of breath and needed to think. Just think.

"What's the matter?" He asked, gently tucking a piece of hair behind her ear.

"I...I don't know. It's just feels ....wrong somehow."

"Kate," Riley whispered. "What I'm feeling isn't wrong. What you're feeling isn't wrong."

She took a step back, moving away from his hand that was still caressing the side of her face. "Riley, I...I just need a moment here."

Riley sighed softly and dropped his hands back to his sides, then walked over to the table to sit down. Kate wrapped her arms around her torso and leaned back against the counter, doing her best to slow down her breathing. What the hell had just happened? Of course, she knew what had happened but she was mortified that her body had betrayed her, seeking the touch of this man who now sat at her table looking at her with concern all over his face.

"What are you thinking about?" He asked.

"Everything," she replied. "You kissed me!"

He nodded. "I did."

"And I kissed you back!" She gasped.

Riley grinned. "Yes. Yes, you did."

"Dammit, Riley. Get that smile off your face! This is serious!"

Suddenly, the smile was gone from his face. What she saw now was the most solemn expression she'd ever seen on him. "That's what I've been trying to tell you, Kate."

Riley stood up and once again walked toward her. She wanted to back up but felt the counter pressing against her lower back and knew there was nowhere for her to go. Not that her legs would have carried her anywhere. Her legs, like the rest of her body, were already beginning its betrayal of her, by responding in anticipation of

Riley's next touch. He stood in front of her, then took her hands in his.

"I know this is serious. Believe me, I know."

She looked up at him, fearful, yet excited she knew exactly what he was going to say. "What do you mean?"

"I mean I am very serious about you. I care about you...very much, in fact."

Kate's stomach did a flip-flop at hearing that. Her heart leapt at the thought that Riley had feelings for her but then, that little voice in the back of her head spoke up again, telling her that this was wrong. She knew she had to ignore her heart and listen to that voice, the voice of reason. "Riley, this is...all wrong. You cannot have feelings for me!"

"I don't see why it's wrong." He tossed her own word back at her and Kate felt a hint of irritation. "We're both adults who are attracted to each other."

"Oh, Riley," she said. He cringed, hearing the condescending tone of her voice. The moment the words were out of her mouth, she wanted to take them back. She knew her tone was laced with condescension and Riley didn't deserve that. "I'm sorry. I don't mean it to sound like that." She watched as his expression relaxed. "It's just that...my age..."

Suddenly, it dawned on him. "Ohhh. I get it. The age difference. That worries you?"

She nodded. "That's part of it, yes. But it's more than that. We're in different stages of our lives. You've got yours completely in front of you. Me? I've already been through so much."

"I realize that. But why should that mean we can't spend time with each other? "

"No." She sighed softly. "It's more than that."

"What then?" He asked.

"Riley, I don't know how to explain this to you without sounding like a parental figure. Believe me, I don't want to do that. But the fact of the matter is, you are still in college. You live with you parents-"

"Just for the summer," he interjected.

She nodded. "Just for the summer. But then you go back to school. You've got another year until you graduate. We're just at different places in our lives." Kate noticed that while he was still holding her hands, he'd stopped caressing her palms with his thumb.

"Kate. I'm well aware of all of that. But based on what just happened, I think we should at least spend some time together. Why can't we just do that?"

"Because it's so complicated," she replied, pulling her hands out of his grasp. He watched as she slowly crossed her arms over her chest.

"Why does it have to be complicated?"

"Look, I don't want it to be. It's not like I have any choice in the matter. It. Just. Is."

Riley could hear the frustration in her tone but he also vividly recalled how she'd responded to him when he kissed her. He knew there was no way he was going to give up – not after she'd responded to him in a way he'd been dreaming of for years. He took both her hands in his own and looked directly in her eyes when he spoke. "Kate, listen. You're talking about things like college and our age difference – things that don't really matter when two people care for each other."

Kate opened her mouth to speak but stopped when she felt his hand on her shoulder.

"Just wait," he said gently. "Let me say this."

She nodded. There was a small part of her that desperately wanted to hear what he was about to say. This part of her was hoping he'd come up with something that sounded completely sane and make her believe that it was okay for her to want to be in Riley's arms again. But, the sensible part of her knew that regardless of what he came up with, it wouldn't be enough to make her change her mind. It surprised to her to realize that even thinking she'd never be in Riley's arms again saddened her. Was there a part of her, growing larger every minute she spent with him, that wanted someone to make it all right for her to spend time with Riley? Surely not. Still, she stood beside him and listened to what he was about to say. She had to force herself to breathe.

"There are always hurdles. But that doesn't mean we should just give up and not even try. Think about it. If everyone who dated just gave up at the first sign of trouble, no one would ever get married or even be together for any length of time. Isn't that what it's all about? Working through those hurdles so two people can be together? Fighting for each other?"

"Riley, I see where you're going with this, but our hurdles aren't your ordinary garden-variety hurdles. Ours are not that our schedules are different or my laugh annoys you or we don't like the same movies. Our hurdles are more like mountains."

He looked at her pointedly. "They're only mountains because you're seeing them that way. The fact of the matter is, any time you date *anyone* you have no idea what you're going to run into. If you think about it, we already know what our issues are. That just might put us ahead of those couples that have no idea what they're going to encounter as they learn about each other. Our differences are laid out right in front of us, ready for us to deal with them...and work through them."

He finished and then stood there in front of her as though waiting for her to see the light. She wondered if she should simply shout, "Aha!" She thought better of it, knowing that Riley was very serious about his thoughts on the matter and as much as she hated to admit it, he did have a point. No one knew what issues they were going to face in the future. And there were always going to be issues. Was it fair to discount a possible relationship just because she thought they might not have anything in common? Was it fair of her to not even give Riley a chance simply based on her own opinion that they were in two different stages of their lives?

She stood in front of him thinking about all he'd said and Riley could tell she was wavering. He also knew he needed to convince her she was right before she realized he had no idea what the hell he was talking about. But screw it, he was desperate. He'd kissed her and wanted to kiss her again. He'd come up with a million theories if he thought it would convince her they should give this thing a shot.

Riley gently removed her hand from where she held it in the crook of her elbow and took it in his own. "If you were to meet someone who was older than me, would you immediately jump to what might happen in a year....or two years?"

She shook her head. As much as she hated to admit it, he did have a point. "No, I guess not."

"Then why can't we just do the same. I just want to spend some time with you. Is that so wrong?"

She looked at him pointedly while trying to figure out the best way to tell him what she was feeling. Her mouth opened and closed several times but nothing she thought of seemed to be the right response. She hated to admit it but Riley was making a certain amount of sense. As if he could see her wavering, he dove back in and continued.

"You don't actually think there's anything wrong with spending time together, do you?" In his mind, the question was purely rhetorical so he didn't wait for a response. Instead, he simply offered a solution. One that he felt certain Kate would agree to. "Let's just take it day by day and not worry about what may or may not happen in two weeks, two months, or two years."

She wanted to agree with him...desperately. Her body was telling her to agree to anything just so that she could be pressed against him again. But her mind was still worried about all the complications. It seemed that little voice wasn't done with her yet.

"Riley..." She sighed heavily, still unable to think clearly, what with him being so close to her and her body practically reaching for his. She wanted him, of that she was certain, but she wasn't quite ready to commit. She still had so many worries.

"Yeah?" He asked, his voice full of hope.

"What about your mother?" She whispered.

His eyebrows came together in confusion. "What about her?"

She practically rolled her eyes, then caught herself, once again knowing that it would be another condescending move. Instead, she exhaled slowly before she spoke. "I don't know if Wendy would like any of this." Kate removed her hand from his and pointed between the two of them.

"Why do you think that? I mean, not that it's any of her business or anything?"

"I don't know. I just have this feeling that she wouldn't approve. Wendy and I? We're friends...very good friends. And I'm just not sure what the rules are for dating your friend's son. It's not like there's a handbook or anything." She grinned, trying to make light of the situation.

"Kate, we're just going to spend some time together. There's nothing wrong with that. "

She grinned at him knowingly. "You say 'spend time together' as though we're going to be studying or something."

"So no studying?" He asked, grinning. "Did you have something else in mind?"

"Riley...." She said in a tone that indicated she was serious.

He chuckled. "Okay, I get it. You're worried about my mother. Honestly? I think she'd be fine with us dating but I really have no idea. Again, not that it's any of her business. But the two of you are friends. And I know she thinks the world of you so why would it matter if you spend time with me?" He raised his fingers and made quotes in the air.

"Well, maybe she wouldn't but don't you think we ought to at least say *something* to her?"

He sighed heavily. "Look, it's not that I don't want to tell her, it's just that I don't see why I should. I mean, if it was anyone else…say someone from school or something….I wouldn't say anything until I thought there was something…serious there." Almost as an afterthought, he muttered, "besides, she's just so involved in every other aspect of my life. I'd like to keep one thing out of her reach."

He looked up to find Kate staring at him knowingly. Wendy's involvement in her kids' lives was something that was much discussed amongst their group of friends. They'd all giggled about it and laughed it off but now, seeing Riley's frustration, Kate couldn't help but feel a twinge of sympathy for someone his age who wanted a bit of privacy from his mother. He hadn't lived at home for nearly three years yet his mother was still heavily involved in nearly every aspect of his life. Wasn't he entitled to just one area to himself away from his mother's eyes?

Riley stood in front of her and turned his head to the side while he looked at her. "Tell you what," he said, formulating an idea in his head. "Since you think other people might have a problem with our ages, let's just spend some time together and keep it between the two of us." He noticed her raise her eyebrows. "Just hear me out. It's not like we're doing anything sinister here. I mean, I wouldn't normally tell my mother about someone I date so this is no different. If things get….I don't know, serious? We'll talk to her."

"I don't know, Riley. It seems like it's all just semantics. Whatever you want to call it, I still don't think it's a good thing."

He sighed. "Look, let's just continue the way things are with me picking up Hadley for practice. If you come to the pool and hang out, great. If I can come over and spend some time with you, even better. If things progress beyond that, and I hope they do," he grinned at her, "then we'll talk to my mother. Does that sound fair?"

Kate sighed heavily. "I'm not entirely sure I'm comfortable with this, but I will say that when I hear you say it like that, it does sound reasonable."

He grinned. "Well, it is. We're just two friends who are spending time with one another, okay?"

Kate still felt a good bit of apprehension but she so desperately wanted to think that this would be all right—that she could spend time with Riley and not have any fallout. Who wouldn't want to spend time with him? But could it be that easy? Could they just spend time together and "see how it goes?" Was that even possible?

She knew beyond a shadow of a doubt that she was going to find out exactly what was possible. Kate looked up at him and grinned. "Are you sure you should major in finance?"

He looked at her with an expression of confusion. Given her abrupt change of subject, Riley thought she might be losing her mind. "Huh? Why?"

"Because you'd make a great attorney. I'll bet you can argue— and win—anything you set your mind to."

"Only if it's something very important to me." Riley said, grasping her hand once again.

Kate looked down at their clasped hands and then allowed her gaze to travel upward to meet Riley's gaze. She sighed softly, feeling her resolve weakening. "I can't believe I'm going say this."

"But," Riley prodded.

"But," she said, meeting his steady gaze. "You win. Let's take it day by day and see how it goes."

"Deal."

"But Riley?"

"Yeah?"

"You've got to promise me something."

"Anything."

Kate saw the intensity in his eyes and it made her heart melt a bit. "We talk to you mother as soon as I feel it's necessary. I don't want to hide anything from her, all right?"

He nodded, then leaned forward and kissed her softly. "So where do we go from here?"

She shrugged. "I guess we just take it day by day."

"Day by day it is," he said, grinning at her.

Chapter 12

Kate lifted her hand to lips, thinking of Riley's kiss earlier. The feeling of his lips against hers seemed to linger and she was unable to erase the memory from her mind—not that she wanted to. She and Riley had spent the better part of the afternoon together, sitting in her living room talking. Although she'd had a wonderful afternoon with him, she was still reeling from the fact that they seemed so at ease with each other. There were none of the awkward silences that she had been afraid of. What had also been surprising was that they didn't spend the afternoon talking about Hadley. Sure, she came up periodically, but most of their conversation was about their interests, movies, and pretty much all the stuff any two people might talk about as they were getting to know one another.

She grinned, thinking of Riley's hand as it rested on her thigh this afternoon. As they'd talked, he'd gently squeeze her kneecap as though letting her know he was listening. Kate loved feeling the warmth of his hand on her skin and even found if she focused on that feeling, she would lose her train of thought, a fact Riley picked up one very early in their conversation and used to his advantage. Although she liked the distraction his hand gave her, she also found she felt a little bit like she was losing her mind since she was practically incoherent when his fingers caressed the delicate skin on the inside of her knee. It wasn't long before Kate placed her hand on top of his so that she'd be able to complete a sentence. They'd chuckled about it, each enjoying the affect one had on the other. From that point on, Kate's hand rested on top of Riley's.

As the afternoon wore on, Kate was surprised – very surprised, actually - to find out they had much in common. It was one of her concerns that had been erased the more she discovered about Riley. Earlier, she had been certain the two of them would have nothing in common and now she knew that her assumption was solely based on their age difference. She was pleased to discover her initial assessment couldn't be further from the truth. Kate discovered that she and Riley enjoyed the same music, both favoring music from the

80's as opposed to some of the cookie-cutter pop stuff that was on the radio currently. When Riley shared his taste in music with Kate, she initially didn't believe him, thinking he was only agreeing with her to prove that they had so much in common. Kate even went so far as to take Riley's IPOD from him and rifle through his playlists. Riley was grinning at her smugly when she handed back the IPOD which was, in fact, practically a mirror image of her own.

It wasn't just music they had in common; there were other things as well. As they spoke, Kate learned that she and Riley shared many common interests. They were both planted in front of the TV for Survivor and turned to Wolf Blitzer for their news. They'd both been glued to TV soaking in every possible detail regarding the Amanda Knox trial and were now thrilled that she'd been exonerated. The Today show was a favorite of theirs as was anything having to do with Law and Order- both spent many a Tuesday glued to the TV set for the marathon that occurred each and every week.

Kate felt herself becoming more and more at ease with Riley as they discovered all of their mutual interests. She hated to admit it to herself but there was a part of her that had hoped there would only be a sexual chemistry between them. That was not the case. She found she could talk to him and share her opinions with him on any number of topics.

And they'd laughed...Oh, how they'd laughed. For the first time in nearly a year, Kate had laughed without immediately feeling guilty afterward. She actually felt as though she were healing. And she was afraid she had Riley to thank for that...very afraid, actually.

This, of course, brought her worries to a whole new level. If there was only a sexual attraction, it would be easy to dismiss it as such. If she were to develop feelings for him...well, that was an entirely different animal altogether. Were to? Oh, who was she kidding? She'd spent one afternoon with him and already had feelings for him.

She sighed and tried to push those thoughts out of her mind. She needed to do what she and Riley had agreed on – take it day by day. No need to mess up something fun with a bunch of feelings. Because that's what this was – just something fun. She was happy, and for the first time in a very long time, she felt like her old self again. When it was time to pick up her daughter, she was surprised to realize she was sad to have her time with Riley come to an end. There was no telling when they'd have time like that again.

Riley had kissed her again as he left her home. It was a bit of a surprise to Kate since they'd not kissed all afternoon. When he reached for her just before she opened the door, Kate once again felt a rush unlike anything she'd ever felt before. When he released her, she couldn't help but wonder if it would always be like that. If so, she'd need to lean against something each time he kissed in order to regain her balance or she'd fall to the floor in a delicious heap. In spite of all this, she still couldn't help but feel that she and Riley were doing something not entirely right. She knew she needed to talk to someone about it, so she figured she'd kill two birds – pick up Hadley and talk to her best friend.

She closed the door softly behind him, then watched him through the blinds as he walked to his car and then drove away. She turned away from the door and, noticing the time, quickly grabbed her pocketbook and drove the short distance to get her daughter.

She pulled up to the house and walked up to the front door. She rang the bell and simultaneously pushed opened the door. "Bethany?" She called. "It's me!"

"In the kitchen!" Came the reply.

Kate walked the familiar path to toward the kitchen, noticing – as she did every time she was here - the stunning details of this beautiful home. Directly in front of the front door was a staircase that wound up to the second level. To her right was a beautifully appointed library with a fireplace that looked as though it got used often. There were bookshelves lining one wall from ceiling to floor and two luxurious chairs on either side of the window. On the other side of the room sat a small desk with a matching chair neatly tucked in. The desk was clean and neat with all the pens placed in an ornate holder on the corner.

She continued down the hall into the kitchen, passing a large dining room on her left. Kate had been to the home too many times to count yet each and every time she came, she found herself speechless. The house was beyond anything she'd ever imagined both in size and décor. Bethany's husband was a leading cardiologist, thus providing them with the income to afford such a large home. Of course, one would never know that Bethany had such wealth. She was the most down-to-earth person Kate had ever met, which was one of the many reasons the two of them hit it off the moment they met. She never flaunted her money as Kate had seen others do. In fact, she almost seemed to want to hide it for fear of making others feel uncomfortable. Bethany seemed to have almost an apologetic air to her when Kate came to the house; almost as though she were embarrassed by the wealth that surrounded her.

Kate reached the kitchen and saw her friend hunched over a tiny piece of pottery. "Hey, whatcha got there?"

Bethany stood up and gave Kate a broad smile. "Something I picked up at Michael's," she said. "Though I had hoped Emily would want to work on it with me. Apparently, sitting in her room texting is waaaay more fun than hanging out with mom."

"Sorry."

Bethany shrugged. "It's all right. I expected it once she hit the teen years. I'm just really looking forward to when she comes back around to liking me again."

"She will," Kate nodded encouragingly. "She will."

Bethany motioned for Kate to sit down at the bar, which was directly in front of the sink and held four tall chairs. Kate pulled out the one on the end and sat down, placing her pocketbook on chair beside her. The kitchen, like the rest of the house, was extremely well-appointed. This room had stainless steel appliances, two ovens, and granite countertops. Kate looked around for a moment, trying to take it all in. Though she'd been here numerous times, she'd grown accustomed to seeing changes each time she came. Despite having four children, Bethany somehow managed to change the décor of her home frequently. Today was no different and Kate looked around, trying to determine what had been done recently.

"Something's different in here."

Bethany looked at her, pleased that she'd noticed. "I did the walls. Do you like it?"

Kate stood up and inspected the walls closely. They were faux painted with a terracotta color that brought out the color of the tiles in the floor. The effect was stunning.

Kate nodded as she rubbed one of the walls gently with her fingertips. "It's beautiful. Faux painting, right?"

"Yeah. I wasn't sure about the color but I think it works."

"Gosh, yes! It looks wonderful! I've always thought I wanted to have something like this done in my bathroom. Who did you use?"

"I did it myself."

Kate turned to look at her friend, mouth agape. "Are you serious? Bethany, this is gorgeous!"

"Really?" Bethany asked. "You think so?"

"I do," Kate nodded. "I really do."

Kate inspected the wall in front of her, rubbing it and loving the feel of the rough patches. Bethany never ceased to amaze her. Of all people, Bethany was someone who could afford to just hire someone to come in and do whatever she wanted. But that was never the case. Bethany had never had someone come in to clean or cook, even when her children were young. The painting was just another example of Bethany wanting to do something herself rather than hire someone to do it. Kate felt a sense of admiration towards her.

Bethany watched as Kate felt the walls of the kitchen, then walk around looking at the kitchen from every angle, nodding and grinning as she took in every nook and cranny. "Really amazing," Kate said, more to herself. Once she'd finished her inspection, she once again sat down in chair at the bar.

"So, how are you? Gosh, I feel like it's been forever since we've had a chance to sit and talk! We need to get these kids of ours to set up more play dates."

"We could ground them if they don't schedule one each week. You know, teach them how to plan ahead?"

Bethany laughed out loud. "I'm totally in. You want a glass of wine? Of course you do." She turned around to face the tiny wine rack on the counter. "Red? White?"

"Whatever you have open."

"Uh-oh," Bethany replied, turning around "I know that sound. What's going on? Hadley's fine, right?"

Kate nodded quickly, eager to erase the worry that came swiftly across her friend's face. "No, no. She's fine. It's me. I've got this teeny-tiny problem…well, it's not a problem really…more of an issue…well, not even an issue, sort of a dilemma….no, no that's not it…"

"Kate…honey? What is going on?" Bethany came over and leaned across the counter in front of Kate.

"I don't even know where to begin," Kate said, sighing heavily. "Beth, let me ask you something."

"Shoot."

"What would you think about me spending time

98

with….someone…" Kate watched Bethany's expression for any hint of disapproval but, for the moment at least, Bethany had no idea what Kate was trying to tell her. "Someone of the opposite sex."

Realization dawned on Bethany. "Ohhhhhhh….," she said. "You've got man problems. We definitely need some wine for this." She turned back toward the wine rack, grabbed two glasses, the wine opener, then poured each of them a very full glass of wine. She placed one glass in front of Kate, then crossed her arms over her chest and tilted her head sideways as though she were in deep thought.

"And as far as your question? No. It is not inappropriate for you to date someone." Bethany came around the counter and stood in front of Kate, placing her hands on her shoulders. "You've been a very good widow for a very long year. No one would ever think badly of you if you were to date someone."

She re-corked the bottle, then moved Kate's pocketbook out of the chair and sat down beside her.

Kate, eyeing the overfull glasses of wine, raised an eyebrow. "You sure you got enough in the glass? I mean, you might be able to fit another drop or two."

"Saves me from getting up again," she replied, waving her hand around dismissively. "Now, tell me all the juicy details."

"I don't even know where to begin! And for the record, there aren't any juicy details….yet." Kate smiled like a Cheshire cat.

Bethany clapped her hands together. "Now we're talking. Just take it from the beginning, all right?" She took a sip from her glass of wine, her eyes never leaving Kate's.

Kate nodded. What was the beginning, anyway? She thought that perhaps the first time she saw Riley would be a good place to start. As she recalled him standing on the side of the pool wearing his tiny swimsuit, she felt the color rise to her cheeks. She took a deep breath before confiding in her friend.

"There's this guy…and he's gorgeous. I mean, drop dead, traffic-stopping gorgeous. I saw him and couldn't take my eyes off of him! Bethany, I tell you, I've never reacted to anyone that way."

"He sounds delicious," she said, taking another sip of wine.

Kate nodded, "He is. So, we get to talking and it turns out he finds me attractive too. Apparently, he's found me attractive for some time and has asked to 'spend some time with me.' Bethany, I swear to God, I thought he was joking or something. I mean, he's gorgeous!"

"Oh, honey, why would that surprise you? You're beautiful!"

"Thanks," Kate replied. "But this guy is breathtaking. Totally not my level. But besides that, there's a whole laundry list of things that make this a bad idea. I mean, it's not enough that we find each other attractive. We're in completely different stages in our lives!"

"Oh, who gives a shit," she retorted, waving her hand around dismissively. "After what you've been through? You deserve to be happy…with whoever you choose to spend time with."

Hold onto that thought, Kate thought. "Here's the thing..," she paused for several moments. "He's much younger than me."

Bethany shrugged. "So?"

"He doesn't have any kids."

"Again, so? Has he met Hadley?"

Kate nodded.

"And how is he with her?"

Kate smiled thinking about Riley with Hadley. "He's wonderful with her. She listens to him, admires him, and hangs on his every word. It's amazing."

"All of this sounds great so I'm not seeing the problem."

"When I say he's younger than me, I mean *younger....* "

Bethany raised an eyebrow. "Define younger."

"He's still in college."

"Oh, wow. Really?" Bethany took a large sip from her glass. "He's not a freshman, is he?"

Kate shook her head. "Senior in the fall."

"Well, that's not so bad. That means he's what…twenty?"

"In a few weeks."

"Hmmm….I still don't see the problem. I mean, you're both aware of the age difference. You're not married. He's not married, right?" Bethany looked at Kate as though expecting the bomb to drop.

"No, he's not married."

"Okay, so you're both single and he's great with your kid. He's an adult and you're an adult but he's…what? Ten years younger than you?"

"Twelve," Kate corrected.

"Twelve," Bethany nodded her agreement. "But, I'm not seeing what the issue is. It sounds like he's a dream. How'd you meet him, anyway?"

Kate paused before speaking. "I met him at the pool."

"Our pool, really? When?"

"I noticed him the first day of swim practice."

"Wow. Where was I? How did I not notice him?"

Kate shrugged. "I'm sure you've noticed him. We all have."

"Okay, now I'm confused."

"Bethany," Kate paused, knowing that once she revealed who it was, things might be different. "He's the swim coach."

"The swim coach? But the swim coach is……Oh. My. GOD!"

"Exactly. So you see where my issue is."

"Riley Morgan? You and Riley?" Kate watched as Bethany's expression went from disbelief to one of pure delight. "Oh my GOD!"

"I know…I know," Kate said. "What am I going to do?"

"What do you mean? You're going to date him. That's what you're going to do!"

"But what about Wendy?" Kate cried.

Bethany looked as though she'd taken a wrong turn somewhere. "What about her?"

"Well, don't you think it's a bit weird for me to date her son? Don't you think she'd think it's weird?"

"Honey, Wendy loves you. Why would she mind if you dated her son? If anything, I think she'd be thrilled. She knows you're a great person, a great mother and a great friend. You'd be great to Riley. Surely that's all that matters."

"I don't know. She's just so protective of her kids. I worry that she'll be angry or upset…"

"Kate," Bethany said, placing her hand on top of Kate's. "I think Wendy would be thrilled to have you date her son. She loves you like a sister!"

Kate pondered that for just a moment or two. "You really think so?"

Bethany nodded. "I do. You're a wonderful, wonderful person that had a terrible loss. You've mourned for a year and now you've found someone who makes you happy. And this someone is great with your daughter? Why would you pass on that? Kate, honey, you deserve to be happy and if Riley makes you happy, then you should be with him."

"But what about when August comes? He's got one more year of school!"

"Why even worry about that? Just take it day by day. If the two of you are still into each other in August, you'll work it out. I really don't think either of you are the type to just forget a relationship but all you can do is live for each day. You of all people understand that sometimes, you only have today."

"God, you sound like Riley."

"Well," Bethany replied, tossing her hair back playfully. "Great minds think alike."

Kate sighed. "I still just don't know about this…"

"What is there to know? You're attracted to him…he's attracted to you. Why not...explore and see where things go?"

"But Wendy…."

Bethany looked confused. "Don't even think about her just yet. She's not going to go with you on your dates, is she?"

"Ha ha. You really don't think she'd have a problem with me dating Riley?"

Bethany shrugged. "I don't see why she would." Bethany began to count on her fingers. "She already likes you. You're one of her best friends. You're completely normal. If anything, I think she'd be happy Riley is choosing to date someone that she already knows. She doesn't have to worry that he's dating some freak."

"Bethany!"

"What?! It's true. There are some crazies out there. I would think Wendy would be thrilled that her son has chosen to spend time with someone who is completely and totally normal."

"But wouldn't it be kind of weird? I mean, if things progress…" Kate couldn't even bring herself to mention the possibility of where exactly things might go. If her body's response to kissing Riley were any indication, there was going to be some severe fireworks.

"Ohhhhh," Bethany replied, completely understanding where Kate was headed. "But come on. Surely she's used to meeting women Riley has slept with."

Kate raised her eyebrows, indicating her differing opinion.

"Look, I admit she treats him like he's a bit of a baby but she can't be completely oblivious to what he looks like and what affect he has on women! Good Lord, the man is GORGEOUS! And he's been at college for three years, out of her line of vision. She can't really think he's a virgin or anything! Can she?"

"I don't know. But I do know that I don't want Wendy to think I'm doing anything sinister here. "

"Sinister? You don't really think that, do you?"

"I honestly don't know. I'm just terrified of pissing her off. She's one of my best friends."

Bethany leaned forward. "Honey, if she's one of your best friends, then she'll want you to be happy, even if it's with her son."

"Her much *younger* son." Kate stated.

"Oh, who give a shit how old he is." Kate looked up at her, startled at the vehemence in her tone. "It's just a number. All that matters is how you treat each other and based on what I know about the two of you, you're both going to be great to each other."

Kate still wasn't entirely convinced. As much as she wanted to explore these feelings for Riley, there was still a small part of her – and getting smaller by the minute – that wondered if she were doing something wrong. "I just don't know..."

Bethany leaned forward just a bit and took Kate's hands in her own. "Look," she said, suddenly quite serious. "You've suffered more than anyone I know. You're husband *died,* for Christ sakes. You've been dealing with your own loss at the same time you've been trying to raise your daughter and run your business. I can't think of anyone more deserving of a bit of happiness in their life and if Riley manages to give you one ounce of what you deserve, well, I for one will be thrilled."

"Thanks, Beth."

She shook her head. "Don't you dare thank me. You deserve it all, honey."

Kate felt much better for having confided in Bethany and told her so.

"So what do you think you're going to do?" Bethany asked.

"Well," Kate replied, smiling hesitantly. "I think I might have to take a chance with him."

"Good for you!" Bethany lifted up her glass to toast Kate and then took a long sip of wine. "I think Riley will be good for you. I for one would love to see the old Kate again."

"What do you mean?" Kate asked.

"You know. The one that smiled and laughed all the time. I miss her."

Kate nodded. "I miss her too." And that was when it hit her. She smiled when she was with Riley.

She thought of the time she'd spent with Riley and remembered the laughter. It had felt so foreign to her but she hadn't realized it was so noticeable to others. Truthfully, she felt as though she'd hidden her feelings from the outside world. Apparently she had not. Well, hopefully now there would be more laughter; much more laughter. Kate carefully took a sip from the still full glass in front of her, then placed it back on the counter gently. Her clumsy hands had broken more than one wine glass on Bethany's granite countertops.

"So now that we've talked about my problems for an hour..." Kate laughed.

"Oh, stop," Bethany replied. "What are friends for?"

"How are things with you? How's Peter?"

"Well, when I do see him, he appears to be fine." She replied dryly.

Kate picked up on the hint of sarcasm in Bethany's response and knew immediately that nothing had changed since the last time she'd been here. She knew from experience that Peter's hours were a source of much irritation for Bethany. Because he was a very successful cardiologist, he worked practically all the time, leaving her on her own for any and all family-related activities. Bethany ran herself ragged trying to make it to every soccer practice, swim meet, parent-teacher conference, and dance recital. On top of all that, Bethany tried to do volunteer at her kids' schools whenever possible. She did all of this without any help from Peter, who was consumed with his patients. While Bethany was thankful she was able to stay home with their four children and understood that her husband was literally saving lives, she frequently confided in Kate that she wished he had a more "normal" job and was able to spend time with his children. It was a constant battle between them, one that Kate had no answers for. She could only provide a shoulder for her to cry on and two ears for her to vent into, so she did that, as often as she could.

"He's still working a ton, huh?" Kate asked.

"Yeah. It never ends. Just when one patient gets better and I think he'll finally make it to a soccer game or something, another patient is just waiting to have Dr. Wellington look at his case." Bethany said 'Dr. Wellington' as though the name itself was worthy of the utmost respect.

104

"And of course, Peter would never consider saying no." She sighed. "The kids are going to be adults and he's going to have missed all of it. Why even have kids if you're not going to spend time with them?"

Kate knew the question was rhetorical so she sat still and waited for Bethany to continue.

"I wish there was some way to find a balance in all of this but every time I bring it up, Peter goes to the extreme. 'What do you want me to do Beth, quit my job? I'll do it, if that's what *you* want. But then we'll have to give all of this up and move into some tiny three bedroom house' he'll say – as if that's *exactly* what I mean." She rolled her eyes. "I mean, does he really need to go there? It's like he's saying if he works sixty hours instead of the hundred or so he pulls in now, we'll be bankrupt. Christ. I give up."

"I'm sorry, Beth."

She nodded. "I'm just thankful I have friends like you who'll listen to me bitch about my life."

Kate smiled. "You know I'm always willing to listen to you bitch. I just wish there was more I could do."

"Could you manage to smack some sense into my husband?"

"If you can't do it, I doubt I can."

Bethany sighed, then took another sip from her glass and glanced at the digital clock on the stove. "Oh my god! Is that what time it is? Shoot, I've got to pick up Brandon from Kyle's house! Let me see if I can round up the girls."

Bethany left the kitchen and Kate heard her walk up the stairs. She smiled as she heard the moans of two seven year olds who didn't want to be separated. Kate took another sip of her wine and looked around the kitchen. She noticed a family portrait on the other side of the room and walked over to get a closer look.

The entire Wellington family, including their golden retriever, was seated on the sand in front of the ocean. All of them were barefoot and wearing jeans with a white shirt which was striking against the golden fur of their dog. The effect was simple yet beautiful. Kate made a mental note to ask Bethany who the photographer was.

This was really the first time Kate had seen the family all together at once, and even now it was only in a photograph. Actually, she could count on one hand the number of times she'd seen

Bethany's husband, Peter. Kate felt a flash of sadness for her friend, knowing she had these beautiful children yet practically had to force her husband to spend time with them. She knew his schedule was hectic, given that he was in high demand, but Kate wondered why he couldn't somehow manage to squeeze in time with his kids. But Dr. Peter Wellington was one of the best. If you or someone you loved had a problem with their heart, you wanted him. Period.

Kate took a closer look at the photo and for the first time noticed how much Bethany's eldest daughter Emily looked like her father. She was nearly seventeen and had the same strong jaw-line and dark hair that her father had. Emily, however, in direct contrast to her father, had porcelain skin that made the nearly black hair one of her best features. It was smooth and shiny and hung to the middle of her back. She was a beautiful girl for sure, but there was something else there as well. Something a bit edgy; a bit rough. Perhaps it was the eyeliner put on a little too thick. Or maybe it was the smile that seemed a bit forced and didn't quite reach the eyes. Whatever it was, Kate could clearly see that Emily was either in the middle of, or just about to enter the throes of rebellion. At that moment, she was glad Hadley was only seven, although she felt a hint of dread knowing that it wouldn't be too long before she was facing the same thing. Teenagers rebel; it's what they do. Like a rite of passage or something.

After Emily, Bethany and Peter had two boys who were about eighteen months apart; Brandon was 14 and Jacob was 13. The boys looked like miniatures of their mother what with their light brown hair and blue eyes. The youngest, Sarah, was Hadley's age and also swam with the Dolphins. Sarah was also one of the few children Hadley played with during the school year since they were in the same grade and had for the past two years, had the same teacher. Sarah looked nothing like either parent. She had a head full of red, curly hair that seemed to have a mind of its own. Her difference in appearance from the other members of the family seemed to lead the path to her own independence. Bethany had often remarked how Sarah was unlike any of her other children, never wanting to do anything her older siblings did, rather choosing to forage her own way into sports and activities.

Kate heard Bethany's footsteps on the staircase and turned just as she re-entered the kitchen. "I love this picture, Beth. Who was the photographer?"

"One of the nurses that works with Peter."

"Really?"

Bethany nodded. "It seems she went to nursing school at the insistence of her parents but really wants to be a photographer." She pointed to the picture. "I think she's got a lot of talent. I don't know if I've ever managed to get all of us to sit still like that! I'll ask Peter for her card, if you want."

Kate nodded. "I'd love it."

"The girls are cleaning up the play room. They should be down in a minute."

"Was Hadley all right?"

Bethany waved her hand in a dismissive motion. "Gosh! Of course she was. She's never a problem. I wish my kids behaved as well as yours."

There was a hint of something in Bethany's tone that led Kate to believe the statement was more than just a flip comment. "What do you mean?" she asked, allowing a bit of concern to creep into her voice. "Sarah has never been anything but polite and well-mannered when she visits."

Bethany sighed. "Yeah, Sarah still minds her manners. It's the others I'm worried about. Emily especially."

"Really? I hope everything is all right?"

"I'm sure it will be. We've just had some issues lately. I'm hoping it's normal stuff…skipping school, sneaking a few sips out of the liquor cabinet. I'm worried, but I'm really hoping it's just growing pains."

"I'm sure it is. Really, Bethany, you have nothing to worry about. Emily's a great kid."

"Thanks for that, Kate. I'm doing the best I can, you know? This is just another thing I need to manage on my own what with Peter working all the time. I just hope this is a phase for her and I'm able to handle it."

Kate felt a twinge of sympathy for her friend. In a strange way, they were both raising their children alone. While Kate was raising her child alone because of a tragedy, Bethany was raising her children alone because her husband just wasn't there. For the moment, Kate wondered which was worse, having someone who could help you, but didn't or not having anyone at all.

She tried to sound reassuring when she spoke, but truthfully, she had no idea if Emily's behavior was normal or not. She just wasn't there yet since Hadley was only seven. "I'm sure it will be fine, Beth. Emily's got the support of her family. She's probably just testing out her boundaries."

Bethany sighed heavily. "I really want to believe that. You're right, though. She is a good kid. Maybe she is just testing me. I mean, what am I going to do? Lock her in her room? I guess to a certain extent, she's got to find her own way. She's practically an adult!"

Kate smiled at that and couldn't help but think of Riley. She supposed most parents did think of their children as adults when they reached eighteen. And Riley was nearly twenty. Maybe things weren't as bad as she initially thought.

Just then, Hadley walked into the kitchen, carrying her bag of treasures. She looked a bit rumpled which Kate correctly assumed was from playing all afternoon. She looked down and smiled at her daughter. "Well, hello there! Are you ready to go?"

Hadley only nodded and Kate knew she was exhausted. Between swimming all morning and then this play date, it would be an early night for her. Then Kate would have to get her up in the morning to do it all again. Minus the play date of course.

"You have all your stuff?' Kate asked. Hadley nodded. "All right, then. Let's go. What do you say?"

Hadley smiled at Bethany. "Thank you for having me."

"You are more than welcome. I'm glad you could come and play with Sarah." Bethany leaned down and gave Hadley a little squeeze.

"Thanks again," Kate said. "Hadley loves playing with Sarah."

"We'll do it again soon…and I'll see you in the morning?"

Kate nodded. "I'll be there a bit later. Riley picks up Hadley and takes her to practice so I can get some work done."

"Oh, that's right! I forgot about that!" She winked conspiratorially at Kate, then looked down at Hadley. "You are one lucky girl. Do you know that?"

Hadley grinned and nodded. "Riley's the BEST!"

Kate smiled at her daughter, then looked up at Bethany. "Well, on that note, I guess we'll head out. We'll talk more tomorrow. Thanks, Beth."

Bethany nodded and walked them to the front door, waving at them they got into the car. Hadley sat in the back seat as though she had been drugged. Kate had to smile. Hadley would refuse to admit she was tired even if she fell asleep on the five minute drive home, which of course, she would. Kate looked in the back seat and noticed Hadley's head leaning on the door. Her eyes were beginning to close ever so gently. She looked forward and began to drive home, anticipating having to carry Hadley into the house.

She drove home in silence – radio off, air conditioner on low – so that Hadley would fall asleep. Kate knew she needed to rest or she wouldn't be any good for practice in the morning. Although Kate hadn't yet fed her any dinner, she knew that Bethany had probably stuffed the girls with healthy snacks all afternoon. Besides, Hadley needed sleep more than she needed another grilled cheese sandwich.

Kate pulled into the driveway, making sure to ease the car gently to a stop. She turned around and smiled when she saw Hadley's curled up as best she could within the confines of the seatbelt. Kate got out of the car, careful to close the door softly, then walked around to the back of the car to get Hadley. She unbuckled her, then pulled her forward onto her shoulder and wrapped her legs around her waist. Hadley barely moved, which cause Kate to giggle.

"No, you're not tired at all," she whispered. She walked in through the garage, closed the door, then walked up the stairs to Hadley's room. "You're getting too big for this," Kate huffed as she reached the top step. On level ground once again, she walked slowly into Hadley's room and laid her gently on the bed. She took the pink, sparkly flip flops off Hadley's feet and tossed them to the floor. After covering her up with the comforter, she slowly crept out of the room backwards, careful not to wake her. When she reached the door, she stood there for a moment and just looked at her daughter. Like most parents, she had always been particularly fond of watching her daughter sleep. She looked perfectly angelic with her eyes closed and her breathing soft and regular. It was hard to believe that this angel lying there so peacefully was the same child who could sass and throw a hissy fit right along with the best of them when she didn't get her way.

Kate crept out of the room, closing the door softly behind her. She went downstairs and made her way into the kitchen. As she opened up the fridge and then the cabinets, she wondered if she were hungry or just bored. Deciding it was the latter; she closed the cabinets and allowed her gaze to drift toward her office. Since it was only seven o'clock, she could probably get some work done. At least she could return some emails and look at a few color schemes for Mrs. Windham. Kate felt a bit of stress work its way into her shoulders as she thought of her most difficult client. Mrs. Windham had strong ideas about what she wanted, the only problem was, she wasn't able to communicate them very effectively. Kate had repeatedly shown her sample after sample of fabric for the chairs she wanted to have re-upholstered but rather than give a definitive yes or so, the woman would offer little direction, choosing to use words like "maybe" and "close." Sometimes there wouldn't even be a word; there was more of a snort of groan, which only further added to Kate's stress. If only she would be given some direction, even a color that the woman liked, Kate would be able to satisfy her. Instead, Kate had absolutely no idea what the woman wanted and was spending more time on these chairs than she'd spend on entire rooms in the past.

Kate walked into her office and turned on the computer. While she waited for it to come to life, her mind wandered back to the afternoon spent with Riley. She smiled, enjoying the flutter in her belly each time she thought of him. She liked spending time with him and he made her laugh. Was that so wrong? She thought about what Bethany had said and it seemed to make sense. Surely she deserved to be happy after all that she'd been through. Still, though, she worried what others might think and how any sort of relationship with Riley other than one of friendship might ripple through their community. And she had no idea how anyone would react.

She felt a bit of boldness work its way into her thought process. Did it matter what anyone else thought ? She knew, though. It did matter. She had never been someone who could easily dismiss the criticisms of others. She'd always done whatever she could to stay on the sidelines and not ruffle any feathers. She was a vanilla type of girl, through and through. And this...whatever it was that was going on between her and Riley, was definitely of the rocky road variety.

She was still on the fence, despite her earlier confidence when speaking to Bethany. She wondered if she and Riley could spend time together and see how things progressed before they make it public knowledge. They didn't have to *hide* or anything. They just needed to keep it between the two of them until Kate was comfortable. She had to think of Hadley and what effect it might have on her. She nodded as she thought of it. It did make a certain amount of sense when she looked at it that way. She knew if she were to date anyone else, she would take her time before announcing her relationship to anyone, especially Hadley. She didn't want her to become attached to anyone only to have them disappear after a few weeks.

Of course, Riley was going to be leaving at the end of the summer. How would Hadley handle that? Kate sighed heavily realizing she could look at this any number of ways and fall on either side of the equation. She suddenly realized she was going to have to do something she'd never before done. She was going to throw all logic to the wayside and simply rely on her heart.

It was then she realized she'd made her decision. To hell with it. She wanted to spend time with Riley, she found him attractive, and he made her laugh. That was all she needed to know. They had almost two months before he had to leave for school and Kate was going to spend the summer enjoying her time with him.

Feeling a renewed energy, Kate sat down at her computer determined to get through her emails. She'd focus on Mrs. Windham's chair problem tomorrow morning after Riley picked up Hadley.

Riley....again a flutter in her belly as she thought of him...all six feet of him. Delicious, that's what he was. Kate knew she was going to taste every inch of him, savoring each moment of the summer. She grinned, then clicked on the first email.

Chapter 13

Wendy knew her son better than anyone so it was only logical that she would be the one to notice.

Riley was in love.

She knew this day would come and had looked forward to it – she only had sons and longed for the day when she'd have a daughter in law. And it went without saying that her daughter in law would be the perfect blend of beauty and intelligence. Wendy had fantasized about it for years now. She would meet the woman Riley was going to ask to marry him and this women and Wendy would strike up a conversation where they'd notice instantly how much they had in common. During some of her more intense fantasies, the woman Riley fell in love with would have lost her mother at an early age (not that she wished that on anyone) and would find in Wendy the mother she'd always longed for. The two of them would plan shopping excursion, always coming home with something for themselves as well as a little something for Riley and the twins.

Once the very important question had been asked and answered in the affirmative, Wendy and this lovely young woman – that she now considered a daughter – would begin to plan the wedding. Wendy would, of course provide the support this young woman would need as a result of the absence of her very own mother. And Wendy, unlike some other crazy women out there, would understand exactly what her role was and not step over the line, staying firmly in the friend/mother in law role instead of wandering into the "I think I'm your substitute mother" arena.

After the wedding, there would be Sunday dinners where the entire family came together to enjoy a home cooked meal. This woman, bless her heart, was not at all skilled in the kitchen and she and Wendy would joke about it with Wendy providing her all the direction she would need in order to cook for Riley and the children that were sure to come. This woman would come over early each Sunday not only because she wanted to learn her way around the kitchen but because she *wanted* to spend time with Wendy. That's how close the two of them would be.

Eventually, that is. As much as Wendy longed for a female addition to her family, she knew it would be at least a few years before Riley made *that* sort of commitment. He needed to finish school, get a job, and establish himself in his field so he could support his family. For now, she would just be excited that Riley had found someone and was happy.

Of course, Wendy wasn't entirely oblivious to the fact that Riley didn't relish being home for the summer. She knew Riley was accustomed to being on his own and preferred it, which was why she had been completely taken by surprise when he made the suggestion to stay for the summer, even if it had been half –heartedly. Her surprise was quickly replaced by excitement at having all her boys under the same roof, if only for a few months. She was so excited, in fact, that she hadn't even asked why he wanted to come home.

Wendy was so proud of all of her children, but if she were being truthful, it was Riley who tugged at her heart just the tiniest bit more. Even from a young age, he'd been so serious. There had never been any doubt in her mind that Riley would be the one to excel in anything he'd set his mind to. Swimming was just one example. Once he chose it, he was unstoppable. If he set his mind to something, he was not going to be deterred. Most mothers she knew would have identified that as a stubborn streak in their child. Wendy did not. Rather the opposite, in fact. She knew the trait would be something that would benefit him as he grew to adulthood. Persistence and determination were two very good traits to have and Wendy wasn't about to squelch those in her son.

Riley had been one of the best swimmers in their hometown and because of this, he'd received a swimming scholarship to Carolina. Wendy and Bill couldn't have been more proud. Not to mention the financial burden it took off their shoulders. Not that they were struggling, by any stretch of the imagination, but they did have two more boys to put through college and neither of them had shown the determination Riley had always shown. Scholarships for either Ben or Tyler were not something they anticipated.

When Riley left for college three years ago, Wendy, admittedly, had had a very difficult time. She wasn't ready to lose the control – if that's what you could call it – of knowing where her son was and who he was with at all times. Though she could text him at any time of day or night, she had always liked knowing he was under her roof and in his own bed when she went to sleep. But she had adjusted, as she knew she would. And maybe, just maybe, she'd cope with the separation of one child by becoming closer to the other two. Luckily, at only seven years old, they weren't old enough to be bothered by her constant supervision. They were still babies, at least in her eyes and she was, in their eyes, still the greatest person in the world. Of course, Wendy knew that it would all change once those hormones kicked in. But for now, she just relished in the fact that she had two boys at home who still needed her.

She glanced at Riley, who was, at the moment, in the pool with Hadley, and felt a pang in her chest. In less than a year from now, he'd graduate college. The chances were pretty slim that he'd move home after graduation. While he was tolerating living at home for the summer, she figured she was cramping his style. He was used to coming and going as he pleased without having to tell someone where he was and when he would return home. Despite the sighs and eye rolls, she insisted on knowing his whereabouts, if only for the next few months.

She wished Bill were more like her with regard to involvement in their children's lives. When she'd told Bill Riley would be coming home for the summer, she expected him to share in her excitement. Instead, he'd only shrugged and murmured "that's nice," as though it didn't matter to him one way or the other. Well, she thought, it may not matter to him but it did matter to her and she was going to make Riley's stay this summer perfect.

She cleaned his room in preparation for his homecoming, stocked the house with all his favorite foods, and of course, cooked his favorite dinner – turkey with all the fixin's – for his first night home. Before Riley had even arrived home, he'd contacted the head coach of the swim team and managed to get himself a position coaching the Dolphins. That hadn't surprised Wendy at all. That was pure Riley; oozing independence and making sure he had a job before he came home to spend the summer. She smiled to herself, thinking how proud she was of him.

She sighed. One more year and then who knew what would happen? And just who was this girl he was so taken with? Was she someone from college or someone he'd met since arriving home?

Wendy, of course, knew what her preference was. Someone close by from a family Wendy knew. That would be perfect. Then she wouldn't feel so much like she was losing her son…she'd be gaining a daughter.

Chapter 14

The next morning, Riley pulled in as usual. Hadley, who had become quite accustomed to the routine by now, sat waiting on the front porch for her ride. Riley parked the car and turned the engine off but Hadley was already running toward the car. As a result, he was only able to stand and wave to Kate.

"I'll see you at the pool later?" He yelled across the front yard.

She nodded and waved. "I'll be there around eleven."

She watched them back out of the driveway and could see Hadley's arms waving animatedly around. She knew she was probably talking Riley's ear off. She smiled and then went into the house to grab a second cup of coffee and get to work.

Two hours later, Kate had managed to return several phone calls and email two quotes, which she felt certain were low enough that she'd be selected to do the work. With the feeling of accomplishment running through her, she decided to head to the pool. When she arrived, swim practice wasn't quite finished so she was able to watch Hadley swim a couple laps. Kate stood on the side of the pool and watched as her daughter came to one end, flipped underwater, and then made her way back to the other side, effortlessly.

"She's really improved this year."

Kate jumped slightly, not having realized someone was beside her. Her body recognized the voice, however, and Kate felt her pulse quicken. "Yeah, she's been practicing all winter." She took a deep breath and released it slowly, trying to calm herself.

"Were you able to get a lot done this morning?"

She nodded. "I sure was. I got through most of my emails and turned in two quotes. It was great. Nice to have a quiet house."

"I can imagine. The twins make a ton of noise when I'm there. I can hardly think!" He grinned. "But, they're cool."

"Yes, they are."

"So, what are you doing this afternoon? Are you sticking around for a bit?"

"I thought I might." She lifted up her book. "I brought this. I'd love to just sit and read for a bit."

He nodded. "Well, I'm going to get back in the water. I'll see you in a bit."

Kate watched him walk over to the side of the pool and jump in, making a huge splash and causing the little boy in the lane to sputter and giggle when he saw Riley come up out of the water beside him. Riley reached over and mussed the kids head, resulting in more laughter. In a matter of moments, three children had abandoned their lanes and were piled on top of him. She couldn't help but chuckle as she watched Riley attempt, halfheartedly at best, to rid himself of the kids on top of him. Shaking her head, she walked over to an empty chaise lounge, spread out her towel, and sat down in order to prepare to read. Just as she opened her book, Hadley came running over to her.

"Mommy! Did you see my flip-turn?"

Kate hadn't, since she had been to engrossed in watching the kids climb all over Riley but she knew, based on the look on her daughter's face, that she couldn't say so. Choosing her daughter's excitement over her own desire to always tell the truth, Kate quickly opted for the route that involved a little while lie. "I only saw a teeny bit of it," she said, placing her forefinger and her thumb about a half inch apart for display purposes. "Will you do it again so I can see the whole thing?"

Hadley grinned, pleased to have her mother's attention. "Sure!" She said, bounding off. Kate made sure she sat and watched at Hadley dove into the water, waving to her mother before she did so, then swam the length of the pool and performed the very difficult (at least by Hadley's standards) flip-turn at the end. She swam back to the other side of the pool and pulled her goggles off. "Did you see, mom? Did you see?"

"I did! It was wonderful!" Kate said, clapping enthusiastically. She watched at Hadley beamed at her, then placed her goggles back on her head and swam off.

For perhaps the thousandth time since Hadley had been born, Kate thought about how glad she was that she had chosen a career where she could have these moments with her daughter. She couldn't even imagine how awful it would have been if she would have chosen something requiring her to work fifty, even sixty hours each week, only to come home each night distracted and thinking of all the work she still needed to get done. No. That had never been for her. Luckily, she had known at a very early age that she someday wanted to have children and perhaps because of that, selected a field that would give her some flexibility.

Kate opened her book and began to read but kept being pulled back to the activity in the pool. Each time she looked up, she saw Hadley either on top of, next to, or being pushed under the water by Riley, all the while with a huge grin on her face. At one point, Hadley climbed up onto Riley's shoulders, then stood up as though he were a diving board. For the briefest of moments, Kate worried that she might get hurt but then realized she was being ridiculous. Hadley was probably safer in the water with Riley than she was on the pool deck. At least if she fell in the water, there would be no scraped knees or elbows. Pool toes, which ran rampant during the first couple weeks of practice when the skin on the kids' toes simply wore away from the combination of the water and those tiny toes constantly walking on the concrete bottom of the pool, was the most severe injury Hadley would get while under the supervision of a swimmer with Riley's background. Feeling somewhat more assured and knowing that Hadley was having fun, she again looked down at her book and began to read.

Kate managed to get through several pages before looking up once again. As was her custom, she scanned the pool in order to locate Hadley. She finally located her swimming toward one end of the pool, then watched as she completed a flip turn and began to swim back toward the other side. She allowed her gaze to move along the length of the pool in search of Riley and found him sitting on the side of the pool watching Hadley swim her laps. As though sensing he was being watched, he lifted his head and looked directly at her. He winked, causing Kate's cheeks to redden involuntarily. She smiled back at him, then slowly returned her gaze downward, trying to resume her novel. Having made eye contact with Riley, even for such a short moment, had such a delicious affect on her, causing her insides to become so jittery that she felt certain staring at the page was simply a farce. She knew she wouldn't be able to recall a single word.

After a few minutes of trying, without success, to resume her reading, she gave up. Her mind was now on something…or someone else. It was one thing to have someone who looked like Riley sitting half-naked on the other side of the pool; it was something altogether much more distracting to know that Riley might be thinking of her as well. She couldn't help herself but imagine the next time they were able to spend some time together, alone.

At this point, Kate knew she wasn't going to get much reading done – she was just too distracted. Although she wasn't reading, she kept her book in front of her as though she was engrossed in the words on the page. Keeping her head still, she lifted her eyes above the book and stole a glance at Riley. She inhaled sharply as she noticed he was seated in the same spot on the side of the pool and was once again looking directly at here. He lifted up his arm to wave at her and then motioned her over to sit beside him. Kate paused for only the briefest of moments, then tossed her book aside and stood up. She walked towards the opposite side of the pool and sat down beside him, letting her feet dangle in the water. Today, the water felt cool and refreshing but she knew that in a few short weeks, the comfortable warmth of June would be replaced by the unbearable humidity of July and at that point, the water would be only a little more refreshing than bathwater.

"Hey," she said, making circles in the water with her feet. They weren't even touching each other, but still her insides began to flutter. She tried to make normal conversation but she found, like usual, her mind was completely useless when she was anywhere near Riley, particularly when he was dressed in so little clothing. "Was practice okay today?"

He nodded. "Sure was. Hadley's a fish, by the way. But you knew that."

She nodded. "She loves to be in the water."

Hadley, who had been playing with Sarah for the past several minutes, noticed her mother sitting on the edge of the pool and swam over. "Mom! Are you going to swim?"

Kate looked down at her daughter and smiled. "I don't think so. I think it's best if I leave the swimming to the professionals." She looked between Riley and Hadley as though to emphasize her point.

"You can swim though, right?" Riley asked, trying to avoid the surprise in his voice.

Kate nodded. "Of course I can! It just needs to be very warm for me to swim."

"Okay, whew! I was afraid I was going to have to give you swimming lessons as well."

She shook her head. "Nope. You can focus your energies on this one," she said, pointing to Hadley.

Riley, in a moment of boldness, leaned over and whispered softly, his warm breath on her ear making her shiver. "I don't know if I need to focus all my energies on Hadley."

Kate turned slowly toward him, finding him mere inches from her. She felt a flutter in her belly – a very familiar feeling by this time – and simply stared at him, mouth agape. When she saw his grin, she responded with one of her own. They both laughed out loud, leaving Hadley in the water, staring up at them, entirely lost with their very adult conversation.

"What?" Hadley asked, looking between the two of them as she treaded water.

"Er...Riley just makes me laugh, honey," Kate replied quickly. She shot Riley a look out of the corner of her eye and saw him looking back at her apologetically. She quickly flashed him a smile, telling him he was forgiven.

"How about I race you to the other side?" Riley challenged. Hadley immediately forgot the laughter of a moment ago and swiftly focused on the challenge at hand, something for which Kate was immensely grateful.

Riley slid off the side of the pool deck and into the water. "I'll talk to you later, all right?" Kate nodded. "I've got to beat this one," he said, splashing Hadley, "to the other side of the pool." Hadley squealed as she pushed off the edge of the pool and headed toward the other side. Riley waited several moments in order to give her a large head start, then took off after her.

Kate watched them, splashing her feet around for a few moments, enjoying the feel of the cool water on her calves. Riley and Hadley reached the far side of the pool nearly together, with Riley beating her by a second or so. Hadley, instead of being saddened at the loss, was thrilled that she'd nearly beaten the coach she idolized. Kate was touched by the display and then wondered how it was that Riley knew what to do. He seemed to place her feelings above his own and was missing that "alpha-male" gene that so many men seemed to have. Riley was genuinely concerned for Hadley's well being, a trait that made him much more desirable in Kate's eyes.

A Ripple in the Water

Admittedly, she hadn't dated much since Todd's death and was completely out of touch with dating and all that it involved. She did, however, have several friends who had re-entered the dating arena since divorcing and it seemed every last one of them had the same complaint – the men they dated seemed indifferent to their children, only tolerating them in order to please their mother. Kate shuddered, thinking of how she did not want to put Hadley through any of that. She knew if she were to ever date someone seriously, it would have to be someone who truly cared about her daughter and wasn't pretending to do so only to gain Kate's affections.

Kate continued to sit on the side of the pool for awhile, watching Hadley swim, if you could call it swimming, that is. Hadley was never far from Riley. If he swam in one direction, she would follow. And Riley, it seemed, enjoyed the attention. He never got irritable or impatient with her. If anything, he encouraged her to play right along side of him in the water. Kate couldn't help but smile as she watched her daughter roughhouse with Riley. She watched at Hadley burst out of the water and placed her hand on Riley's head, making an attempt to push him under water. She succeeded, but Kate suspected it was only because Riley allowed her to do so. As he went under, he grabbed Hadley's feet and pulled her under the water. Hadley came up out of the water along Riley, both of them giggling and spurting water.

It was then that Kate realized that she was actually enjoying her summer, which she'd never anticipated. After last year, she had been worried that summertime would always bring forth bad memories for her. She was glad to see that was not the case. Thanks to Riley, she was able to spend some time each day working and then spend time with Hadley in the afternoons. Real, quality time. Not the half-assed time she'd been afraid of – her watching Hadley from a distant table, perhaps another room even, filled with stress, trying to meet her deadlines while cultivating new clients. She knew she had Riley to thank for that. If it weren't for him, she would be that parent who sat on the side of the pool working while their kid did anything in their power to attract their attention and failed ninety-nine times out of a hundred.

Kate splashed the water on her thighs, arms and back, relishing the feeling of the cool water swooshing over body parts that had gotten warmed under the sun. Feeling cooled off, she stood up and

Donna Small

walked back over to her chair, fully intent on making some progress
on the novel she was reading. She chuckled, thinking that while she
may get some work done each morning, she wasn't going to get very
far into her book if Riley stayed at the pool each day. He was just so
damn distracting!

She managed to read a few pages, even becoming immersed in
the story for a few moments. She was seated near enough to an
umbrella to be in the shade but her feet were receiving a good bit of
sun, which felt deliciously warm. She turned to her right side,
hearing a scraping noise and saw Riley dragging a chair closer to
where she sat. He situated the chair in the full sun and plopped
himself down. "What are you reading?" He asked.

She noticed that he'd wrapped a towel around his waist, leaving
his chest exposed. She looked up and shuddered as a fissure of pure
sexual attraction ripped through her. Somehow, the sight of his
exposed chest in combination with the towel wrapped just below
made Kate immediately lose all train of thought, including the name
of the book she was reading. Actually, she would have been hard
pressed to remember her name at the moment. As a result, she found
she had to look down at the cover in order to answer him.
"Uh...Before I Go To Sleep."

"Oh," he said. He leaned back against the lounge chair and
stretched his legs out in front of him. He laced his fingers together
and placed them behind his head. "Is it any good?"

"I have no idea," she muttered, staring at his muscled torso.

"Huh?"

Kate blushed as she realized she'd spoken out loud. "I, uh...It's
good. I'm not that far into it but so far, it's good."

Riley leaned forward and reached for the book, grazing her hand
with his as he did so. As skin met skin, Kate felt that familiar longing
from deep in her belly; a feeling that she was becoming more and
more accustomed to. She watched as he read the back cover and then
handed it back to her. "It looks interesting. Let me know what you
think when you finish."

"Okay."

"So, what do you two have going on later?" He asked.

"Nothing, really. Why?"

"Well, I was hoping I could swing by later...if that's all right
with you?"

122

Kate was momentarily taken by surprise, followed immediately by a ripple of excitement in her belly. "Er…sure," she said.

"Great," he said, smiling at her. "I bought some new goggles at The Swim Shop and the owner gave me an extra pair to try out. I thought I'd bring them over so Hadley could see if she liked them. I ran out of the house this morning in such a rush that I completely forgot to grab them."

"Well, of course you can bring them over but I hate for you to make a special trip. If you want, you can just bring them to practice tomorrow."

"Kate," he said, eyeing her pointedly. "I want to swing by your place."

She heard the emphasis on the word 'want' and blushed, realizing exactly what he meant. "Oh," she said, looking down at her lap, feeling a mix of excitement and terror.

Besides her own feelings of trepidation, she had to admit she was still worried about what Wendy and some of the other moms might think. Surely, her friends would be happy for her, right? Oh hell. She had no idea. She was on her own for this one.

Riley noticed her silence and looked at her, concern evident on his face. "Is that okay?"

She looked over at him. "Of course it is."

"Is something wrong?"

"No. It's just…I don't know Riley. All of this is just happening so fast."

"Well, I don't have to come over."

"No, no. I want you to come over. I guess I just need to get my bearings together. You know, get used to all of this. It's been a very long time since I've had a guy 'stop over.' It's just going to take some getting used to."

"Don't worry. I'll help you." He grinned at her wickedly.

She smiled back at him, feeling a bit more at ease with whatever it was that was going on between them, though she wasn't ready to put a label on it just yet.

"Great. I'll see you later, Kate." He winked at her, dropped his towel on the chair, then bounded off to the deep end of the pool. Kate sat transfixed as she watched him dive into the pool and swam underwater to the opposite end, never taking a breath. He rose up out of the water near Hadley and shook his head, ridding himself of the water.

Kate slowly exhaled. This would definitely take some getting used to. Her body's reaction to him was something she'd never encountered before. She really needed to get a grip on herself before she started to have some serious feelings for him. After all, he was only here for the summer. A mere eight weeks or so! Then he'd head back to college – and still had a year left. He'd be at school with young, beautiful co-eds and she'd be here in Lancaster doing all the mundane things she did every day.

She felt an odd pang in her stomach that felt an awfully like a pang of jealousy. It couldn't be, could it? But it was. Just the thought of Riley spending time with young, bendy co-eds was enough to turn her green with envy.

Good lord, if she was already feeling jealous, she was in serious trouble.

With a small sigh, she looked down at her book yet again, but she knew at this point, it was just for show. It could have been written in Chinese for all she was going to get out of it. Still, she managed to sit there and look vaguely like someone who was engrossed in a novel for the better part of an hour. Hadley finally came out of the pool and announced she wanted to go home. Kate was actually glad to leave the pool, given the amount of distraction she felt when Riley was near…and wearing practically nothing.

A ripple of excitement ran through her knowing that she would be seeing him later. She might have to tell him to wear a snowsuit when he came over or she wouldn't be able to think. She giggled. It wouldn't matter what he wore. She'd still find him attractive. The man just radiated masculinity, which Kate found extremely appealing.

"What are you laughing at?" Hadley asked. She looked confused, as though she'd missed the punch line of a joke.

"Nothing. I just thought of something from earlier," she replied. "Why don't you tell me about practice?"

Hadley began chatting about the day's practice. As she listened to her daughter talk, she was amazed that a seven year old could grasp so much. She spoke about how her arms weren't straight enough for one stroke, but too straight for another. She mentioned times of swimmers in comparison to her own and basically detailed the drills they'd gone through today. Kate nodded at the appropriate intervals but knew so little about the strokes her daughter was learning, that she found she couldn't even ask a question. They drove home with Hadley chattering the entire way and Kate nodding and "umm-hmming" until they arrived in front of their mailbox

Kate stopped the car and rolled down Hadley's window. She unbuckled herself and reached through the open window for the mail and then tossed it on the front seat. Kate quickly glanced at the pile and determined they were mainly bills and not worthy of further attention from her. She pulled the car into the driveway and Hadley bounded out, dragging her towel on the ground behind her.

"Pick up your towel, PLEASE!" Kate yelled after her daughter. She watched at Hadley rumpled the towel into a ball and instinctively Kate knew she'd find it at the bottom of the stairs.

She reached into the backseat and grabbed their pool bag, then carried it into the kitchen and placed it on the counter. Realizing she was starved, she began to look in the fridge for something to eat. She found a couple of slices of turkey in the drawer so she pulled them out and rolled them up with some cheese.

"Can I have a snack?"

Kate turned around to find Hadley in an 80's prom dress that was several sizes too large for her. Just for something to do, Kate had begun taking Hadley to the local Goodwill store in search of …well anything, really. Kate would peruse the store looking for anything she could use or take apart and use pieces of. Occasionally, there would be a table or chair of some sort that would have 'good bones' as she liked to say and Kate would have a vision of what the table or chair would look like with another stain or stripped clean. Hadley, on the other hand would spend her time wandering through the formal dresses, fingering each one to feel its shiny silkiness. Hadley had fallen immediately in love and looked at her mother with such hope that Kate simply couldn't say no. On that particular day, Kate left with an end table and Hadley left with a new dress. As they continued to visit the Goodwill, Hadley's dress collection grew. Kate kept telling herself she was going to find the time to alter the dresses to fit Hadley but she never seemed to find the time to do so. Besides, it seemed Hadley liked to have her dresses too long. She'd spent hours walking through the living room and up and down the stairs with her dresses flowing behind her, swinging them side to side and smiling each time she heard the swish of the fabric on the hard wood floors. Other times, Kate would peer into her bedroom to find Hadley standing in front of the full-length mirror, swinging the train of the dress around her like a cape. Seeing her daughter's imagination in full force like that swiftly erased any guilt she had about not finding the time to alter the dress.

Today, Hadley had chosen a hot pink concoction that had yards and yards of tulle around the bottom. The bodice, which Kate assumed was supposed to be snug, was held up around Hadley's too small torso with one of Kate's scarves. Wrapped around Hadley's shoulders was a pale pink pashmina that had sat unused in Kate's closet since it had been purchased nearly two years ago. The effect was dazzling, though only to a mother's eyes. Kate reached for her camera.

"Now, this is a beautiful outfit you've put together. I've got to get a picture of this one!" Kate said, reaching for her camera.

Hadley rolled her eyes at her mother but once the camera was lifted and ready to snap, she smiled broadly and placed her hands on hips and cocked her head to one side, presumably to showcase her best feature. Kate had to stifle a giggle.

"Now you may have a snack." Kate said. She placed the camera back on the counter, then reached in the fridge for an apple. "How about an apple with peanut butter?"

"Sure," Hadley replied. She swept up the train of her dress and swooshed over to the table to sit down.

Kate sliced up the apple and then scooped some peanut butter into a tiny bowl, then placed it in front of Hadley. "I'm going to take a quick shower, all right? If the doorbell rings, come get me, all right?"

"Who's coming over?"

"Riley. Something about some new goggles for you or something."

"For me? Really?" Hadley looked like she'd just won a million dollars. Kate had to struggle to remember a time when such small things made her smile like that. Then it came to her.

Yesterday. She smiled like that yesterday...*With Riley.*

Chapter 15

She walked into her bathroom and turned on the shower. Was it really so simple? Though she wasn't ready to admit it, she did feel more like old self when she was with Riley. Maybe Bethany was right. Maybe it was time to move forward. She still felt a tiny pang in her stomach when she thought of Wendy. How would she feel if knew Kate was dating her son? Surely, their friendship had to mean something? Wendy did like her after all. She certainly wouldn't have a problem with Kate's moral character or anything like that. Kate hadn't dated anyone since Todd had died. And Wendy had been pushing Kate to get out there and even put herself on one of those on-line dating services. Surely, this was much better than that.

The more Kate thought about it, the less anxious she felt. Maybe she had been overthinking this somewhat. Bethany certainly didn't see a problem with it so maybe she was just being oversensitive. And if Bethany didn't see a problem with Kate dating Riley, maybe the others wouldn't have a problem with it either. Bethany normally had a good grasp on what the other moms were thinking and how they'd react to particular situations.

Kate turned off the water and stepped out, wrapping herself in a fluffy, white towel. She dried herself off, then grabbed some shorts and a t-shirt to put on. As she reached for one of her favorite, well-worn shirts, she stopped. Should she put on something different? Maybe something a bit nicer? She turned to look at herself in the mirror. And what about her hair? She fingered her dark hair, which fell to her chin in soft waves. Should she blow dry it and style it? And what about makeup? If Riley was coming over, should she put on makeup?

God, she was exhausted just thinking about all of it! In the end, she decided that she was just going to wear what she'd normally wear if it were just she and Hadley. Riley found her attractive? Well, he could find her attractive in her favorite t-shirt.

She heard a chair screech across the kitchen floor and knew

Hadley was finished with her snack. "You okay, honey?"

"Yup. Can I watch TV?"

"Sure." Kate walked into the living room, preparing to turn on the TV for Hadley, when she saw her lift up the remote and point it at the TV to turn it on. Kate raised her eyebrows seeing her daughter complete the task. How was it that she had to read the seventeen manuals that came with the TV in order to learn how to turn it on and her seven year old just picks up a remote as though she was born with the knowledge of how to work it? I give up, Kate thought, then went back into her room.

Seeing the stuffed laundry basket, Kate figured she'd throw in a load of laundry. She got it started, then walked through the living room to check on Hadley. She rumpled Hadley's hair as she went past her but she was so engrossed in ICarly that she didn't even move. Just as she was about to step into her office, she heard a knock at the door. She felt her pulse quicken knowing it would be Riley who was on the other side of it. She'd barely changed direction when Hadley leapt off the couch and ripped open the door, hitting the wall with it.

"Riley!" She squealed. "I'm so glad you're here! Mom said you have some goggles for me?"

Riley leaned over so he was eye to eye with her. "I do. That is, if you think they'll help you with your dives."

She nodded solemnly. "It will."

He stood up and laughed as he looked at Kate. "Well, there you go," he said, motioning to Hadley.

"Let me see those," Kate said, reaching out her hand. Riley dropped them in her palm and she inspected them. "Okay, Hadley. Why don't you tell me why these goggles will help you with your dives." Kate looked at Riley and winked.

Hadley took the goggles from her mother and looked at them with a discerning eye. She turned them over in her palm and then bent them in half as though testing to see how flexible they were. "Ummmm....they're very bendy!" She said at last. Hadley smiled up at her mother and Riley, pleased to have come up with an answer.

Kate had to stifle a chuckle. Keeping a serious expression on her face, she looked down at her daughter. "Well, if they're so bendy, then I think we need to buy them for you." She looked up at Riley. "Can I get her some at The Swim Shop?"

"Actually, you can have these. Mr. Williams gave them to me on loan."

She nodded. "Perfect. I'll swing by there tomorrow and pay him for them."

"Thanks mom!" Hadley took off toward the living room, clutching her goggles.

"I doubt she'll lose those." Kate said, noticing her daughter's tight grasp on the goggles.

"Why do you say that?"

Kate looked back at Riley. "Well, you brought them for her. Just knowing that you selected some goggles for her will be enough to make that pair a treasured item."

"Wow. Really?"

"Don't look so surprised. It's like that for all the kids on the team. They all adore you and Hadley's no different. You're great with them. You know that, right?"

He shrugged. "I'm just doing what I think will work."

Was he actually embarrassed? Kate had to smile. Yet another quality she needed to add to her list of things she found attractive about him. Not only was he great with all the kids on the swim team, but he was humble about it. "Well, come on in. You want a soda or something?"

"Sure," he replied, following Kate into the kitchen. "So, what did you two have planned for tonight?"

"Nothing really. I was going to head into the office and see if I could get through some emails but that's about it. I'm actually pretty caught up with work – thanks to you – so I'm not stressed about trying to get stuff done."

Hadley poked her head into the living room and looked at Riley. "Wanna watch a movie? "

"Uhh…" He glanced at Kate, unsure of what his response should be.

Kate noticed his discomfort and was quick to jump in. "What did you have in mind, Hadley?"

Hadley looked down at the floor to think about her selection. After several moments, she looked up abruptly, clearly having come up with a suggestion. "How to Train Your Dragon?"

"Ooooh," Kate replied. "That's a good one. Why don't you get it for me and I'll put it in the DVD player." Hadley skipped off, thrilled to be watching her favorite DVD. Kate looked at Riley. "You don't have to stay and watch this, you know."

Riley stood up and walked over to where she stood. "I know I don't. I want to."

"You can't be serious." She felt his hand graze hers.

He leaned in closely and Kate could feel his breath on her ear. "If it means I can spend the evening on your couch, I'll watch anything."

Kate released a slow breath, trying to calm her nerves. Riley would be spending the evening with her and Hadley watching a movie. Well, wasn't this very ordinary of them? Surely, Riley had better things to do with his time. She watched as he walked into the living room and made himself comfortable on the sofa. Kate placed the DVD in and sat on the other side of the sofa, far away from him. Hadley plopped down right in the middle of the two of them and looked at her mother, then Riley. She seemed to decide that he was the more comfortable of the two and curled up against him, tucking her legs underneath her. Riley wrapped his arm around Hadley's shoulders and settled himself in, pulling her just a bit closer to him.

Kate felt her heart melt just a little bit.

The three of them watched the movie in silence for a bit, then Kate decided she should probably order some dinner. It was still pretty early in the swim season and she knew Hadley wouldn't last much later than 9 o'clock or so. Kate phoned in an order of pizza and when it arrived, Riley insisted on paying for it, which made Kate feel a bit uneasy. He noticed her discomfort and asked her about it when the two of them were in the kitchen putting the slices on plates.

"Kate," he said. "Does it really bother you that I bought the pizza?"

She sighed heavily and shrugged. "Yes...no...Oh, I don't know."

Riley laughed out loud. "Well, I'm glad we got that cleared up."

"I don't know what it is. You already do so much for me, what with taking Hadley each morning that I figure I should buy the dinner."

"Next time, all right?" She nodded. "Let me do things for you, Kate. I want to. This is just a stupid pizza but I want to do so much for you."

He was looking at her so earnestly that she couldn't speak. He enveloped her into his arms for a brief moment, then pulled her back to look into her eyes. "Let's eat. I think Hadley's only got a little while before she falls asleep. Then I've got you all to myself."

Kate felt a shiver of anticipation work its way up her spine.

Together, they carried plates of pizza into the living room and ate in front of the TV, which was something that was rarely, if ever allowed. Hadley was thrilled beyond belief to be able to watch her favorite movie with a plate of pizza on her lap. And like Riley's prediction, Hadley didn't last long. She was fast asleep by 9:30 and missed the final thirty minutes of the movie. Kate gently lifted her up and carried her upstairs. She tucked her in and then gently closed the door behind her before returning downstairs.

Riley was seated on the couch with one arm resting along the back of it. The spot beside him appeared to be a nice fit for her so she sat down beside him and leaned back against him. He wrapped his arm around her shoulder, pulling her even closer to him. Within moments, the heat from his body radiated through his clothing and hers, warming her.

They sat in silence for several moments with Riley gently caressing the skin on Kate's arm, leaving a trail of warmth wherever he touched.

"God, I love being here with you."

She turned around and looked at him, surprised by the emotion she heard in his voice. "You really mean that, don't you?"

He raised his eyebrows. "Of course I do. Why would you question it?" He was smiling gently.

She looked away from him, afraid of showing her insecurities. "It's just that you're so...well, look at you."

"No," he said, lifting up her chin with his finger. "Look at you. You are intelligent, beautiful, kind, sexy...you're the whole package, Katharine Penner. And I for one am thrilled you've chosen to me to spend time with."

Riley fingered a loose lock of her hair, then tucked it gently behind her ear. Kate felt her insides turn to mush. As his lips met hers, she had one last coherent thought...

This was no ordinary summer romance.

Chapter 16

The next morning, Kate lay in bed long after her alarm went off. Her thoughts continued to bring her back to the previous night. It was uneventful really; just a nice night at home watching a movie. Oh, who was she kidding? Last night was about as uneventful as Hadley's first day of school. Last night was...unforgettable. If she had any doubt as to Riley's feeling for her, they were now gone.

Kate heard the faint humming of the coffee maker turning on and shortly thereafter, the delicious scent wafted down the hall into her room. Feeling the tug of her addiction, she tossed off the covers and began to make her way toward the delicious aroma. Just as she reached the door to the kitchen, she heard a soft knock on the front door.

Of course, Riley would choose today to show up earlier than normal. When Kate opened the door, she couldn't mask her surprise. She felt a moment's embarrassment since she'd only been up for a few minutes and still had on the ratty t-shirt she slept in – and pretty much nothing else. Her hair was still rumpled from sleep and she felt certain her face was still puffy.

God! She was not ready for this yet! She needed time to prepare herself for these early morning meetings. While she wasn't someone who normally needed hours to prepare herself for visitors, she would have at least liked to have had the opportunity to brush her teeth. Thinking of her possible morning breath, she took a step away from him.

"Riley!" She said. "You're early!" Subconsciously, she pulled the t-shirt down to cover her bottom, embarrassed at being caught in her current state of undress.

He stepped into the foyer and puller her close, gently patting her bottom with his hand. "I know I'm early," he whispered into her ear. "I was sort of hoping I'd find you like this."

"I'm a complete mess!"

"I think you're adorable," he said, nuzzling her neck. "An

adorable, sexy mess."

Kate pushed him away playfully. "Come on in. Hadley's still asleep. You want some coffee?"

"Sure." Riley sat down at the table and looked at her with a devilish grin on his face. "You sleep okay last night?"

Kate looked at him and noticed his expression. "Yes...what's with that look?" She asked, pointing to his face and making a circular motion.

"I hardly slept," he replied, his expression turning sheepish. "I had a lot on my mind."

Kate placed a cup of coffee on the table in front of him and sat down. "Oh, all right. I had a lot on my mind as well." She smiled shyly.

Riley reached over and took her hand in his own. "I have to tell you....I can't seem to get you out of my mind."

Kate felt her insides becoming all warm and buttery.

"I don't know what it is about you, Kate, but I just can't stop thinking about you."

As if on cue, a sound from above their heads told them that Hadley was now awake. Kate did not want her daughter to walk into the kitchen and find her dressed as she was (or undressed, as the case may be), holding hands with Riley. She gently pulled her hand away from his. "I'm going to go put some pants on."

He chuckled. "Good idea," he said, grinning. Riley allowed his gaze to follow her uncovered legs as she walked out of the kitchen.

From above his head, he heard Hadley banging around in her room. He assumed she was looking for her bathing suit or her flip-flops but it sounded like she was tumbling all over the floor. After a few moments, he heard her stumble down the stairs and into the kitchen. Her hair was matted on one side and sticking straight up on the other and her eyes were barely open. "I'm hungry," she said. She peeked out from under the lashes of one eye obviously expecting to see her mother. When she realized it was, in fact, Riley who was seated at the table, she opened her mouth in surprise, then a look of panic swept across her face. "Am I late for practice or something?"

Riley shook his head. "Nope. I just got here early this morning. I wanted to talk to your mom."

"Oh," Hadley replied, as though it were normal for Riley to be at her house this early in the morning.

Kate, now fully clothed, walked back into the kitchen and saw her rumpled daughter. "Morning, sleepyhead. Do you want some breakfast? We've got plenty of time before you need to leave." Kate stood up and made her way to the cupboard. "Do you want a pop-tart?"

Hadley's eyes lit up. "Really? Sure!" She said, bouncing over to the table and pulling out the chair beside Riley.

He looked down at her. "Eat up," he said. "Big practice today. Tomorrow night's meet is against the Sharks."

Kate turned around in surprise. "Already?"

"Yeah….it comes quick, doesn't it?" Riley looked down at Hadley. "You ready? You've got fly tomorrow, remember?"

Hadley nodded, her mouth stuffed full of strawberry frosted deliciousness. She took a sip of milk, then swallowed. "I'm ready!"

"What time does she need to be there tomorrow?" Kate asked.

"Warm-ups start at five," Riley replied. "The Sharks have a large team so, unfortunately, I think it's going to be a long night."

"Ugh. I think it's going to be pretty hot, too."

"You'll be there, right?" Riley asked, looking up at Kate expectantly.

Kate nodded. "I'm the seven/eight team parent."

Riley laughed out loud. "Oh, right. I forgot about that. Brenda and her volunteers."

Hadley stood up and finished the last sip of her milk. She walked over to the sink and placed her cup and plate on the counter. "I'm going to get my suit on," she said as she bounced out of the room and up the stairs.

Riley stood up and walked over to Kate, who was leaning against the counter. He placed his coffee cup behind her, letting his hand rest on the counter. He placed his other hand beside her on her other side, in essence trapping her right where she was. He looked down at her and smiled. "Good morning," he said, coming very close to kissing her.

She playfully batted him away. "Riley," she whispered, nodding toward the stairs. "Hadley…" His smile didn't waiver.

"You think she'd mind if I kissed you?"

"I really don't want to find out!" she replied, holding back laughter. "Now behave!" She scolded.

"Yes, Ma'am," he replied, nearly choking with laughter.

"Ohh....you did NOT just go there!" Kate placed her hands on her hips and looked at him sternly, though her smile told Riley she was about to burst into laughter. "Don't you even start with the Ma'am crap."

"Yes, Ma- Hey!" Riley ducked at Kate took a swing at him, aiming for his head. She missed and Riley deftly swung her around and into his arms so that she was leaning back looking up at him. Before she even knew what was happening, Riley quickly kissed her on the lips. Kate tried to maintain a stern look but found that once his lips touched hers, she lost all train of thought.

Riley slowly lifted Kate back up to her normal, upright position. His hands lingered on her hips as though he was unwilling to let her go, which of course, he was. "You'll be at the pool later? Maybe swim for a bit?"

She nodded. "Sure, I can do that. Hopefully, some magical fabric will appear for Mrs. Windham and I can be done with her stupid chairs."

"Mrs. Windham....isn't that the rich lady with the big house over off Trelawn?

Kate nodded. "The one and only."

"She still hasn't found anything she likes? Haven't you been working on her stuff for awhile now?"

Kate sighed heavily. "Yeah...I'm beginning to think she feels the longer it takes, the better the end result."

Hearing Hadley approaching from the top of the stairs, both moved a respectable distance apart from the other, neither one ready to explain things to a seven year old. Riley looked at Kate and grinned shyly, realizing they'd both done the exact same thing. Kate raised one eyebrow in reply.

"Hey, Sweetie!" She said. "You ready for practice?"

Hadley nodded. "Come on Riley!"

He turned to her and raised his eyebrows. "I'll see you later, right?"

She nodded and was rewarded with a wink.

Kate sat down at her computer with the intent of going through all her emails and at least organizing them into some sort of order; quick answers, things she needed to think about, and ones that needed follow up. She was also determined to find the perfect pattern for Mrs. Windham. Once her emails were reviewed, spent the better part of an hour reviewing every sample of fabric she had in her office. She finally located a piece of fabric that, for some reason, she'd kept from one of her first projects. She'd designed a library the old Walker house. The family had been in the same house for generations and was completely averse to any change. As a result, the fabric she'd used looked like had been first used in the early 1800's. Although she thought the fabric was hideous, she wondered if it just might work for Mrs. Windham. She tucked the fabric into her briefcase, meaning to bring the swatch to the Windham home on her way to the pool. At this point, she had nothing to lose since she'd shown the woman nearly every fabric she had on hand. This was altogether too much work for one chair.

Glancing at her watch, she noticed that it was nearly time for practice to end. She felt satisfied with the work she'd gotten accomplished this morning and actually felt up to driving to the Windham house on her way to the pool. Regardless of the end result, Kate knew it wouldn't matter. She'd gotten a lot done today and the sense of accomplishment would carry her through the day.

Kate pulled up the Windham house – mansion really – and clasped the fabric to her chest. She looked around as she did each and every time she came here. The immaculate landscaping, the pristine columns in front of the house, the perfectly manicured lawn...everything around her spoke of wealth and power. She walked up the wide, brick steps and knocked loudly on the large, double doors. Almost immediately, the door opened and Kate was ushered in by Edward, Mrs. Windham's personal assistant. Each and every time Kate came to the house it was the same; she would knock and then immediately the door would open, as though Edward simply stood there all day, just waiting for someone to come for a visit. Kate thought surely he had the most boring job ever, since Mrs. Windham hardly ever went anywhere.

She was ushered into the parlor – there was really no other word for it, what with the stiff, uncomfortable looking furniture, ornate moldings and decorative figurines tucked into every corner– and Edward motioned for her to have a seat. She sat down on the edge of the couch stiffly, afraid of upsetting any of the knick-knacks that surrounded her. On the table in front of her, there must have been a hundred or so tiny porcelain rabbits. On each table beside the couch

Kate sat on, another fifty or so. The mantle, as well as the other tables, was littered with an enormous collection of these tiny rabbits. Kate had to stifle a chuckle. This was by far the oddest collection she'd seen in this room. On previous visits, there had been a collection of antique thimbles, baby rattles, and ornate bells. There had even been one visit where the tables were littered with skeleton keys, which Kate found just creepy. This was what Edward probably spent his days doing; changing out the items Mrs. Windham had collected during her eighty-odd years.

She heard the sound of heels crossing the hard wood flooring of the front hall and looked up to see Eleanor Windham enter the room. Kate stood immediately, both out of respect and because it had made clear to her it was expected by the elderly woman. While she had never been told to do so, Kate had witnessed others do the same when she first came to the house. The effect was startling, to say the least, and from that moment on, Kate was trained to do the same.

Mrs. Windham, despite having lived a long life, still retained all of her faculties. She strode into the room as if she owned it, which of course, she did. Kate often thought that she entered every room with just the same attitude. An attitude that comes from years of people doing exactly as you tell them to, most likely because everyone around you worked for you in some capacity. At the very young age of seventeen, Eleanor Banks had married the eldest son of the town's wealthiest family. When Quentin Windham met his bride at the altar, she quickly became the envy of every young girl in Lancaster, both because of Quentin's wealth, but also because he was considered by most to be the most handsome young man in their small town. Though her family had not been destitute by any means, marriage into the Windham family secured her future.

Although she'd never worked outside the home, Mrs. Windham had always dressed as though she had someplace fascinating to go. Today was no exception. She was an old school woman from the south – born and bred. Kate had never had the courage to ask if she'd been a debutante or some other antiquated, outdated tradition, but Mrs. Windham's posture, manners, and delicate mannerisms spoke of years of training.

Today, she wore a delicate pink suit with low heels. As usual, small pearls adorned her ears and a pearl necklace peeked out from between the collar of the silk shirt she wore underneath her jacket.

On her left hand, the largest diamond Kate had ever seen rested. The ring had obviously been given to her some time ago when there was more than just skin and bones there. Now, the ring would continuously slide around her finger, which led to Mrs. Windham constantly fiddling with it to ensure it was in the correct spot on her finger.

The elderly woman sat down in the chair across from Kate and rested her hands in her lap. She looked at Kate without saying a word, almost as though inspecting her for any changes since their last meeting. Initially, this practice had made Kate uncomfortable, now she knew it was just part of the process and she sat, waiting for Mrs. Windham to complete her inspection and begin their meeting.

Today, however, the inspection lasted a bit longer than usual and Kate began to feel just a bit of discomfort. She looked down into her lap, doing her best not to fidget.

"Yessss…"

Kate looked up expectantly. "Pardon?"

Mrs. Windham pointed a long, slender finger in the general direction of Kate. She swooshed it around as though holding a paintbrush to a canvas. "There's something…..different today."

Kate shook her head and smiled pleasantly. "Different? Nothing's different. It's just the same old me."

"No," she said firmly, shaking her head. "I can tell. I just need to put my finger on it." She folded one arm across her chest and tapped a finger to her cheek.

Kate felt quite uncomfortable being subjected to such scrutiny. She quickly looked away from the old woman's piercing gaze and reached for her bag.

"I think I've found something you might like," she said as she pulled the newly discovered fabric out. "I found this in my office and I think it might be just what you're looking for." She removed the swatch of fabric and moved to lay it on the table in front of her. Realizing there was no room due to the rabbits, she instead held it up in front of her. "What do you think?"

Mrs. Windham leaned forward, inspecting the fabric. She reached out one of her hands and rubbed the fabric between her thumb and forefinger. "I don't know if this is exactly what I was thinking…"

Kate suddenly felt as though if this fabric didn't work, nothing would. She knew she needed to convince Mrs. Windham that this would be the right choice. She took a deep breath and leaned forward another inch or so. "Mrs. Windham, I certainly don't want to overstep my boundaries here..."

"Go on..." she replied, looking up at her over the rim of her eyeglasses.

Kate stifled a grin as she tried to convince the white lie out of her mouth. "I think you should take a close look at it." The elderly woman leaned forward, following Kate's direction. "Do you see this color here?"

She nodded her reply.

"This is the exact color Queen Elizabeth used for her napkins when she hosted the president."

Mrs. Windham gasped. "Really? Well that is something," she said, leaning forward even closer to the fabric.

Kate knew she only needed to seal the deal since Mrs. Windham was clearly hooked. Lucky for Kate, she'd overheard one of the grandchildren speak about Mrs. Windham's love of anything British. Kate figured a tiny white lie couldn't possibly hurt. After all, the Queen may very well have used the same color for her napkins.

White is a very popular color for napkins, after all.

Mrs. Windham leaned back and sat upright, clapping her hands to her thigh. "Well, if it's good enough for the Queen, it's good enough for Windham chairs. Well done, Katharine. You may proceed."

"An excellent choice, Mrs. Windham," Kate replied as she placed the fabric back into her bag. She didn't want to give the fickle woman any chance to change her mind. She stood up and placed her bag on her shoulder. "I'll get to work. The chairs should be done by the middle of next week."

"Excellent! Now, my dear. Let's get back to you." Mrs. Windham leaned back against her chair, crossed her arms over her chest, and resumed her earlier inspection.

Kate sat back down, realizing she had not yet been dismissed.

"As I said earlier, there is something different about you. Now what is it, exactly?"

"I'm not sure, Mrs. Windham. There's really nothing different to speak of."

Suddenly, the elderly woman snapped her fingers. Her huge

diamond spun around as a result of the motion. For the moment, she ignored the fact that her diamond was on the palm side of her hand. "I know what it is!" Mrs. Windham leaned forward as though about to reveal some deep, dark secret. "You've taken a lover!" She exclaimed, clapping excitedly. Kate wasn't sure whether she was clapping for Kate or for herself for solving this "puzzle."

"Goody for you!" She sat back in her chair, seemingly pleased with her assessment. Kate sat across from her, momentarily stunned.

"I...uh...No. I don't have a ..." she looked around to be sure no one was listening. "...lover! Mrs. Windham, please!"

"Oh, dear. It's quite all right. Really it is. In my day, of course, that sort of behavior was frowned upon. But now? Well, it's really quite the thing to do, isn't it?" Mrs. Windham's expression was one of pure delight. "I only wish I were younger now. It's such a fun time to be young."

Kate was stumbling over her words. Not only was she very uncomfortable with this conversation, but she had not, in fact, taken a lover. Sure, there was some mutual attraction between her and Riley and there had even been some...well, a kiss or two, but they weren't *lovers,* for God's sakes. And it wouldn't do her any good to have Mrs. Windham thinking she had taken one on.

"Mrs. Windham," she said, somewhat exasperated. "Is there anything else you need me to do? I really should get to work on your chairs."

She gave Kate a knowing look. "All right, dear. You go ahead and work on those *chairs.*"

Kate sighed heavily. "Oh, honestly Ma'am." She stood up. Dismissal or not, this conversation was over. She grabbed her bag and walked pointedly toward the door.

Mrs. Windham sat still in her seat. When she spoke, it was as if Kate was still seated on the couch in front of her since she didn't turn her head at all. "It agrees with you, Katharine. I've never seen you look more lovely."

Kate paused for the slightest of moments as she reached the front door. She heard what Eleanor had said, she just didn't want to acknowledge it. Edward was beside the door, waiting to open it for her. As she caught his eye, he raised his eyebrows. "Oh, stop," she said, causing Edward to chuckle softly. Kate couldn't help but smile – Edward knew exactly what his boss was like.

Chapter 17

Kate drove to the pool slowly and found she was unable to rid herself of the conversations she'd just had. Well, it really wasn't a conversation, more like an accusation. She glanced at herself in the mirror. Was it really so obvious?

She was still a bit frazzled when she arrived at the pool. Luckily, Hadley was too busy swimming with Sarah to notice her mother set up her towel on a chair near the deep end of the pool. Just as she sat down, Bethany walked over and sat down on the end of the chair next to her.

"Hey, Kate," she said. "What's up?"

She sighed. "I just came from the Windham place."

Bethany held up her hands in front of her. "Say no more. You have my sympathies. Have you gotten any further along on her chairs?"

"I did," Kate replied. "But that's not the half of it. You better get comfy."

Bethany slid herself back on the chaise so she was seated only a few inches from Kate. "Do tell," she said solemnly.

"Beth, Mrs. Windham basically congratulated me for 'taking a lover.'"

"What?!" Bethany hissed. "You did NOT tell me that! When did this happen? Geez, I just saw you what…two days ago? I need all the details."

"Bethany!" Kate hissed. "I have not 'taken a lover!' The idea is just ludicrous!"

"Oh." Bethany looked crestfallen. "Well, what happened? I thought you were attracted to Riley."

"I was. I mean, I am, but that's beside the point."

"No," Bethany replied. "I think that *is* the point."

"You know what I mean."

"Okay, okay. So, what's the matter? I'm not following. You're upset because…."

Kate sighed heavily. "Because Mrs. Windham thinks I've taken this lover! She said she 'noticed something different about me.' What am I going to do?"

Bethany shook her head. "Nope. Still not following."

"Do you notice anything different about me?"

Bethany looked at Kate, turned her head sideways and looked her over from head to toe, as though completing a thorough inspection. "Not really, no."

"Well then, why would Mrs. Windham say that?"

Bethany shrugged. "Maybe she just noticed you seemed happier or something."

Kate thought about that. "That makes sense. I mean, Riley did come over early this morning so maybe I was a bit chipper when I went to her house."

"Riley came over this morning?"

Kate looked over at Bethany who was grinning from ear to ear and obviously waiting for all the sordid details. "Wipe that look off your face, Beth. Nothing happened. He just came for coffee and to pick up Hadley. We only spent only a few minutes with each other."

"'Came for coffee,' huh?'" Bethany smirked. "Is that what it's called nowadays?"

"Oh, Stop. Nothing happened!" Kate hissed.

Bethany made a very expressive frown. "Oh, poop. I was hoping for a little more...I don't know...steam?"

Kate snorted. "Well, that's not going to happen with a seven year old running around. That's something I'm just not comfortable with regardless of how attracted I am to Riley."

"Well, I may be able to help you with that tiny detail."

Kate raised her eyebrows. "What do you mean?"

"Well," Bethany began, barely concealing a giggle. "Sarah wants Hadley to come over for a sleepover."

"Sarah does? And who, may I ask, put this suggestion into your daughter's head?"

Bethany looked down at the ground and shrugged. "I'm sure I have no idea." She looked back up at Kate and grinned. "So...Friday night work for you?"

Kate laughed out loud. "You do realize you are an accomplice to all of this, right?"

"And I'm completely fine with that." Bethany sat up and leaned towards Kate, her expression changing to one of complete seriousness. "I told you the other day; I want the old Kate back. I miss her."

Touched by her friend's words, Kate could only manage one word. "Thanks," she whispered.

Bethany looked pointedly over Kate's head. "You've got company," she said as she stood up.

Kate followed Bethany's gaze and saw Riley walking toward them. She couldn't help it and her face broke out into a huge grin.

"All-righty then," Bethany said, seeing the look on her friend's face. "I'll see you later."

"Bye Beth." She barely even glanced at Bethany's retreating figures since her gaze was focused on the man walking toward her. Riley's gaze met Kate's and didn't waiver as he made his way to the chair Bethany had vacated only moments before.

"Hey," he said softly.

Kate noticed that his tone was more intimate now. She realized it was a tone he'd begun using since they'd kissed. The knowledge that only after mere days she and Riley had something that was just between the two of them gave her a warm feeling in her belly. She didn't want to admit it, but she liked the feeling of having something for only the two of them, even if it was something as insignificant as the tone of his voice. She wondered if she had a special tone she used for him as well.

She looked at him splayed out on the chair beside of her and once again took in his near perfect form. It very nearly took her breath away. She wondered if she'd ever get used to seeing him sitting beside of her like this. She wondered if she'd ever get used to the idea that he had feelings for *her*. It was surreal.

"Practice go okay?" She asked.

"Yeah. I think Hadley's going to do really well tomorrow night. Her times on the fly are getting better and better. I'm sure she'll place in the meet."

"Really?" Although Kate loved her daughter desperately and thought she was the most wonderful kid on the face of the planet, she certainly wasn't one to think her child excelled at everything. Hadley had struggled with swimming for so long that Kate knew in order for Hadley to place in a meet must mean that Hadley's hard work was paying off. "Oh my god. She'll be thrilled to get a ribbon."

Riley smiled, then his expression turned somber. "So, listen."

Uh-oh, Kate thought. "What is it?"

"I've got to enter all the information for all the swimmers tonight. I'm not sure how long it's going to take."

Kate nodded, not sure where he was headed with this.

"I was hoping I could come over tonight and we could spend some time together but I'm thinking this might take me awhile."

"Oh," she replied, feeling more disappointed than she wanted to feel so early in their…relationship?

Riley seemed to sense her disappointment and leaned forward. "I'm really sorry, Kate. I had already entered the information for everyone but I was just told that they don't have any information for our team. I need to enter all the kids' information again in order to print out the heat sheet. Once it's all in, I can just move the kids around for their events."

"Don't worry about it. It's fine," she said, forcing her tone to mask her disappointment.

"Good," he replied and Kate could see he was visibly relieved, which both excited her and terrified her. She knew she was already feeling more for Riley than she thought was possible.

And she most certainly wasn't ready for it.

Chapter 18

"Hadley!!! Put your suit on! We're going to be late!" Kate stood at the bottom of the stairs, waiting impatiently for her daughter to appear. Instead, Hadley's voice bellowed from what Kate assumed was the inside of her room.

"I'm coming!" Kate giggled as she heard the exasperation in her daughter's tone.

Moments later, Hadley came down the steps tugging her swim suit over her shoulders.

"Do you have your goggles?"

"Yup."

"Okay, I've got snacks and some water...Do we need anything else?"

Hadley shook her head. Kate smiled at her daughter in the new bright red suit. Though she spent most of her days swimming, her body still retained the softness that was typical of most seven year olds. Kate knew that in the blink of an eye, Hadley would develop curves and breasts and subsequently lose all of her baby fat. For now, though, Kate relished the fact that her daughter filled out the team swimsuit with a round tummy as opposed to a flat, taut one.

The suit the team wore was a typical one piece with a hole in the lower back. Though the swim team managed to get a discount, the cost normally ran around $50.00. While Kate normally preferred swimsuits from the likes of Target, she felt that the amount of time Hadley spent in the suit over the course of the summer made it a worthwhile purchase. She also held out hope that the team would vote to keep the same suit for more than one year, although it had yet to happen. The cost of purchasing a new suit, in addition to joining the team and the pool membership fee added up, and with only one income, well, she needed to watch just where she spent her pennies.

"I've got your towel. Let's go." Kate said as she ushered Hadley out the front door.

Kate walked quickly in front of Hadley, hoping to get her to move quicker than her normal "Hadley pace," but of course, Hadley was oblivious to her mother's efforts. When they reached the car, Kate tossed the overflowing bag into the back seat and then got in the driver's seat, coughing at the heat that surrounded her. She turned the car on, letting the air conditioner blow for a moment before backing out of the driveway, knowing she needed as much A/C as possible before spending the evening beside a pool but not being allowed to go in it.

Kate was excited about the swim meet for more than one reason. Of course, seeing her daughter swim and actually having a chance to win a ribbon was thrilling but she hadn't seen Riley since yesterday at the pool. Just like he told her he would, he'd spent most of the night preparing for the meet, entering all the swimmers into the system to produce the heat sheet – the listing of all the events and the swimmers for each event. Kate was still feeling a bit unsettled from her realization that she actually missed Riley after not seeing him for an entire day.

They arrived at the pool to find the parking lot nearly full. Kate quickly glanced at her cell phone, concerned that they were late. They were not. Evidently, everyone was excited about the first meet and wanted to arrive early. Hadley unbuckled and opened the door before the car was turned off.

"Hadley, wait please. I need to get the bag." She smiled as she heard a very loud sigh from her daughter who was extremely anxious to get to the pool. She tossed the bag over her shoulder and began to make her way through the rows of cars with Hadley skipping excitedly behind. When they reached the sidewalk, Hadley ran in front of her, too anxious to wait for her mother, who was lugging all the necessary items.

Kate entered the pool and walked over to where the team was. Hadley was engrossed in a conversation with a few of her teammates. As she looked for a spot to put her bag down, she felt it being lifted from her shoulder. She looked up in surprise to find Riley standing beside her, holding the bag. "Hey," he said.

"Hey yourself," she replied, smiling at him.

The two of them stood there for only a moment or so but in that moment, she knew that he'd missed her as well. Riley placed her bag down next to a chair and then stood back up, leaning closer to her. "You're here all night, right?"

She nodded.

"Good. I like that you're close by." He whispered into her ear.

Kate couldn't help but smile.

"Kate! Riley!" Both of them turned at the sound of their names and saw Bethany coming toward them with Sarah in tow. "Are we late?"

"No," Riley replied. "I think everyone's just excited about the meet and got here early. You're fine."

"Whew! I thought for sure Sarah was going to miss her first event."

"That reminds me. Here's your heat sheet." He handed a group of papers that had been stapled together to Bethany and then to Kate. "Both Sarah and Hadley are swimming in five events and they're swimming a relay together."

"Oh, God," Kate said, "Hadley's going to be wiped after this!"

"I'm sure she can handle it. I'll see you two later, all right? I'm going to make sure everyone has a heat sheet." Kate looked down at her heat sheet in order to avoid watching him walk away.

"Is Hadley nervous?"

"I don't think so. More excited than anything."

Bethany nodded. "Sarah's the same. Though I have to tell you that she's only trying to get all this done so tomorrow will come quicker. She's sooo excited about the sleepover!"

Kate grinned. "I haven't even told Hadley yet. If I did, she'd spend the next day asking 'can we leave now?' and I'd lose it."

"Well, I'm sure it won't be long before-"

"MOM!! I'M SLEEPING AT SARAH'S TOMORROW?"

Kate laughed. "And there it is." She turned toward her daughter and nodded. "You sure are!" She watched at Hadley and Sarah hugged and jumped up and down with pure excitement. Kate would never understand the thrill of sleeping at someone else's house. The thought of sleeping in someone else's bed instead of her own held no appeal to her whatsoever.

"Sorry," Bethany said, cringing.

"Don't worry about it. I don't expect them to keep it a secret. They're too excited."

"I'm going to get Sarah marked up. I'll see you in a bit."

Kate went about the process of finding Hadley's name in the six or so pages of events. She highlighted each of them, then wrote the event number, stroke, distance and lane placement on Hadley's arm in black Sharpie. While there was a team parent for each age group that was responsible for gathering the children and putting them where they needed to be, having it written on their arms was yet another safety measure. Plus, it got the kids started on the process of learning where they needed to be and when they needed to be there. Because of the huge demand for Sharpie's, Kate usually purchased a pack of them before each meet. It never failed that someone would forget to bring a Sharpie and once it was out of her hands, there was a pretty good chance that she'd never see it again.

It was always sort of hectic at the beginning of each meet. Inevitably, there was always a parent or two who couldn't read the heat sheet or didn't know how to mark their kids' arms. Because of this, those that were familiar with the process ended up grabbing any child who wasn't cover in black Sharpie and writing their events on them, with much thanks from their parents.

After this initial rush of getting the events written on all the kids' arms and then lining up the children she was responsible for the first few events, Kate stood off to the side and took a breather, feeling the heat for the first time that evening. Already, there was a line of moisture trailing down her chest and soaking her sports bra. Unfortunately, it was only going to get worse.

She looked over at the pool to make sure the kids she'd just lined up were still in their spots, waiting for their event. As she did so, she stole a glance at Riley, who, as though feeling her eyes on him, turned and looked at her. He grinned, then turned back to the heat sheet in his hand, checking to make sure all his swimmers were lined up. Kate smiled in return and felt color rise to her cheeks. She had to admit, but this feeling that came with knowing someone was thinking of you was something she could get used to. She liked knowing that she could look across the pool or a room and Riley would glance back at her and smile. It made her feel special, which was something she hadn't felt in a very long time. She was used to being Hadley's mother, nothing more.

The swim meet lasted the usual four hours, which was very long when standing in 90 plus degree heat. It was also long for the parents who had swimmers scattered throughout the events. It wasn't out of the ordinary for a swimmer to swim in one of the first events and then one of the last, meaning that child's parents were there the entire time. Admittedly, meet nights were a long, arduous process, but Kate knew Hadley loved swimming so she did it without complaint.

The Dolphins lost the meet but the morale of the team was still very high. They came closer to winning the meet tonight than any other time before. Partly because of the close score and partly because it was the first meet of the season, the kids decided to jump in the pool. As soon as that was completed, they decided it only made sense if they pulled the coaches in afterward. It wasn't long before most of the parents decided to jump in. Kate was waivering on whether or not to jump in but that was decided for her when Hadley came over and grabbed her arm and began to pull her toward the deep end. Kate began to laugh, knowing she would let her daughter pull her into the pool despite not having the strength to do so. However, before she was tugged even a few steps, strong arms lifted her up and walked her toward the pool. She looked up at Riley and laughed, realizing he was going to toss her in. Instead, he simply walked over to the edge of the pool and stepped in, taking Kate with him. She rose up out of the water, sputtering and laughing at the same time. Because she was in the eight foot section of the pool and wasn't the best swimmer, she found she needed to hold onto Riley's shoulder – a fact that she felt was just too convenient for Riley not to have planned for.

The water, though only marginally cooler than the air outside, still felt wonderful after four hours of standing in the heat. She hung onto Riley's shoulder, for the moment forgetting they were surrounded by nearly sixty children and most of their parents. Kate looked at him and smiled; the certain smile that had become the look they shared between each other.

"So, coach, great meet tonight," she said.

"Thanks," he said, keeping his eyes locked with hers.

Kate figured she'd better get out of the pool before she felt an irrepressible urge to start frolicking with Riley. She splashed him playfully as she swam to the side.

"You getting out?" He asked, giving her frown that she knew was meant to be playful.

"Afraid so. Hadley's probably wiped. If there's practice tomorrow, I'd better get her home and into bed."

He swam over to the side and held on beside her. "Mind if I swing by later?"

Kate felt a rush of pleasure as well as the color rise to her cheeks. She nodded.

"Great. I've got to put the ropes and the flags and stuff away so...maybe an hour or so?"

"Perfect," she said.

"Riley," came a voice from on the deck. Kate looked up to see Wendy standing there. Instinctively, the two of them moved apart just a bit. Because they were in the water, the movement was soft and fluid as opposed to jerky and sudden and Kate couldn't help but feel a twinge of guilt run through her knowing she was hiding something from her friend. "Are you coming home? Hey Kate."

"Hi Wendy," Kate replied while bobbing in the water.

"Nah," Riley said to his mother. "I think I'm going to head out for a bit."

"Well, all right," she replied, her tone indicating it wasn't all right with her. "Hopefully, I'll be asleep when you get home so I'll see you in the morning."

Kate lifted herself out of the water and stood dripping on the side of the pool. "It's a good thing I've got extra towels. I should be pissed at you!" She smiled and leaned over Riley, who remained in the pool.

"You would, but I'm just too cute, right?"

"Oh, yeah. That's *exactly* what it is," she said, rolling her eyes. "I'm going to head home. I'll see you later."

Riley winked at her. "Later."

Kate gathered up her things then began to look for Hadley. She couldn't help it but she had a grin on her face that she couldn't get rid of. It seemed Riley had that effect on her. She found Hadley in a makeshift cabin that the girls had made out of lounge chairs that were turned on their side and upside down. The girls had draped their towels over and under the chairs and they were huddled inside the space they'd created. Kate leaned over the contraption and pulled one of the towels back.

"Hadley," she said, as the girls shrieked in surprise, "come on. It's time to head home."

Hadley sighed heavily as she moved to crawl out of the chairs and grab her towel. "All right," she huffed.

When Hadley stood upright, Kate draped her arms around her shoulders. "You swam great tonight. I'm really proud of you."

"Thanks, mom," she replied, beaming.

The ride home was mostly quiet and Kate knew that Hadley was spent. Luckily, she'd packed plenty of things for Hadley to eat between her events so there wouldn't be the hassle of dinner when they got home. Of course, Kate felt certain that after swimming all her events, Hadley wouldn't make it up the stairs to her room, let alone eat something before she collapsed. She managed to get Hadley out of her wet bathing suit and into one of Todd's old t-shirts, just a few of her father's items Hadley had insisted on keeping. While she initially had wanted to rid the house of all of his clothes in an effort to promote healing, she gave in and let Hadley have her wish, thinking it might not be the worst idea for Hadley to sleep in her father's old t-shirts. Hell, she had no idea if it was right or not. All she knew was that it made Hadley feel better so she opted to try it. She was winging it, anyway.

After tucking Hadley in, Kate went downstairs and took a shower. She needed to rid herself of the feel of chlorine on her skin and in her hair. She put on a clean tank top and a pair of shorts, then combed her wet hair, leaving it to air dry. She was just hanging her towel over the rack when she heard the knock at the door. She smiled, thinking that only someone with two younger brothers would know to knock rather than ring the doorbell when there was a child asleep in the house.

She took a deep breath, then walked through the living room and opened the front door.

Chapter 19

Kate opened the front door and felt a flush of warmth the moment her eyes met Riley's.

"Hi," she said.

"Hi." He glanced over her shoulder towards the stairs. "Where's Hadley?"

"Upstairs sleeping. She's practically unconscious."

The moment the words were out of her mouth, Riley swept her up into his arms and planted a kiss on her lips that left her breathless. He pulled back and looked down into her eyes. "You sure this is okay? Me coming over, I mean. I realized I sort of put you on the spot earlier…"

"Riley," she said, placing a hand on his arm. "It's fine. I'm glad you came over."

He looked visibly relieved. "Good. I was a bit worried." He pulled her close to him once again and nuzzled her neck. "God, you smell good."

She chuckled. "Come on in," she said, stepping aside. Riley walked into the living room and as he passed her, Kate got a faint whiff of him and she realized she was beginning to like the smell of chlorine. She followed him into the living room and sat down beside him on the couch, tucking her legs underneath herself so she could face him. She put one arm on the back of the couch and rested her head on her hand.

"So…" She said, unsure of what exactly she was going to say. She was stunned to realize she was actually nervous!

Riley looked at her and smiled. "You all right?"

Kate chuckled softly. "Yes. It's just that this," she pointed to Riley and then back to herself, "is going to take some getting used to. Having these handsome men show up on my doorstep at all hours of the night is wreaking havoc on my sleep schedule." She grinned wickedly at him.

He raised one eyebrow and grinned back at her. "Men? What

men are showing up on your door?"

"Oh, I lose track..." Kate said. She suddenly realized she was flirting with Riley and she had to admit, it felt good. Feeling a bit bold, she reached up with one hand and ran her fingers through his hair. Though he'd been in the pool within the last hour, his hair was surprisingly soft. Slowly, she worked her hands through his hair, massaging his scalp. Riley released a small groan and closed his eyes, leaning into her hand.

"I could get used to this."

Kate continued to massage his scalp, then worked her way onto his shoulders and upper arms, loving the feel of his skin beneath her fingers. Riley's breathing became slow and steady and for just a moment, she began to think he'd fallen asleep.

As though reading her mind, he sat up. "Don't worry. I'm not going to fall asleep. I wouldn't waste my time here with you by sleeping."

Kate found she had no response. She wasn't accustomed to someone being so open with their feelings and truthfully, it was throwing her for a loop. Riley was exposing his heart to her, unafraid of what might happen. He was so vulnerable and that both thrilled and saddened her. Thrilled for the emotion she knew he was feeling for her and at the same time saddened to realize he was able to feel so much and with such reckless abandon because he had never experienced loss as she had. She knew she cared for Riley; very much in fact. But she also knew that as a result of her loss, she would need to keep her heart protected for just a little bit longer.

They sat on Kate's couch for some time, enjoying the time they had with each other. After several moments, Kate began to wish they could have more time like this, alone, just the two of them. It struck her then that she'd forgotten to tell Riley something.

"I just thought of something." Her brow furrowed slightly, making a tiny groove in the middle of her forehead. Riley resisted the urge to reach up and smooth it out for her, not wanting her to feel any amount of stress.

"Oh yeah?" He asked. "What's that?" As he looked into her eyes, he noticed she suddenly looked uncomfortable or nervous – he wasn't sure which – and began to feel a bit of apprehension. He sat silently next to her, almost afraid to move while he waited for her to speak. With each passing moment, she seemed to become more uncomfortable. He felt his apprehension turn to near panic and silently urged her to just say whatever was on her mind. Though honestly, he was constantly afraid she was going to change her mind about him and explain that all of this – this time spent with each other, the rush of emotions – was all a big mistake. He'd had feelings for Kate for so long and now that they'd finally been able to be let out, he wasn't sure he'd be able to tuck them back inside so easily. They were out now, with a mind of their own. He was falling for her, and falling hard. He swallowed, waiting for her to tell him what was on his mind.

"Hadley's having a sleepover tomorrow night with Sarah."

Riley nodded, yet unaware of the sleepover's implications and still nervous about what was to come.

"Well," Kate asked, smiling hesitantly, "do you have any plans?"

He shrugged. "What...for tomorrow? No, not really. I mean we've got practice in the morning, but that's about it. Why?"

When faced with actually talking about her plans for tomorrow night, she became tongue-tied. It seemed she couldn't make herself speak the words. "Hadley's sleeping over at Sarah's house..."

"Uh-huh..." He responded, not understanding.

Kate had to chuckle as she realized she practically needed to draw him a map. "She won't be here tomorrow night....all night." She paused, waiting for it to sink in.

Riley was looking at her, clearly not understanding where Kate was alluding to. After several moments, his eyes lit up and he grinned. "Ohhhhh...you mean....."

"Maybe you'd want to come over tomorrow night? We could have dinner and..."

"Just the two of us? You mean..." Relief flooded though him. He felt like leaping up onto the couch a la Tom Cruise but instead remained seated, trying to grasp what she'd just said.

She leaned over and kissed him on the lips. She pulled back and looked him dead in the eyes. "That's exactly what I mean."

Riley looked at her strangely. "Are you actually going to cook?"

Kate laughed out loud. "Don't look so surprised! I have managed to keep Hadley alive for the past seven years. I'm certain I can manage *something.*"

Riley leaned forward and kissed her gently on the lips. "That sounds incredible. But are you sure?"

Kate nodded, feeling more certain with every passing moment. Despite wanting to take things slowly, she of all people should have known you can't control your heart. It always seems to have a mind of its own. She wanted Riley, desperately, and thanks to Bethany, she would have an entire evening with him. "I'm sure."

He reached for her hand, never taking his gaze from hers. "You're so beautiful," he blurted. The moment the words were out of his mouth, he wished he could pull them back it. It wasn't that he didn't mean the words – God, how he meant the words – it was that he was still terrified that this whole situation would somehow vanish before his eyes. He feared his feelings for her were moving too fast for her and was afraid he might destroy this situation they found themselves in. In spite of her invitation for the following night, he still felt as though Kate were a frightened kitten that would run away if he moved too quickly. But when he looked at her, he found she wasn't frightened at all. She was smiling back at him, which to him made her all the more beautiful.

"Riley," she said softly, then reached out and ran her fingers through his hair. "What am I going to do with you if you talk to me like that?"

"I will talk to you like that all day, every day if it means I can spend every waking moment on this couch with you."

Kate's hand rested on his cheek. She was still, save for her thumb, which began to caress the side of his face. Slowly, he leaned into her hand. He pressed his hand over hers, then moved their hands together so it was over his mouth. Ever so gently, he kissed the center of her palm, keeping his gaze locked on hers. He smiled as he felt her shudder.

"I'm so glad you're here," she said as she leaned forward. He reached for the side of her face and gently pulled her toward him. As their lips met, Kate felt her bones turn to jelly. Her last coherent thought was that she was thankful she was seated on the couch. Had the two of them been standing, her legs would not have held her up.

Chapter 20

The next morning, Riley was at the door a bit early, which Kate noticed, was becoming quite a habit of his. She opened the door and looked at him and then the clock over the sink.

"Gosh, you're early! Hadley's not even dressed yet."

He grinned. "Oh, bummer. I guess I'll have to kill a few minutes." Before Kate knew what was happening, Riley had wrapped his arms around her, lifted her up off the ground and then placed her back down on the front porch. He reached behind her and closed the door, then pulled her into his arms and began to kiss her. When he finally pulled away, Kate was breathless.

"Good morning," he said.

"Good morning to you," she replied, lifting a finger to her lips. "Is this going to become a habit for you?" She grinned at him.

He nodded. "It's a habit I hope I never break myself of."

From inside the house, they heard Hadley shouting for her mother. "I guess we should head back inside. You want a bagel or something?"

"Or something," he replied, grinning.

She smacked him on the shoulder as they walked into the house. Hadley was rummaging through the cabinets in search of breakfast.

"What do you want for breakfast, sweetheart?"

"Do we have any more pop-tarts?"

"Umm…I think so." Kate began to rummage through another cabinet in search of the elusive pop tart. Normally, she would push Hadley to have something a bit more substantial for breakfast since she was going to be swimming for the better part of two hours. But today, given the events of the previous night and the plans they'd made, she was happy to dole out something sugar-filled to her daughter. After all, she got a treat, why shouldn't Hadley? She chuckled softly.

"What's so funny?" Hadley asked.

"Nothing, Sweetheart," Kate replied. She stole a glance at Riley, who was looking at her with eyebrows raised and a grin on his face. She tried to look sternly at him but instead, felt color rise to her cheeks. "Come on, eat up. You've got practice."

Hadley opened the silver package and sat down at the table. Kate poured her a glass of milk and set it down in front of her. She turned around and found Riley staring at her.

"What?" She stage whispered.

"Why don't you come to the pool later and bring lunch? We can hang around for a bit and you can swim."

Upon hearing this, Hadley whipped around. "Really? Mom, will you swim with us?"

Kate looked sternly at Riley, making an attempt to chastise him. "I really don't have a choice now, do I?"

He grinned and shook his head. "We'll meet you there in a couple of hours. Come on Hadley. Let's head out."

"Okay." She bounced up out of her chair as though a spring were under her and ran to put on her flip flops. "Ready!" She said, pulling her towel around her.

Riley smiled at her, then looked back at Kate. "So, we'll see you later."

She smiled back at him. "I'll be there."

Kate watched the two of them as they walked out the front door. Hadley was a ball of energy, skipping and hopping the entire way to the care. Kate had to giggle watching her daughter walk beside this man. His height made Hadley look so much smaller than she actually was. Once Riley's car was out of sight, she turned and headed back to the kitchen. She poured herself another cup of coffee and then sat down at her computer to begin her day.

Nearly two hours later, Kate arrived at the pool with a bag of snacks in her hand. Experience told her that it was impossible to have enough food in the house during swim season. Kate just hoped that what she brought would feed both Hadley and Riley for the hour or so she planned to stay at the pool.

She found an empty chair easily since most of the families were leaving after practice. Kate had always found it odd that the pool seemed to empty after practice, but without fail, each day at eleven o'clock, the pool would empty, leaving only a few die-hard kids in the water. Of course, Hadley was one of the few children who never wanted to leave the pool and if Kate had allowed her to, Hadley would be up for sleeping on a raft in the pool overnight.

She spread out her towel on the chair and had just sat down when Riley approached. She looked up at his tan body, which was barely decent in his tiny competition swimsuit. She felt her pulse quicken and had to stifle a gasp. It seemed each time she saw him, she was blown away at how attractive he was and her body responded in kind. At least now, knowing he knew she felt that way, she didn't have to hide it, from him at least. The other pool members – well, that was a different story altogether.

"And what do you think you're doing?" He joked.

"Relaxing, why?"

He shook his head. "Oh, no. You're getting in the water with us."

Kate was just about to tell him she wanted to sit on the deck and relax but then she realized she would rather be in the cool water with him. The thought of being in the pool with Riley was simply too tempting to pass up. Just then, Hadley walked up behind him.

"Are you going to swim?" She asked.

"I think I am," Kate replied.

Hadley grinned at her, walked back to the edge of the pool, and then pulled her goggled over her face in preparation for jumping into the deep end. She jumped in, cannonball style, making a huge splash. When she came up for air, she was grinning from ear to ear.

Kate stood on the side of the pool and shook her head. She looked at Riley and smiled. "She's a fish! It's a wonder I ever get her to come home!"

They walked over to where Hadley had jumped in and Kate sat on the side of the pool, letting her feet get used to the water. The water was still relatively cool, since it was only the third week in June. Still though, she would have liked to have a few moments to prep for total immersion. Unfortunately, Hadley began to splash her almost immediately after she sat down, causing her to shiver. Realizing the only way to win this battle was to get in the water, Kate slid off the side and went under, chasing Hadley. She came up for air in front of Hadley and playfully, dunked her under water.

"I love it when you swim with me!" Hadley squealed. She wrapped her arms around her mother and the floated peacefully for several moments.

Riley, who had been watching from the deck, stood up and dove into the pool, coming up for air next to them. Hadley laughed out loud, causing Kate to giggle. The three of them played for a bit, then Kate figured she might as well swim some laps. She was a bit out of practice but managed to complete a few without drowning and without choking down too much chlorinated water, two feats that pleased her to no end, given the fact that the only time she swam was during the first few weeks of the summer. Once the novelty wore off, Kate resumed her spot in the chair and made it a goal to read all the magazines that had accumulated at her house during the year.

After swimming for about an hour or so, Kate realized she was hungry so she decided to resume her position on her towel. Once Hadley and Riley realized Kate had brought food, they were right behind her. They got to their chairs and Kate opened her cooler, revealing a smorgasbord of sandwiches, chips, and fruit.

"Hey, Hadley!" Kate looked up to see Marissa, another little girl on the swim team and one of Hadley's closest friends standing at the end of Hadley's chair. "Do you want to play? My mom got me some new dive sticks."

Hadley looked over at her mother. "Can I?" Kate nodded, then watched her skip off with Marissa.

Kate couldn't help but feel a bit of unease. Marissa's mother was a bit of a gossip and Kate wasn't sure how this little picnic of theirs would look to another parent. Of course, it was what it was. They were just eating some sandwiches. Surely, you couldn't read too much into it, could you? She frowned as she watched Hadley skip across the pool deck with Marissa.

"What's wrong?" Riley asked.

Kate nodded her head toward Hadley and Marissa. "Marissa's mom is somewhat of a gossip."

He looked toward the other side of the pool where Marissa's mother sat. "And you're worried about what she might say?"

Kate nodded.

Riley turned to look at her. "I don't understand. Why is it such a big deal?"

Kate looked at him pointedly and waited for him to understand.

"Ohhhhhh," he said, finally realizing what it was that Kate was worried about. "You're worried about the age thing again, right? I don't get why this is such an issue? If our ages were reversed, it wouldn't be a big deal."

She rolled her eyes at him and frowned. "No, if you were my age, you'd be high-fived by all your friends. I'm just a…a… cougar."

He laughed out loud. "You're kidding, right? If anything, I'm the cougar. I kissed you, remember?"

It was Kate's turn to sigh. "I don't think it matters who kissed who. It only matters that I'm old enough…"

"Don't say it. You are NOT old enough to be my mother."

"Okay, older sister."

"Better. Much better." He had a satisfied look on his face and Kate wanted to smack it off him.

"You know. This isn't funny."

He turned to look at her. "I know it isn't. Look, I really don't think you should worry about this. We're spending time with each other, and that's all there is to it. Who cares what anyone else thinks?" He was looking at her and waiting for her to agree with him. Though she knew he had a point, there was still a tiny part of her that felt there was still cause for worry.

"Look, in theory you're right. But this is real life and people just wouldn't understand. Not yet, anyway. I just need some time to get used to this before we broadcast it, I guess."

"Mom?" Hadley interrupted them. "Marissa wants to know if I can have a sleepover."

"Well, when?" Kate asked. "You're sleeping over at Sarah's house tonight so it will have to be another night." She looked at Marissa, who was standing beside her daughter. "Did your mother say it was okay?"

Marissa nodded, then turned to point to her mom who was sitting on the other side of the pool. "She's right over there."

Kate stood up. "It's fine with me but let me go over and check with your mom, all right?"

Both girls hugged and jumped up and down. Kate smiled at them, then turned to Riley. "I'll be right back."

She walked over to where Marissa's mother sat. " Hey, Holly. How are you?"

"I'm fine, Kate. How 'bout yourself?"

Kate nodded. "I'm good. The girls just wandered over and asked about a sleepover. You okay with that?"

"Sure. Hadley's always so well behaved. And having Hadley

around means I don't have to play with Marissa." She joked.

Kate smiled and nodded knowingly. "Believe me. I completely understand. Hadley's sleeping over at Sarah's house tonight but any other time is fine with me. That is, if you're sure Hadley didn't invite herself." Although Kate had spoken to her daughter about not inviting herself anywhere, she wasn't under any illusion that Hadley actually *waited* for an invitation, at least when it came to sleepovers. Sure, the invites came but not nearly as often as Hadley would like, which was nearly every day. As a result, Hadley would often suggest to friend that they have a sleepover. Much to Kate's embarrassment, the sleepover would inevitably involve Hadley sleeping at someone else's house.

Holly laughed. "No. Though I am familiar with that. Marissa does it all the time. But Hadley's clean this time. Marissa's been asking since the first practice."

"All right. Just want to make sure, you know?"

Holly nodded. "Sure. Is that Riley over there?"

Kate suddenly felt exposed and very uncomfortable. "Er…yeah. I brought some sandwiches for us. He's been such a big help to me this summer, helping me with Hadley and all."

"Oh, right."

"Yeah, he picks her up in the mornings and brings her to practice. I figured the least I could do was bring some lunch." Kate knew she was rambling but she felt the need to fully explain what she was doing. Although she knew it wouldn't have much effect on what Holly told everyone she came in contact with. Kate just wondered exactly what their picnic looked like from the perspective of an outsider.

"I saw you swimming earlier. How's the water?" Holly was looking at her as though she was the only suspect in a murder case and was waiting for her to confess. Then again, maybe she was just reading into her questions. Maybe Holly just really wondered how the water was. Sheesh! She was driving herself crazy with paranoia.

"The water's great. I swam a few laps then realized how out of shape I was."

"Oh, Kate, Don't be silly. You look great! Those of us that have had three children are the ones that need to worry about our looks." She giggled in the way that women do when they're telling you how awful they look but want you to tell them otherwise. Kate didn't disappoint.

161

"Holly, come on! You look great! In fact, you're even thinner this year than last."

Holly looked down at her midsection, smoothing it out with her hands while she sucked in. As she did so, Kate could make out her two lower-most ribs and had to stifle a chuckle. "Really? Do you think so? I have been trying to eat healthier, get a little exercise…"

Kate was nodding absentmindedly, wondering how quickly she could leave this superficial conversation. It wasn't that she didn't like Holly; in fact, she liked her very much. She just never had time for these types of inane conversations where people stood around complementing each other and not really meaning it. Kate knew that deep down, Holly was just itching to ask about Riley. Sure enough, once she was done clenching and unclenching her thighs in order to check their firmness, she returned to the topic Kate wished she could avoid.

"So, Riley's sitting for you this summer?" Kate nodded. "I'm sure Hadley loves that. All the kids just love him. And he's such a good sport. Whenever I see him, he's got at least five kids climbing on top of him." She leaned forward, as though about to share some deep, dark secret. And of course, she was. "Lucky kids, huh?"

Kate chuckled uncomfortably as Holly continued.

"And you've got him all to yourself, you little devil, you."

Kate was desperately in need of a change of subject. Out of some higher power, Hadley came running up to the two of them dripping wet. Kate could have kissed her.

"Mom! Come watch me do a flip!"

She looked at Holly and shrugged. "I guess I'm being summoned. I'll see you tomorrow?"

"You bet," Holly replied. "Look at your schedule and then we'll figure out when we can do the sleepover."

Kate nodded and smiled, then followed Hadley over to the other side of the pool, where she and Marissa were tumbling in the water, clearly enjoying the buoyancy it provided. She watched for a few moments, cheering and clapping as required, then went back to her chair where Riley was still munching on the last of his sandwich.

"You want to swim some more?" He asked.

She shook her head. "Nah, I think I'll just read a bit. You go ahead." She reached into her bag and pulled out a book, opening it up without so much as a second glance toward Riley. Only moments ago, there had been playful banter and sexual tension. Now there was an awkward silence between them. Riley stared at her for a moment, then leaned forward.

"What's the matter?" He asked.

"Nothing, why?"

He tilted his head as he looked at her. "You seem upset."

Kate sighed heavily and slapped the book against her thigh. "I'm not upset. I'm just...Oh, I don't know what I am."

Riley looked at Kate as though inspecting her for some clue as to what had made her become upset. After a few moments a thought occurred to him. "What did she say?" He asked, nodding toward the other side of the pool.

"Nothing really. Just some offhanded comment about how the kids climb on you."

"Huh?" He asked, clearly confused. "Why would that get you upset?"

Kate paused, unsure of the best way to explain it to him. "It wasn't the fact that she said the kids were climbing on you. It was that she made a snarky comment about it."

Now Riley grinned. "Oh...I see. You're not jealous are you?"

Kate smacked him on the shoulder with her book. "Don't be ridiculous! I'm not the jealous type."

"Then what?" Riley was back to looking confused.

"It's like there was...sort of an undercurrent in the conversation. I don't know. It was like she was trying to insinuate something."

"And that bothers you," he said and Kate noticed a hint of sadness in his voice.

Kate sat up and leaned forward, wanting to comfort him yet aware that eyes were on them. "I just don't want to advertise this yet," she said, pointing to the two of them. "Before we tell anyone, I want Wendy to be told. I think it's the right thing to do. Once we talk to her, then I don't care who knows. I don't want your mother to find out something and think we were...I don't know, hiding this from her?"

"I know you're right." He sighed heavily. "It's just that...well; she's in every aspect of my life. I just want to have something to myself. But it is frustrating for me to sit here and pretend that I'm *just* the person who drives Hadley to practice."

Kate smiled tenderly. "Riley, you're not '*just*' anything. I hope you know that." He nodded and she continued. "This is all so new to me and I need want to make sure I handle this the right way. I'd hate for anything to happen to my friendship with your mother. I owe her so much."

Riley nodded his understanding.

She continued. "It's very important to me that she hears about this," she pointed to the two of them and noticed Riley grin as she did so, "from us. I think it would hurt her if she were to find out about her friend dating her son from some gossip mommy on the swim team. And Holly is the biggest gossip-monger there is."

As she sat back, she wondered if she and Riley were there yet. Was it time for the two of them to talk to Wendy? The thought terrified her. She knew she had feelings for Riley; feelings that were more than just some passing fling. She was beginning to look forward to his visits and miss him when he wasn't able to stop by. And yes, there was a small part of her that wanted to show everyone that they were a couple, if that's what was happening here. But most importantly, she needed to have Wendy's blessing. And in order to get that, she and Riley were going to have to tell her themselves…before someone else did.

"You know…" She said, her voice trailing off as she thought about this whatever-it-was between she and Riley. "Maybe it's time we talked to Wendy." Kate looked at Riley and raised her eyebrows. "What do you think?"

He smiled, then leaned forward, elbows on his knees in order to look directly in her eyes. Kate felt a shiver run through her as she caught his eye and wondered if she'd ever get used to having those green eyes look at her with such intensity. "Kate, as much as I need to keep something from my mother, I will tell whoever you want, whenever you want if it means I can walk anywhere I want with my arm draped around your shoulders."

"Well, good." She said, tearing her gaze from his, knowing that unless she did so, she'd melt into a puddle right there on the pool deck.

Riley nodded. "I'll talk to her this weekend. We're still on for tonight, right?"

Kate felt a flutter in her belly. *Tonight.* Riley would be coming over tonight and Hadley would be spending the night at Sarah's house. God bless Bethany.

"Oh, yes." She said, meeting his gaze with a look she hoped told him all she was feeling. "We are definitely on for tonight."

Chapter 21

Kate checked Hadley's bag to make sure she had all the necessities – toothbrush, toothpaste, pajamas, sleeping bag – which of course were all missing. Apparently, if you were to ask Hadley, all you needed for a sleepover were a few stuffed animals and your entire collection of Polly Pockets. Kate put the missing items in Hadley's bag and the brought it downstairs where she was waiting anxiously by the front door, holding her pillow and favorite blanket.

"Can we go now?" She asked.

Kate looked at the clock. They would be about a half hour early. Knowing Bethany wouldn't mind, she nodded. After all, Bethany would understand that Kate wanted to get home and get ready for her evening with Riley – whatever that entailed. It had been forever since she'd had…well, whatever this was and wasn't sure exactly what she needed to do to prepare.

Ever since she'd made these plans with Riley, her pulse had been racing, and not in a good way. Truth be told, she was terrified. She hadn't been with a man in well over a year and she was afraid of disappointing Riley. Besides worry about her own lack of practice, there was the tiny matter of her body not looking as it did when it was twenty, which she assumed, was what Riley was accustomed to viewing. Though she loved Hadley more than anything in the world, her stretch marks were at all pleasing to look at. She said a silent prayer that Riley was someone who'd agree to keeping the lights off.

She texted Bethany to let her know they were on their way and within moments, she responded with a smiley face and several exclamation points. Kate chuckled, causing Hadley to look at her strangely.

"We can go now," Kate said to her daughter. "Do you have everything?"

"Yup," Hadley said, hopping up and down. "Let's go!"

"All right."

She drove the short distance to Bethany's house and when she pulled into the driveway, she laughed out loud when she saw her friend standing on the front porch. Kate knew she was going to give her a pep talk and she realized she could use it. She put the car in park and Hadley jumped out of the car and ran into the house, nearly knocking Bethany over in the process. Luckily, Bethany was accustomed to such behavior and laughed as she caught Kate's eye.

Kate slowly walked up to the front porch and hugged her friend. "What the *hell* am I doing?"

Bethany pulled out of the embrace and held Kate's shoulders. "You are living again. That's what you're doing. Now go home and get ready for your date."

"I don't know if I can do this, Beth."

"Of course you can. You want to, don't you?"

"Oh my *God!* Of course I *want* to. What if I'm awful at this? It's been so long since I've…"

Bethany smiled knowingly. "You'll be fine. And I don't even think you can be *bad* at it. Besides, he's probably nervous too."

"I doubt that," Kate snorted. She took a deep breath, straightened her spine and nodded. "All right. I'm heading home. I'll see you in the morning."

"Can't wait!" Bethany giggled, causing Kate to roll her eyes. She stepped off the porch and walked to her car, waving to her friend over her shoulder.

"Details! I'll want details!" Bethany called after her.

Kate drove home slowly, wondering for perhaps the thousandth time if she was making a huge mistake. She felt a wave of sadness deep within her and realized that if her feelings for Riley were wrong, she didn't want to be right. The thought of not being with Riley caused her more anguish than she cared to admit. She cared for him, truly cared for him, which scared her even more than not being with him.

Good lord. Was this even possible? What exactly were these feeling she had for him? Could she be falling in love with him? She shook her head. She couldn't be. It was impossible! It had only been, what, a few weeks? Sure, she'd known him for a few years but she'd only *known* him for a much shorter period of time. No, there was no way she was falling in love with him. It wasn't possible. She sighed.

Of course she was. She was falling in love with Wendy's son.

"Shit," she mumbled.

Once home, Kate cleaned up the kitchen and living room. She had picked up a roasted chicken earlier and now put it into the oven to re-heat. She poured herself a glass of wine and took a sip of it, letting the warmth of it slide down her throat. She walked into her bedroom closet, still carrying the glass of wine and tried to select an outfit. While she didn't want to look as though she was trying too hard, she certainly didn't want to look as though this were just an ordinary day. It was anything but. Besides the fact that she was about to spend the night with another man – the first one since her husband, she was also going to spend the night with a man she was nearly certain she was falling in love with.

There was no doubt about it; she was terrified.

She took a large sip from her glass and selected a pair of black shorts and a silk top. She nodded, feeling like the outfit gave the exact impression she wanted to give – casual, but with a hint of something special.

Kate laid the clothes out on the bed and then turned on the shower. She took her time, making sure to rinse and repeat, rubbing her legs with her hands to make sure they were free of stubble, and then coating herself with thick, scented body lotion. When she at last turned the water off, her skin was smooth and soft, and begging to be touched.

She got dressed slowly, taking sips from her glass occasionally. Kate stood in front of the mirror and combed her shoulder length, dark hair. She worked her fingers through it so it would fall as she wanted it to across her eyes but still look as though it was effortless. Her hair had a slight wave to it and for once, she was thankful for it. As it dried in the coolness of her air conditioned home, it would form loose waves that would curl delicately around her face. Kate hoped Riley would tuck one of those loose curls behind her ear as he'd done the first time he kissed her.

She looked in the mirror and nodded. She was ready. Well, as ready as she was ever going to be. Kate turned from the mirror and made her way into the living room. As she sat down on the couch to wait, she wondered if she should wait on the front porch instead. She stood, then paused. Would she appear too eager if she were to wait outside? Maybe she should just sit here on the couch.

She sat down again. What about the TV? Should she put it on? Leave it off? What about music? Should she put on some easy-listening? Would setting the mood appear cheesy? Kate sighed, then flopped back on the couch.

What the hell had she gotten herself in to?

Just then, she heard a soft knock on the front door. Their first night together was about to begin. Slowly, she stood up and walked to the front door.

Okay, she thought. *Here goes....*

Chapter 22

Riley stood on the other side of the door, hands shoved into the pockets of his khaki shorts. Kate realized he was just as nervous as she was and she felt all her apprehension evaporate. It was going to be all right. They looked at each other and grinned, understanding the other felt exactly the same. Riley leaned across the threshold and kissed Kate gently on the lips.

"Nervous?" He asked.

"Not anymore," she replied, reaching her arms up and wrapping them around his neck. "Now I'm just glad you're here."

"I'm glad I'm here too." He stepped in and took Kate into his arms, kicking the door closed behind him. He lifted her up off the ground and held her so they were face to face. Kate instinctively wrapped her legs around his waist and placed her hands on the side of his face.

"Hi," he said, grinning at her.

"Hi, yourself," she replied as she pulled him closer and kissed him deeply.

Riley carried Kate into the kitchen and sat her on the counter. She kept her legs wrapped around him, unwilling to let go of him for even an instant. He pulled away from her and looked her in the eyes. He placed his hands on either side of her face and then traced one loose curl along the side of her face, then tucked it behind her ear. She shuddered.

"I love it when you do that."

Riley wound his hands in her hair and pulled her closer, taking her mouth in his. He nibbled the outer edges of her lips before nudging them apart with his tongue. He heard a soft moan escape and it made his pulse race. He pulled her even closer. His hands returned to the side of her face and he pulled away momentarily to look at her. Riley felt certain this was all a dream and had to make sure it was real.

It was. He saw the passion in Kate's eyes and knew he was going to take her right here on the counter unless they stopped.

Riley reached around behind him to untangle himself from Kate's legs, then took a step back and placed his hands on Kate's shoulders.

"What is it?" she whispered, her face a mixture of confusion and sadness.

He saw the disappointment in her eyes, which was the last thing he expected to see. She had no idea the effect she had on him. "Kate," he said, grinning knowingly. "If I don't stop, I'm going to have my way with you right here on your floor."

She smiled. "Now why on earth would you want to use the floor when I have a perfectly good bed just down the hall?" Kate hopped down off the counter and in a moment of boldness unlike anything she'd ever done before, she stood up on her tip-toes and kissed him deeply on the mouth. "Follow me," she said as walked out of the kitchen.

It was Riley's turn to stare at her, mouth agape. He shook his head, then quickly followed her into the bedroom.

Kate stood at the foot of the bed, suddenly nervous. As Riley entered the room, she suddenly realized that this would be the first time a member of the opposite sex other than her husband had ever been in the room with her. Her one moment of boldness had vanished and was replaced with an all too familiar feeling of self-consciousness. She smiled shyly at him as he came to stand in front of her. He took her hands in his own and slowly, lifted each one to his mouth and kissed her palm. The sensation made her shiver.

She stepped closer to Riley and placed her hands on his shoulders. Slowly, she felt her way down his chest and across his abdomen, feeling his muscles quiver beneath her touch. Knowing she had this effect on him made her feel powerful and confident at the same time. She grabbed the bottom of his t-shirt and pulled it out from his shorts. She slid her hands underneath the fabric and slowly massaged his stomach and chest, until finally making her way around to his back. She held his gaze the entire time, watching his eyes close and open repeatedly with the sensation of her hands rubbing his torso.

Slowly, she lifted his shirt up and over his head, revealing his powerful chest. She couldn't help but gasp. She'd seem him shirtless many times before but now he was here in her room and she could touch and taste as she'd longed to do. She broke his gaze and brought her lips to his chest, kissing across the expanse of it. Riley groaned and placed his hands on her shoulders, pulling her closer. He rested a portion of his weight on her, feeling his legs nearly give out beneath him as she kissed and caressed his chest.

"Wait," he said, gasping for air. "I need to see you."

Kate stepped back slightly and reached for the bottom of her tank. "Let me," he said. Kate nodded and let her hands fall to her side. Riley watched as his hands worked their way down her sides until they grasped the bottom of her shirt. Slowly, he pulled it up and over her head. She stood before him, naked from the waist up.

"My God," his voice was thick with emotion. "You are so beautiful."

"Riley," she whispered. "Come here."

He grinned at her and took her into his arms and lifted her. Once again, she wrapped her legs around his waist as he carried her to the bed and laid her gently down. He looked down at her and was overcome with emotion. He could scarcely believe that the woman he'd desired for so long was right here with him, *wanting* him. Slowly, he placed the full weight of him on top of her and captured her lips. She moaned and lifted her hips to meet his. He groaned and knew he wasn't going be able to wait much longer. Kate felt it as well and reached for his shorts, sliding them down over his hips and pushing them off with her feet. Once she had freed him of his clothing, she reached for her own and peeled them off.

She looked up at him, full of passion and desire. "Riley, please," she begged. He saw the look in her eyes and groaned.

As he slid into her, her last coherent thought was that she no longer feared she was falling in love with Riley.

She loved him. Completely. There was no turning back now.

They lay together on top of the comforter, wrapped in each other's arm. Riley came up on one elbow and looked down at her, concern for her all over his face.

"What?" She asked.

"Are you okay?" He looked at her sheepishly. "I think I got a little bit carried away. I wanted to take my time but…"

She smiled as she realized he was worried about her. "Riley," she said, placing a finger over his lips to silence him. "I'm more than fine. I'm wonderful. And if you recall, it was me who led you down the hall."

He grinned, then leaned down and gave her a kiss on the lips. "Kate," he said.

She noticed that his voice had taken on a more serious tone. She immediately became nervous.

"What's wrong?" She asked, suddenly well aware of her feeling for him and how vulnerable she's become. She'd been out of this world for so long that she'd forgotten how much it could worry and uncertainty there was in a new relationship. She gripped the sheet closer to her.

Riley sat up and swung his legs over the side of the bed. He sat for a moment looking around the room as if trying to locate something. After a moment, he found his shorts and put them on.

"Riley, what are you doing?"

He turned to look at her. "I just don't want to be sitting here naked when I tell you this."

Kate felt panicked. Did she just invite this man into her bed only to be told moments after that he was dumping her? God! She was such an idiot! How could she be so stupid as to think someone like Riley could fall for her? She sat up and pulled her knees into her chest, making herself as small as possible. "What do you need to tell me?" Her voice was smaller than it had ever been and Riley looked at her strangely.

"Kate, I don't know how to tell you this. I know we said we'd take it day by day and it's only been a couple of weeks or so, but-"

"But what?"

He turned to look at her. "I'm... in love with you. I can't stand the thought of being without you for even one minute." Riley grinned at her. "I love you, Kate. More than I ever thought possible."

Kate exhaled loudly and then collapsed back onto the bed. "God, Riley, you scared the shit out of me. For a minute there, I thought..."

"You thought what?"

Her eyes welled with tears at the thought of being without Riley for one minute. She sat up and looked at him. "I love you too, Riley. So much. I can't believe it, but I do. I don't care about our ages or about the fact that I have a child or that you have one year left of school. I've never felt this way before and-"

Riley covered her mouth with his own, kissing her roughly. "I think I need to get these shorts off again," he growled.

"Quickly, please," Kate replied, giggling.

Kate dozed, forgetting about the dinner she'd planned to serve. She woke after a few hours, when the scent of burnt chicken wafted down the hall to her bedroom.

"Dammit," she said, untangling herself from Riley's limbs. He barely stirred. She smiled at him as she pulled on a t-shirt and padded her way to the kitchen. The turned the oven off and stood back, not even daring to open the oven door. She knew that dinner had been ruined; there was no need to see the evidence.

She turned to see Riley walk sleepily into the kitchen. He put his arms around her and nuzzled her neck. "What's wrong?" He asked, yawning loudly.

"I burnt our dinner."

"Huh?"

Kate leaned over and turned on the light inside of the oven. The two of them peered inside and saw a very well done chicken that neither thought would be edible.

"Whoops."

"Well," Kate said. "I can call for a pizza."

Riley came up behind her and wrapped his arms around her, burying his head in the crook of her neck. "I'm not hungry for food," he said.

Kate turned around and melted her body to his. "Well, *that* I think I can manage."

Riley, seemingly effortlessly, lifted her up and carried her back to the bedroom.

Kate woke the next morning having slept a full ten hours, well…minus the times she had been woken up during the night. She giggled, realizing how much she relished the stamina of the man she loved. Perhaps there was a little something to dating a younger man, she thought.

She rolled over on to her side and watched Riley as he slept. The sheet covered only the bottom half of him, leaving his chest exposed. Kate found herself staring at the exposed area and felt her pulse quicken. Would she ever get used to seeing him like this, she wondered? She took her hand and placed it on his chest, making slow, languished strokes across the expanse of it. She loved the feel of the smooth skin and ripple of muscles underneath. Her heart thudded in her ears. God how she loved this man. It terrified her how much she felt for him.

Her hand continued to stroke his chest and as she watched, his lips worked their way into a smile, yet his eyes remained closed. Movement just beneath the sheet told her he was awake, very much awake, actually. His hand came up from beneath the sheet and took hold of hers. In one deft movement, he had climbed on top of her, holding her captive. He held her hand pressed to the bed above her head as he began to kiss her face and neck, then slowly working his way down. Kate's breathing came in short, raspy breaths as his tongue darted in and out, making her writhe with pleasure. When at last he entered her, Kate knew she'd never been loved like this.

Riley's lovemaking seemed desperate somehow and Kate felt the same. Her hips rose up to meet his again and again until at last, they came together in one final moment of ecstasy. Riley's collapsed beside Kate breathing heavily. "I love you," he gasped.

"I love you, too."

After a few moments, their breathing returned to a somewhat normal rhythm and Kate thought Riley seemed to be abnormally quiet. Much too soon for her taste, he rolled over to the other side of the bed.

"Everything okay?" She asked.

"Yeah," he said, sitting up. "I was just thinking about what you said yesterday."

"What's that?"

"You wanted to tell my mother about us."

Kate nodded.

"I definitely think I should have that talk with her now...today, as a matter of fact."

"Good," she replied. "I want her to hear about this from us." Kate lifted herself up onto one elbow and looked down at Riley. His hair was mussed up from sleep...and not from sleep, making him look somehow rugged and handsome. "You hungry? If you recall, I burned our dinner," she said, smiling. "I think I can manage to make some eggs, though."

"That would be great," he replied, reaching for his shorts. "I'll make the coffee."

Riley put on his shorts and Kate threw on a t-shirt and the two of them walked hand in hand to the kitchen. Riley got to work on the coffee, managing to find the coffee and the filters in her cabinet, which Kate scrambled some eggs and made some toast. When they finally sat down to eat, the both realized they were famished and ate their breakfast without speaking. Afterward, Riley grinned at her. "I guess we were hungry, huh?"

"Starved." Kate replied, grinning back at him.

"So what time do you need to get Hadley?"

"Sometime this morning. Probably around eleven or so."

"What would you think about the three of us doing something later? Maybe a movie or something?"

"You mean...." Kate let her voice trail off, wanting Riley to answer her unspoken question.

"I mean, I'd like it if we could talk to her about us...if you're ready for that." He reached for her hand. "I know this might be soon for you and if you're not ready to tell Hadley, I understand."

Kate smiled. "Riley, I'm ready to tell her. I love you. I'll tell Hadley and anyone else that comes along." She paused, frowning just a bit.

"What?" he asked, noticing her expression.

"I think I should probably tell her when it's just the two of us. I mean, she loves you and all but I think it might be better if it's just us. I don't want her to feel as though she needs to act a certain way because you're there." She looked up at him, her expression filled with worry. "I hope you understand."

He nodded. "Of course I understand. Why don't you talk to her and see how it goes. If all goes well, text me and I'll come over and we can watch a movie or something."

"I'm sure Hadley will be fine with this...turn of events," Kate said, grinning. "But I'll let you know for sure. I'll run to the grocery store on my way home and get us something for dinner. Maybe tonight I won't be so *distracted...* " She looked at him pointedly. "... and we can actually eat something."

Riley had the decency to look embarrassed, which made Kate laugh out loud.

"I'm going to get my clothes." He said, color slowly creeping into his face.

She watched as he stood up and placed his dish into the sink. A thought suddenly occurred to her. "Ummm...Riley?"

"Yeah," he said, turning around.

"Out of curiosity, where did you tell Wendy you were sleeping last night?"

He leaned back against the counter. "I said I was going to spend the night at a friend's house."

"Oh," Kate replied.

"Was that wrong? We are friends, right?"

She smiled. "We are most definitely friends. I just don't want her to think I've betrayed her in any way. Promise me you'll talk to her today, all right?"

Riley came back and kneeled in front of Kate, taking her hands in his. "I promise. I'll talk to her and my dad. But don't worry about it. She loves you. She's going to be thrilled."

Kate nodded, desperately wanting to believe that everything would work out for the best. But deep down, there was still the tiniest feeling of dread that someone would take issue with this new twist in her relationship with Riley,

She smiled at Riley, pushing that nagging thought from her mind. Things would be fine. They just had to be.

Chapter 23

After Riley left, Kate cleaned up the bed, which looked like there had been a wrestling match on it. She smiled, memories from the previous night flooding her senses. Kate knew he loved her. She felt it every time he touched her. Riley was someone who wore his feelings on his sleeve, which was something terribly appealing to Kate since she was someone who rarely let her feelings show. She knew Hadley would be thrilled with the announcement that her mother was dating Riley. If she had to guess how much her daughter looked up to Riley and loved being around him, she'd guess that Hadley, when told of their relationship, would probably ask when he was going to move in. Well, Kate thought, that was one move that would have to wait. Riley had one more year of college. As the realization that he'd be leaving in little more than a month hit her, she felt a pang in her stomach as she realized that she'd hardly be able to see him while he was at school. She and Hadley were here and he would be more than an hour away. She shook her head. She couldn't think about that now. They'd only just gotten to this point and now she was looking painfully ahead to the time when he would no longer be around. She pushed the thought from her mind. It was just too painful to think about.

Kate took a quick shower, then headed over to Bethany's to pick up Hadley. She pulled into the driveway and started to walk up to the front door when it opened and Bethany stepped out, closing the door behind her.

"Oh. My. God!!!" She screeched.

Kate feigned innocence. "What?" she asked.

Bethany crossed her arms over her chest. "Let's just say I can see *exactly* what Mrs. Windham saw the other day. You have taken a *lover*." She let the word 'lover' ooze off her tongue slowly, relishing both syllables.

"Is it that obvious?"

"Oh, honey," she said as though speaking to a child, "there's definitely a difference. You're smiling ear to ear. Oh, and you might even be glowing. Come here. Let me get a good look at you." Kate stepped onto the front porch and stood in front of Bethany, who grasped her upper arms and look her over from head to toe.

"What exactly is it you're looking for?"

"No idea...but I'll know it when I see it." After several moments, Bethany's eyes locked on Kate's and she nodded, apparently satisfied with what she saw. "There it is!"

Kate raised an eyebrow. "There what is?"

"The glow of a woman in love! You've definitely got it!"

Kate giggled. "You know what? I'm fine with that."

Bethany squealed loudly, causing Kate to cover her ears. Just then, the front door opened and Peter, Bethany's husband peeked out.

"Everything okay out here?" he asked, his shiny head glinting in the sunlight. Ever since Kate had known Bethany and Peter, he'd been bald...or some level approaching it. Because he was only in his early forties, the sight of his perfectly round head always surprised her.

"We're fine. Just a little girl-talk," Bethany replied, shoo-ing him away with her hands.

Peter nodded, then shut the door softly behind him.

Kate raised her eyebrows and turned back to her friend. "Peter's home? On a Saturday morning?"

"Don't get too excited. He's got a tee-time in about an hour. He'll be leaving in ten minutes or so."

"Oh," Kate replied. Once again, she felt a rush of sadness for her friend who was, for all intents and purposes, raising her four children alone because their father was too busy to be bothered. Bethany however, was used to Peter's non-involvement and turned back to Kate the moment the front door closed.

"Come on in. I want to hear everything!" She opened the front door and led the way down the hall toward the kitchen. "Coffee?" She asked, turning to Kate.

She nodded. Moments later, Bethany placed a steaming cup of coffee in front of her along with an array of artificial sweeteners and creamers. Kate took her time preparing her coffee, knowing that Bethany was about to burst with excitement.

"Well?" She asked. "Things went well, I take it?'

Kate looked at her friend and felt tears spring to her eyes. "Bethany, I-"

"Oh, honey," she said, sitting down beside Kate. "What is it?"

"Bethany, he loves me," she said.

"Well, of course he does," Bethany replied, sounding absolutely certain.

"And I love him. So much it scares me. Is this crazy or what?" She shook her head. "No. Absolutely not. Totally normal and sane."

Kate smiled. "He's going to come over later after I talk to Hadley. I thought it might be too soon but I gotta tell you, Beth. I've never felt like this before. It's so...odd. I thought we'd have nothing in common but there's just so much. And I'm so comfortable with him."

"And the sex?" Bethany prompted, grinning like a Cheshire cat. She placed her elbows on the counter and rested her chin in her hands, waiting expectantly for Kate to answer.

"The sex..." Kate's mind drifted back to the previous night. "Oh My God. The sex!"

"I knew it!" She said, slapping her thighs with her hands. "I knew it would be fabulous!"

Kate nodded. "Fabulous doesn't even begin to cover it. We just...fit together so perfectly." Bethany watched as Kate bit her lower lip. "I can't help but worry about what Wendy will think."

Bethany waved her hand around dismissively. "Don't you worry about her. She's going to be thrilled. Why wouldn't she?"

"And you don't think some of the other parents will think this is...sinister?"

"Where do you come up with this stuff? Sinister? No way." She shook her head vehemently. "But who cares what anyone else thinks. All that matters is that you love him and he loves you. You just worry about that little girl of yours who, by the way, is going to be thrilled that her mom is dating the swim coach...and someone who truly *enjoys* spending time with her."

"Speaking of my little girl...was she okay for you?"

Bethany rolled her eyes. "Now you know you don't even have to ask me that! I haven't even seen her or Sarah since dinner last night. The two of them have been holed up in Sarah's room all night! I even got to watch a movie in its entirety. Any time you want Hadley to spend the night here, just tell me. That little munchkin is welcome here anytime."

"Thanks, Beth."

"I mean it, Kate. Any time you want a little alone time, you just let me know." Bethany winked.

Kate chuckled. "You know, I just may take you up on that."

"Please do." She reached over and hugged Kate. "Now let's go see what those girls are up to."

Kate managed to get Hadley home and in the tub. Although she was swimming every day in enough chemicals to stop an outbreak of e-coli, Kate had learned the hard way that if she didn't scrub Hadley's hair at least three times a week with special shampoo to rid the hair of chlorine, her hair would develop a green hue to it. She also knew that whenever Hadley was in the tub, she liked to talk with her mom and Kate thought it might be a good opportunity to talk to her about Riley. She hated to do it without him here but realized it might be better for Hadley if he wasn't there during their talk. She didn't want Hadley to feel any pressure to be polite or not be comfortable to show her true feelings about the fact that her mother was dating someone. Kate figured the best situation would be a one on one session with her daughter.

Once Kate had Hadley's hair lathered up for the second time, she opened the door, hoping they'd both come through the other side unscathed.

"Did you have a good time at Sarah's house?"

Hadley nodded. "Did you miss me, mom?"

"I sure did. But you know what?"

Hadley looked up at her expectantly.

"Riley came over for a visit."

"Oh, cool." She replied, splashing one of her dolls around in the water.

Kate frowned. This was going to be more difficult than she thought. She slowly rinsed the soap from Hadley's hair, watching as the sudsy water slid down her back and into the warm tub water. Once Kate felt as though Hadley's hair was free from the shampoo, she reached for the towel that had been left out beside the tub.

"Come on, sweetie. Let's get you out of the tub."

It took a little bit of prodding but Kate managed to get Hadley out. It never ceased to amaze her that getting Hadley into the tub took an exhaustive amount of pleading but once in the water, she didn't want to get out. Kate certainly understood the desire to stay in the water – Hadley practically grew gills in the summer – but what was so different to a child being in the tub as opposed to the pool? Sure it was smaller and the water was warm, but so what? Water was water, right? This past winter, getting Hadley to take a bath had become so difficult that Kate had resorted to allowing her to wear her swimsuit and even her goggles. That ruse, however, only worked a couple of times then it was back to bribery and cajoling in order to get her daughter wet.

Kate dried off Hadley then helped her put on her sundress.

"Wow," Hadley said when she saw her mother pull out her favorite dress. "I get to wear my sparkle dress?"

"You sure do. Today is a special day."

"Really? Are we going to the zoo?"

Kate chuckled. "No, sweetie. We are not going to the zoo. But Riley is coming over later." Not exactly the same thing but in Hadley's case, it would have the same effect.

"Can we get Chinese food?"

"We'll see," Kate replied, thinking that might be a better option than trying to cook dinner. At least if she ordered something, it would be edible. Even on her best days, there was no guarantee that anything she put in or on the oven would turn out the way it was supposed to. She put the dinner menu on the backburner, so to speak, and tried once again to talk to Hadley about Riley.

"Hadley, honey?" Once her daughter looked up at her, Kate continued. "Mommy wants to talk with you about Riley for a minute."

"Okay."

"You like Riley, right?"

"Sure."

"Well, mommy likes him too." Kate said hesitantly, waiting for Hadley to explode.

"Well of course you do!" Hadley said, smiling.

Kate realized her daughter didn't really understand what she was trying to say. God, this was more difficult than she thought! Then she thought of an analysis even a seven year old could understand. "You know how on ICarly, Freddy likes Sam but he *really* likes Carly?"

She nodded.

"What if I told you I liked Riley like that?"

"You like Riley?"

"Yes Hadley. I do."

"Is he your boyfriend? Are you going to marry him?"

In that instant, Kate knew she had been allowing Hadley too much TV time. She made a mental note to cut that time in half.

"No, honey. I'm just going to spend some time with him because I like him. Is that okay with you?"

"Sure. Can he still bring me to swim practice?"

"Of course he can!" Kate replied, grinning.

"Oh," Hadley said, "Okay." Kate brought her daughter close to her for a quick snuggle and chuckled as she realized all Hadley was worried about was whether or not her "cool ride" to swim practice was going to continue.

"So, it doesn't bother you that I like Riley?"

Hadley turned her head to the side and pondered the question. Kate had to stifle a giggle when she saw how seriously her daughter was considering the question. Finally, she looked up at her mother. "Nope. Does he like you?"

Kate smiled. "Yes honey, he does."

"Okay."

Okay? Was that it? Just 'okay' and the conversation was over with? How in the world, Kate wondered, did she end up with the most unflappable child ever? Then another thought entered her mind...would all her adult friends react the same as her daughter? At least Bethany had. Perhaps the others would follow her lead.

"Okay, then. Let's get you dressed. I think Riley wants to come over later."

"Can we watch a movie?"

"Sure," Kate replied, chuckling. "We can watch a movie."

Kate texted Riley to let him know he was cleared to come over. When she received his smiley-face emoticon in return, she knew he'd be arriving shortly. He showed up within the hour and Kate met him at the door. She opened it and stepped outside on the front porch, closing the door behind her. She wrapped her arms around his neck, nearly toppling him over.

"Whoa! What's this for?" He asked, pulling her closer to him.

"Because you're so wonderful."

"Well, I know *thaaat*..." he replied, only to receive a sharp poke to his stomach. "Oof! Is there anything a bit more specific you'd like to share?" He grabbed her hand to prevent another slender finger in his belly.

Kate pulled away and nodded. "She's not even the slightest bit phased by it. You know, I have to admit, you might have been right about this all along. Maybe no one will have a problem with it."

"What was that?" Riley asked, grinning. "Did you just say I was right?"

"Maybe," she replied, grinning.

"I told you. No one cares if we date. I'll talk to my parents tonight when I get home so my mother doesn't find out from the...what was it again? Oh, Right. The Gossip Mommies."

Kate finally felt as though the weight had been lifted from her shoulders. If her best friend and her daughter didn't seem to mind she was dating Riley, surely others would feel the same. She grinned at Riley and took his hand. "Come on," she said, opening the door. "Hadley wants to watch another movie with us."

"Yes, ma-" He began, grinning.

"Don't say it," Kate said, looking back at him sharply and cutting him off. Riley laughed when he saw the glint in her eyes.

Chapter 24

Despite being at the pool all week, Hadley felt the need to go to the pool on Sunday afternoon. Kate loaded up the towels, sunscreen and a few snacks, and drove the short distance to the pool. Once they arrived, she sprayed Hadley with sunscreen, thoroughly coating all exposed areas despite her protests.

She had hoped Riley would come to the pool and spend time with them today. He'd been so busy over the past few days that she hadn't had any contact with him other than texts. Even those were sporadic. She didn't mind, though. Sure, she missed him but she also knew that he was reviewing the swimmers times and trying to determine who would enter which events for the championship meet, which was only a few weeks away.

The one nagging thought that Kate continued to have was whether or not Riley had spoken to his parents. Thought she knew he had been busy, she also hoped he'd managed to find the time to speak with them. She couldn't rest easy until she knew the conversation had occurred. It was only moments after Hadley hit the water that Wendy arrived with the twins in tow.

Well, she knew her questions would be answered in a moment.

As Wendy came through the gate, she spotted Kate and lifted her chin in greeting. With a nod of her head, she indicated she would join her and heaved her bags further up her shoulders and headed in the Kate's direction. Seeing the armful of bags filled with towels, snacks, and toys, Kate felt a pang of sympathy for Wendy knowing she had to go through the process of packing and unpacking nearly every day for *two* growing boys. She stood up; attempting to help Wendy with her load but Wendy grinned at her and then dropped the bags where she stood, several feet away from the chair she was heading to. One of the bags toppled over, spilling out plastic toys in a four foot perimeter. Tyler and Ben grabbed several of the dive sticks and jumped into the water.

"Don't worry guys," Wendy said to their heads as they

disappeared under the water. "You go ahead and swim. Mom will get all this stuff." She flopped down into the chair beside Kate and grinned at her. "Can you believe I do this every day? I must be out of my mind."

Kate felt an immediate rush of worry for Wendy but it was quickly tempered by the heartfelt chuckle she heard her release as she looked at her boys splashing each other in the water. Kate smiled as well. "I think all parents are a bit out of their mind. Isn't that why wine was created?"

"Ah, yes," Wendy replied knowingly, "the beloved mommy-juice. Something I find I look forward to on days like today when I am overworked and underappreciated."

Kate nodded. "I'm familiar with the concept. Anything I can do to help?"

"Do you want to take two seven year old rambunctious boys home with you for a week or so?" Wendy asked, grinning. Seeing Kate look of mock horror, Wendy continued. "Didn't think so."

"While I may not be willing to take those two home with me," Kate said, pointing to the twins, who were now climbing on top of each other, "I will provide an ear or two for you to use for venting."

"Thanks." Wendy got up and moved one of the bags closer to where she sat. She pulled out a towel and laid it on the chair, then sat down heavily. She groaned softly as she eased herself back and put her feet up. "I guess I didn't realize how much my feet hurt until I put them up."

"Mom!" Both women looked toward the sound of the voice and saw Ben approaching the end of his mother's chair. "You forgot to spray me!"

"Me too," said his brother, who was only a few feet behind him.

"Can you guys spray each other? Just this once?"

Ben shook his head in disgust. "I don't want *him* to spray me!"

"Me either," Tyler replied, sticking his tongue out at his brother. "He gets it all goopy." Kate chuckled at the two of them. They were the best of friends one minute, and practically enemies the next, almost as though a switch had been flipped. She was momentarily thankful she had only one child and didn't have to referee her children's arguments constantly as she felt certain Wendy had to do.

Wendy sighed heavily, then leaned forward. "Oh, all right, you two…"

Kate placed her hand on Wendy's arm. "I've got this," she said.

Wendy looked at her appreciatively and leaned back against the chaise, closing her eyes. "Boys," she said from beneath nearly closed eyes, "Miss Kate is going to spray you with sunscreen, all right?"

"Okay," they said in unison. Both boys quickly assumed the customary position - feet spread apart, arms wide, head lifted toward the sky and their eyes squished tightly closed. Kate sprayed both from head to toe careful to get the part in their hair, knowing it was a spot often missed.

"Turn, please," she said, making a circular motion with her index finger. She smiled as both boys turned around, teetering on stiff legs, then faced away from her so she could spray the other side of their bodies. When she felt as though she'd covered them thoroughly and both were safe from the sun's rays, she nodded. "There. You're free to go."

Both boys hooted, then jumped into the deep end together, their earlier annoyance with each other having quickly faded.

"Unbelievable."

"What's that?" Kate asked, turning around.

Wendy pointed to the deep end, where Tyler and Ben were splashing each other mercilessly and having a great time. "The two of them are like an old married couple. They hate each other, they love each other, hate each other, love each other. Who can keep up?" She smiled at them. "I'm so glad they have each other. Poor Riley didn't have anyone to play with at home. Sometimes that makes me sad when I think about it. All he had at home was his mother and I can assure you, I'm not that much fun."

At the mention of Riley, Kate felt a tiny flutter in her belly. Though she tried to prevent the memories of the other night from coming into her brain, almost immediately she was flooded with images of herself and Riley in a tangled heap. It seemed her body had a mind of its own when he was concerned and at the mere mention of his name her pulse quickened. As the color rose to her cheeks, she wondered once again if he'd spoken to his mother about the two of them yet. Kate rightly assumed he had not since it would have been the first thing out of Wendy's mouth the moment she laid eyes on Kate.

A nagging feeling crept into her belly.

Kate adjusted her position slightly so that she faced Wendy.

"You shouldn't worry about that. I think it's just as good for a child to have one on one time with their mother."

"You're probably right. Though, I'm sure we're bound to do something wrong with our kids at some point. It's probably inevitable that they'll end up on a couch in therapy somewhere."

"God, I can only imagine what I've done to mess up Hadley."

"You, my friend," Wendy said, turning towards Kate, "are the only person I know that is completely and totally normal. I don't even think I've ever seen you yell at Hadley. That is probably the only child in Lancaster that will turn out normal. We're all messed up. Every last one of us." She laughed out loud. "I could tell you stories of me trying to handle those two." She nodded toward the deep end where Tyler and Ben were swimming the width of the pool instead of the length.

"Just because you've never seen me yell doesn't mean it never happens. I've just learned to control myself while out in public." Kate leaned back against the chair and stretched out, enjoying the warmth of the sun on her skin. It wouldn't be long before it would be too hot for her to tolerate and she'd have to hide completely in the shade or submerge herself in the pool water that she was certain wasn't going to be the least bit refreshing.

"I wish I could say the same. Some days? I feel like all I do is yell. That's when I call Bill at the office and force him to come home early and take over."

"Aaaahh...I remember doing that. The good ol' tag-team parenting." Kate closed her eyes, thinking of Hadley's early years – no time to sleep, no time to eat, no time to shower... "It goes by so fast, though."

"Yes, it does," Wendy said, nodding slowly. "You just can't stop it, can you? She said, glancing at the twins. "Say," she continued, "have you done much thought about joining one of the on-line dating sites?"

Kate, momentarily stunned at the abrupt change of subject, felt her mouth drop open. "Er..no, not really, no..."

"Well, why not?"

"I, uh..." Kate had no idea to respond and prayed for something to distract Wendy. Experience told her that when she had something she wanted to talk about, there was no stopping her.

"Now why do you look like that? Don't you want to meet

someone? You might even want to have another child."

Kate nearly choked, but managed to force a cough out in order to cover her shock.

Wendy was lost in her own world now, leaving Kate to sit beside her and stare while she planned out the rest of Kate's life. "I mean, surely Hadley would love to have a little brother or sister. And you know, on-line dating doesn't have the stigma it had when it first started. It's completely accepted now. Lots of people are doing it and meeting their soul-mates? Just think!" Wendy clapped her hands together. "You meet someone, things move along – much quicker now than they did when we were in college, mind you – and before long, you're picking out another wedding dress....and a flower girl dress for Hadley, of course...."

Kate was becoming dizzy. Wendy was sitting here planning her entire future and had no idea Kate was involved – very involved, actually – with her son! She pursed her lips together. She was going to *kill* Riley when she saw him next.

Wendy chatted incessantly for several minutes. Kate did her best to block out the conversation but managed to pick up a snippet here and there. For once Kate was thankful Wendy had the ability to keep herself occupied by talking while at the same time remain completely oblivious to the discomfort and lack of attention of those around her.

"Since we're talking about new relationships..." Wendy said, leaning forward conspiratorially. "I'm pretty sure Riley's met someone."

"Really?" Kate replied. Her voice came out as a strangled squeak.

Wendy looked off into the distance, still oblivious to Kate's discomfort and giggled as she thought of her son. "That boy has been walking around the house on cloud nine for a couple of weeks now. I'm not sure who she is but she had a hold on Riley's heart like I've never seen."

Despite the over ninety degree heat and near one hundred percent humidity, Kate felt herself grow cold. She was beyond uncomfortable. What was she supposed to do now? Should she confess and tell Wendy that she was this mysterious woman? She felt the pressure of being between a rock and a hard place. If she were to tell Wendy about her relationship with Riley, he might be upset with her since they'd decided he was going to speak to his parents. On the other hand, if she remained silent, only to have Riley speak with her later, she would realize Kate knowingly kept her mouth shut while Wendy went on and on about Riley's new girlfriend.

Unsure of which was the lesser of two evils, Kate simply sat there while Wendy chatted incessantly.

"I can't wait to meet her! Course, I can't push the issue. You know how boys are. They like to think they came up with the idea all by themselves. So I'll just have to wait until Riley figures out that he should bring this girl over to the house to meet us." She clapped her hands together again. "I'm just so excited! I tell you Kate, I've never seen him like this before."

She leaned back against the chaise with a large sigh and Kate could tell Wendy was content with latest turn of events. Kate bit her lower lip, wishing desperately Riley had been able to talk to his parents. Now, Kate feared, the fact that she'd sat there while Wendy spoke of Riley's new relationship and Kate said nothing could easily be interpreted as her attempt to hide their relationship- something she didn't want to do. If anything, she was bursting inside. She wanted to tell everyone she knew that they were together. She wanted to walk into the pool holding Riley's hand and give him a kiss as he left her side regardless of where they were or who they were with.

Kate glanced at Wendy out of the corner of her eye and saw that her eyes were closed. For the moment, Kate relaxed, knowing that Wendy would be silent for some time now. She did her best to direct her attention towards Hadley but found her attention was directed otherwise.

Riley had just walked into the pool.

He stepped through the gate, met Kate's eyes with a huge grin, then began to walk toward her.

"Riiiillleeeeeee!"

"OOOF!" As he neared Kate's chair, he was tackled by two little boys who looked remarkably like him, only shorter. He scooped up each of them in one arm and carried them over to the steps of the pool. He walked down the steps and then, seemingly effortlessly, tossed them into the water. They squealed in delight. "That'll teach you to tackle me!" Smiling, he turned around and walked back over toward Kate and Wendy.

"Hey mom, Kate," he said as he approached the two women.

"Here, sit down with us," Wendy replied, motioning to the empty chair beside her. "Are you all done with the championship line-up?"

He nodded. "Yeah, finally. Now that it's done, I'll have some free time."

Riley glanced at Kate over his mother's head. She looked back at him, then pointedly at Wendy, trying to communicate to him that he needed to speak to his mother...and quickly. He responded with an apologetic nod, then looked back at his mother. "Are, uh...you and dad going to be home later?" He asked, looking back at his mother.

"Your father wanted to stop by Jessica's office this afternoon. She had an open house this past weekend at the Twin Oaks property. But he'll be home for dinner."

"Oh, right." Riley said, nodding. Jessica Park was the realtor that handled sales for all of the houses his father's company built. Though the houses were still moving, the economy had taken its toll and Riley knew his father kept a close watch on how each open house went. "Well, I'll be around later so I'll catch up with you guys then."

"All right," Wendy said as a smile work its way onto her face.

Riley stood up. "I'm going to see if I can torment some seven year olds."

Both women watched Riley walk toward the deep end of the pool. Once he was out of earshot, Wendy looked at Kate, a huge grin fixed on her face. "See? I told you!! It's going to be tonight! I'll bet he's bringing this mysterious girl over tonight!"

Kate knew she couldn't sit there beside Wendy and not tell her. She had to assume Riley would understand the position she was in. Well, she hoped he'd understand. Kate knew she had no choice.

She had to tell her.

"Er...Wendy," Kate began, sitting up. "I think there's something I should-"

"MOMMY!" Instantly, Kate recognized the sound of the voice and the terror that accompanied it. She looked over to where the scream came from and saw Hadley hobbling toward her holding her hands over one knee. Even from this distance, Kate could see the blood dripping down her shin. Riley was beside her, guiding her toward her mother. From the look on his face, one would think he had been the one who'd fallen.

"Oh my God!" She jumped up and ran over to her daughter. "What happened? Are you all right?"

At that moment, Hadley burst into tears. "I fell on the pool deck," she sobbed. "Can we go home?"

"Of course we can," Kate replied, hugging her daughter. She looked up at Riley and he nodded. She hoped that nod was shorthand for 'I'm going to talk to my parents very soon.' "Here," she said, motioning to her chair. "Sit down on mommy's chair."

Riley knelt down in front of Hadley. "I'll see you later, all right?"

Hadley sniffed and nodded. Kate took one of the towels and wrapped it around Hadley's knee, tourniquet style, then quickly tossed her items into her bag. She looked at Wendy, who had been watching to make sure Kate didn't need any help. "I've got to take her home."

"Of course," Wendy replied, nodding. She then looked at Hadley. "I hope you feel better."

Hadley looked at Wendy and nodded but then quickly hugged her mother's legs, burying her face into her thigh. "Can we go now?" She asked, looked up at her mother.

Kate nodded. "Let's go."

As they walked out of the pool area, she looked back and saw Riley standing there watching them, concern written all over his face. She knew he was worried about Hadley since she so rarely asked to actually leave the pool and perhaps thought her injury might be serious. Kate knew from experience that at the first sign of blood, her daughter became practically an invalid and the only thing that would make her feel better would be lying on the couch for the rest of the afternoon while her mother waited on her hand and foot. As much as Kate hated to play into Hadley's injury and make it seem worse than it was, there was a part of her liked the fact that only mommy's TLC would make her better. And Kate had never been one to turn away from mother/daughter cuddle time. She'd text Riley later to let him know Hadley was all right.

Of course, she hoped he'd be unavailable because he'd be talking to his parents.

When they walked into the house, Hadley plopped down onto the couch and pulled a blanket over her, transforming herself into a soft, tiny mound. Kate made her a sandwich and let her eat it front of the television, which was all part of the 'Mommy TLC protocol.' She let her lounge on the couch for the evening and then when she noticed her eyes drooping before her normal bedtime, she decided it was time for Hadley to go to bed. To her surprise, Hadley went upstairs without an argument.

Once Hadley was tucked in and sound asleep, Kate headed back downstairs with the intent of opening up a bottle of wine and catching up on her never ending supply of emails. She supposed she should be thankful for her exploding inbox, since it meant her business was doing well, but she found she wasn't able to muster up the energy required to filter through them all. Instead, she opted to curl up on the couch with a glass of wine and a book.

After staring at the same page for several minutes, she heard the sound of a car in the driveway. "Thank God," she said, tossing her book onto the couch.

She walked over to the front door and opened it, smiling as she recognized both the car and the gorgeous man who got out of it.

Riley walked up to the front door and looked at her sheepishly, hands thrust in his pockets. "I...uh...thought I might swing by. See if you were doing anything," he said. "And check on Hadley, of course."

She laughed. "Come on in. She's asleep, and she's fine. Didn't you get my text?"

"Yeah," he said sheepishly. "But I thought I should come over and see for myself."

"Go upstairs to her room if you want. But she's out cold." She closed the door behind Riley as he stepped into the foyer.

"You all right?" He asked.

She knew exactly what he meant and once again, Kate was surprised at how well Riley knew her. She stepped into his arms. "I'm much better now."

"Good," he said, planting a kiss on her forehead. "I felt awful when I got there today. When I saw my mom sitting there next to you, I knew it was going to be a rough afternoon."

She crossed her arms over her chest. "It was pretty stressful. I even started to talk to her myself when she began to tell me she could tell you've met someone. But then Hadley fell and we had to leave..."

"My mother said *what?!*"

Kate chuckled softly. "She told me she could tell you've met someone. Apparently, you don't hide your feelings at all when you're at home." She looked up at him and grinned. "Which is fine, by the way. I don't want you to hide anything. So you've got to talk to her."

"I will. I promise," he said, pulling her into his arms. "When I get home, all right? I was sort of hoping I could stay for awhile." He nuzzled his face in the crook of her neck and began to plant tiny kisses on the delicate skin there.

"All right," she replied, wrapping her arms around his neck. "I *guess* you can stay."

Chapter 25

Despite his best intentions, Riley wasn't able to speak with his mother until Monday afternoon. Between her schedule with the twins and his with swim team practices, there hadn't been a free moment. But this was important to Kate, so he was going to find the time….today. As he sat in the kitchen, he thought about his mother's behavior over the past few weeks and couldn't help but smile. She'd never been one to hide her feelings and it was obvious she knew something about what was going on with him. Though he much preferred to keep this small part of his life from his mother's prying eyes, he knew it was time he told her – if only to make Kate feel at ease.

Of course, he wasn't entirely sure how much detail he was going to give her. Just the basics, he thought. Any more than just an overview would surely send his mother into a tizzy. She could fill in the blanks all by herself. He did *not* want to go there. For all he knew, his mother probably thought he was a virgin! Three years away from home and he hadn't had sex? Right. The problem, of course, was that his mother spent a good amount of time in the Land of Denial. She'd hovered over him all his life and knew she had trouble "cutting the cord." He'd hoped living away at college would help her with letting go but instead she only clung to him tighter each time he came home for a visit. When he'd been notified of the internship last summer, he'd been immensely relieved that he wouldn't have to go home and face her attachment again. This summer, though…well, her hovering was a very small price to pay for the benefit of spending his entire summer with Kate.

The more he thought about the conversation he was about to have, the more insignificant he thought it was. It really wasn't a big deal…at least it shouldn't be. This was more of an information session for his parents. Nothing in his life was going to change. He loved Kate—more than he ever thought possible. But that fact didn't change anything in his life, especially now. He knew if he was going to have any sort of future with her, he needed to continue on with everything he had planned for his life. Once he had his degree and got a job, he and Kate could make their relationship more serious...and more permanent.

He heard the squeak of the back door and turned. Wendy came in, tapping her bright yellow gardening shoes against the doorway to rid them of any dirt. She pulled off the clogs and placed them on the mat just inside the door. Riley didn't understand his mother's desire to grow things in the backyard, particularly in the sweltering heat of the summer, nor did he understand her desire to wear such hideous shoes. He cringed each time she put on those brightly colored things that seemed to light up on their own. He chuckled softly, looking back down at the kitchen table. After he'd managed to stifle his laughter, he looked up at his mother. Her face was streaked with sweat and dirt, her clothes were smeared with dirt and she was leaning back with her hands on her hips in order to stretch out her back. One might think, having looked at her for only a moment, that she was in agony, having spent time outside in the heat tending to her garden, but her eyes shone and she looked exhilarated.

"Hey, mom," he said.

At the sound of his voice, she looked up. "Oh! Riley, I didn't know you were home. Everything all right?"

He smiled. He must have been with Kate more than he thought for his mother to think something was wrong if he was home. "Everything's fine. Just thought I'd hang out at home for a bit today."

She looked at him as though considering if he had an ulterior motive, which of course, he did. Her scrutiny made him feel a bit uncomfortable so he quickly tried to divert her attention elsewhere. "What's for dinner?"

"Your dad's going to grill some steaks. Are you sticking around? Or do you have other plans..." She said 'other plans' as though Riley were going to be out doing some sort of top secret CIA ground reconnaissance work. She held his gaze while grinning at him. Riley began to fidget under her scrutiny.

"Umm...I don't really have any plans so I guess I'll hang around."

Wendy nodded. "Great. It'll be good to have you...for a change."

He looked back at his mother to find her grinning at him. He chose to ignore her look knowing it was merely a way to ask about his love life without speaking of it. Instead, he got up, turned to face the stove and opened the oven. "Baked potatoes, too?"

Wendy smiled, knowing baked potatoes were one of Riley's favorites. "Grab me another one from under the counter, would you? I'll put one in for you."

Riley reached into the cabinet next to the stove, pulled out the bag of potatoes, and grabbed the largest one he could find. He handed it to his mother, knowing she would spend several minutes cleaning it off in the sink. Wendy stepped over to the sink and began her ritual of washing the dirt of the potato. As Riley watched, he wondered how the skin of the potato stayed on, given the amount of scrubbing his mother was doing. "Your father should be home soon. I'll have him start the grill and then we'll eat."

"Cool. I wanted to talk to both of you about something, anyway."

Hearing this, Wendy turned and smiled. "Really? Is this conversation going to be about what I think it's about?"

"What do you think it's about?" He asked, grinning. Riley purposely walked over to the fridge and opened it in order to avoid meeting her eyes. He rifled through the contents, trying to find something to snack on until dinner was ready. Knowing his mother normally did the weekly grocery shopping on Friday's, he didn't expect to find much in the way of sustenance after a weekend of having the entire family home for meals. He settled on a bag of raw baby carrots.

She grinned knowingly and crossed her arms across her chest. "About why you've been walking around here on cloud nine for the past few weeks."

Riley shoved two carrots into his mouth. "I've been walking around on a cloud?" he asked, crunching loudly.

"Oh, come on! You know you have. Something...or *someone* had kept you in a good mood for some time now."

He grinned at her, relishing in his mother's frustration. "What do you mean?" He asked, tossing another carrot into his mouth.

"Riley," she huffed. "You know *exactly* what I mean. Now come on...tell me what's going on." She sidled up next to him and lowered her voice. "We don't need to wait for your father. I'll fill him in later. Who is she? Do I know her? Is she from around here? How serious are you?"

He held his hands up in front of him. "Whoa, whoa! Calm down, mom. Sheesh." He turned back toward the fridge in order to put the bag of carrots away. He took his time, selecting a few from the bag before closing it. He could practically feel his mother's impatience. "Yes, yes, and very," he said, placing the carrots back in the vegetable drawer.

Riley turned back around to find his mother standing there with her mouth open. "How serious," she asked after several beats.

"As serious as I've ever been about someone," he replied, closing the refrigerator door.

"Oh. My. God!" She said, clapping her hands together. "I knew it! So who is she? Do you know her from school?"

"No," he replied. "She's from here."

"Here? You mean Lancaster?" Seeing his nod, she continued. "Well, who is she?" Though Wendy was trying to reign in her emotions, she was quickly becoming frustrated with this exchange, as well as Riley's obvious avoidance of answering even the simplest of questions.

"Kate," he replied, shoving another carrot into his mouth.

Wendy frowned. "Kate? Hmmm…Kate…Kate…" She tapped her finger against her chin, trying to think of who this 'Kate' might be. Finally, she looked up at Riley. "Kate who?"

"Kate Penner," he replied.

"Very funny, Riley," she deadpanned. "Seriously. Who is she?"

"Mom," Riley replied, sighing softly.

Wendy stood in the middle of the kitchen and stared at her son. He watched as the realization slowly dawned on her. Her expression changed from confusion to understanding, and then finally, anger. She pursed her lips together into a thin line and her eyes formed tiny slits. Riley waited several moments, expecting her to say something…anything, but instead, she just stood there seething, while she glared at him from underneath hooded lashes.

She opened and closed her mouth several times, trying to figure out which thought to express first. Her mind was a jumble of confusion and anger and she was having difficulty determining which emotion she was feeling was the dominant one. "Katharine Penner? You're serious? But she's…she's…" Her voice trailed off. "I don't understand. You? And Kate?"

Riley rubbed his face with his hand. He knew his mother well enough to know when she was about to lose it and today was one of those days. And he was not in the mood for this. Not that he ever was, but today? He wanted her to be happy for him. Instead, she had such a look of shock and anger on his face that he felt himself steeling for an argument. Despite his own anger brewing inside, he forced himself to respond to her in his most normal, non-confrontational tone. "Yes mom. Me and Kate."

"I...I don't understand. But how? I mean...did you...did she?...Oh hell, I don't know what I mean." Wendy turned away from her son. "What did she do to you?" She asked, looking down into the sink.

Riley stepped back as though he'd been slapped. "What are you talking about?"

"She must have done something? What did she say to you? Did she force you?"

"Force me to what?" A feeling of disgust came over him and he felt his stomach turn over. "You can't be serious!" Wendy turned around and Riley saw the hardened look on his mother's face. "You are serious. Jesus!" He raked his hand through his hair.

Automatically, she corrected her son, momentarily forgetting about the larger issue at hand. "Don't say that."

Riley ignored her reprimand and bulldozed on. "Do you realize what you're saying? You actually think that Kate had to somehow coerce me? Or...or..." He swallowed hard, the saliva in his mouth turning bitter. "Force me?"

"Riley! Are you actually going to stand there and take her side? Good lord, this is worse than I thought." She rubbed her temples with her fingers as though a migraine were coming on. "There are no sides. No one has done anything wrong here. Kate and I care about each other."

"Pffft." Wendy waved her hands around dismissively. "It will pass."

"Mom." Riley's voice had taken on a steely edge, causing Wendy to stop and look at him. "My feelings for her aren't going to change. Her feelings for me aren't going to change."

Wendy looked at her son and for the first time, noticed his look of determination. She nearly laughed out loud at his stupidity and warped sense of reality. He really had no idea how things worked. She knew he was living in a fantasy world while he was spending time with that woman. "How *exactly* are you going to continue this *relationship* when you're at school? You've got another year still. Or have you forgotten that? Were you simply going to drop out? Well, I won't have it! You are going to finish your education! I don't care what you think you feel for that woman!"

"Oh my God," Riley muttered. He looked up and met her gaze. "How can you even say that? It's like you don't know me at all! Of course I'm going to finish school! I'd have to be an idiot to quit now." At the sound of the word 'idiot,' Wendy snorted. Riley looked up at her pointedly. "Look, I'm going back to school. Kate knows I'm going back to school. That doesn't change anything between us."

"Really," she said, sarcasm creeping into her tone. "So you're just going to go back to school for what? Ten months? And then come back here and resume this….this…" She waived her hands around in front of Riley. "Whatever it is you two have going on? Is that what you think?"

"Yes," he replied. "That's exactly what I think. Geez, mom! You're acting like I'm a child, for God's sakes!"

"You are a child! You're MY child! And she was my FRIEND!" Wendy's voice broke on the last word.

"Was? How can you even say that? Kate is one of your closest friends! Why are you acting like this?"

"How could she do this to me?!" Wendy wailed.

"To you? How did his turn into being about you? This is between me and Kate. I only told you because Kate insisted on it." Riley sighed heavily and raked his hand through his hair. "I should have kept my mouth shut," he muttered.

Wendy was sobbing now. "I can't believe this is happening! Do you have any idea how much this hurts me?!"

Riley shook his head in disgust. "I can't even talk to you when you're like this." He turned to leave but stopped at the sound of his mother's voice, which had now oddly become very calm.

"What did she say, Riley, to make you think you were in love with her? Oh, God. You're not in love with her, are you?"

He turned back toward his mother, crossed his arms over his chest and fixed a steely gaze on her, waiting for her to realize how asinine and idiotic her question was. Did she really think he'd be having this conversation with her if he *didn't* love Kate?

"Oh, Riley. You don't even know what love is." She spoke

dismissively, as though his feeling for Kate weren't real, as though they could be changed with the wave of her hand. "How can you be so sure?"

The sound of the front door opening and closing told the two of them that Riley's father, Bill, was home. Riley felt relief wash over him. Maybe his father would be able to talk some sense into her since she refused to listen to anything Riley had to say. His father had always been the only one with enough patience to deal with his mother's craziness.

"Thank God," Riley muttered as his father walked into the kitchen. Dressed in well-worn khaki shorts, a polo shirt, and flip-flops, his father looked more like a college student than someone who spent his days traveling from job site to job site, supervising the construction of any number of houses and well over one hundred employees.

As Bill stepped into the kitchen, he immediately sensed something wasn't right. Wendy stood on one side of the kitchen, her face streaked with tears. Riley stood on the other side, hands on his hips and brow furrowed with anger.

"What's going on here?" Bill asked, looking from one to the other.

Wendy nodded toward Riley. "You might want to direct that question to your son."

"Riley?" He asked. "What is it?"

"Nothing's wrong, dad. Mom's just being melodramatic." He rolled his eyes to further communicate his annoyance.

"Riley," he said, using a tone he'd not used since Riley was around fifteen.

He shrugged. "Sorry, but it's the truth." He looked up to find his father looking very impatient. Riley was quick to continue. "It's just that she's overreacting....as usual," he muttered.

"Why don't you tell me what's going on." Bill said, taking a seat at the table. He sat down heavily, as though expecting to hear news that was about to destroy his family.

"I'm seeing someone." Riley said.

"Okaaayyyy..." He said, looking from Wendy to Riley, clearly not following where this was heading.

"Dad," he said hesitantly. "I'm seeing Kate. Kate Penner."

"Todd's widow?"

"Don't call her that." Riley said.

"Riley," Bill replied, using once again a tone of warning. He sighed. "Fine. Hadley's mother."

"Yes," Riley huffed. "Hadley's mother."

Bill looked at his son as though inspecting him. "How serious is this?"

"Bill!" Wendy shouted. "Have you LOST YOUR MIND?!?! Your son is involved," she made quotation marks in the air with her fingers, "with an older woman….a much, much older woman. Who cares how serious he is?! It's not going to continue!!! Unless, of course, you think this is a good idea and want to pat him on the back or maybe give him a high five."

"Wendy, I'm just trying to figure out what we're dealing with here." Wendy tossed her hands up in the air and let them fall to her thighs, clearly exasperated. Bill chose to ignore his wife for the moment, accustomed to her dramatics and looked back at his son. He motioned for him to continue.

"We," Riley pointed to his parents, "aren't dealing with anything. This doesn't concern you. I only told you because Kate felt we should. She was worried about your-" he looked pointedly at his mother, "reaction. And like an idiot, I told her she had nothing to worry about it. I told her you'd actually be happy for us since the two of you were such good friends. I can see now that telling you was a HUGE mistake. Kate was right all along."

"Kate?" Wendy screeched. "What does *that woman* have to say about all of this?"

"'That woman?' So, now she's 'that woman?' Mom, are you serious?" Riley had just about exhausted his patience with his mother.

"Fine," Wendy huffed. "What did *Kate* say?"

"She wanted me to tell you about us so you didn't feel as though we were sneaking around behind your back."

"THAT'S EXACTLY WHAT YOU'RE DOING!!" She screeched.

"Okay, hold on for just a minute," Bill said, standing up and moving to stand beside his wife. "Riley, what exactly is going on."

"Kate and I are seeing each other."

Bill nodded slowly, appearing to ponder what his son had just told him. "You're seeing Katharine Penner." Riley nodded. "I take it you two are serious about each other?"

Riley nodded. "Very."

Wendy sighed loudly. "How can you be serious when you're going back to school in six weeks? You are *not* quitting school. I simply won't have it!"

"Can you please talk to her? She won't listen to anything I have to say," Riley pleaded, throwing in an eye roll for good measure.

"Don't even try," Wendy said, fixing a steely gaze toward her husband. She looked back at Riley. "So, are you? Going to quit school?"

Riley's matched his mother's sigh. "Are you even listening to me? Of course not! I've got one year left! Do you honestly think I'm going to just quit? Geez! It's like you don't even know me at all."

"Well," Wendy sniffed. "Maybe I don't know you the way I thought I did." She turned and walked out of the room.

"Dad," Riley said, giving his father a pleading look.

"Let me talk to her, all right?"

Riley nodded.

"But tell me something," he asked, leaning against the counter. "You're serious about this?"

"I love her, dad."

"And Kate? Does she feel the same?"

He nodded. "She does."

Bill crossed his arms in front of his chest and took a deep, calming breath. He met his son's eyes and waited several moments before speaking. "Riley, there's a child involved here. A very young child. That's a lot of responsibility. Are you sure you're ready for this?"

"Dad!"

He held his hands up in front of him in a show of surrender. "Look, I'm just asking. That's all. If you want me to go to bat for you with your mother, I need to know where you stand on all of this."

Riley nodded his understanding. "All right. Maybe this whole thing is a bit crazy…maybe I don't know *completely* what I'm getting into…"

"But…" his father prodded.

"But… I love her, dad. And I love anything that comes with her, especially her daughter."

A Ripple in the Water

"And what does Hadley think of all this?"

"She's fine with it. Kate told her everything us last week."

Bill nodded, still pondering the situation. "Well, how do you think Hadley's going to feel when you leave for school? I'm guessing she's pretty attached to you."

Riley smiled at his father. "Yeah, she is. But I don't think it's because I'm dating her mother. I think it's because of how she knew me first...you know, swim coach and all. And besides, she knew I was going back to school in August."

Riley looked patiently at his father, waiting for the next in a series of questions he felt certain were some sort of a test. He crossed his arms over his chest and leaned back against the counter.

He looked into his son's eyes and saw such a fierce look of determination that Bill nearly laughed out loud. It was a look that Bill himself had perfected when he was about the same age...the look he had on his face when he told his father how serious he was about Wendy. "All right."

"All right?" Riley asked. "What do you mean, 'all right'?"

Bill groaned, resigning himself to what he knew was going to be an uphill battle. "I can't believe I'm going to say this but...I'll talk to your mother."

"Do you think you'll be able to talk some sense into her? You know, convince her that Kate isn't some...I don't know..."

"Don't worry," Bill replied. "I've been dealing with your mother for quite some time. She just needs some time to get used to the idea. I'm sure it's just the initial shock of your announcement, that's all."

Riley sighed heavily. "I don't see why it's so shocking to her. I mean, she knows Kate – has known her for years."

"That's exactly it," Bill said, clasping his son on his shoulder. "Your mother has only known Kate as a friend. It's something entirely different for her to know her as your girlfriend. Your mother just needs to connect the dots; that's all. Give her some time, all right? She'll come around."

Riley knew his father was right. His mother would come around. She was just shocked at the moment. She'd come around. He exhaled slowly, feeling the tension leave his shoulders.

Just a little time. That's all his mother needed. Just a little time.

Chapter 26

Kate looked down at her phone for perhaps the hundredth time and wondered why she hadn't heard from Riley yet. Her brows came together as she felt a tinge of worry but she quickly brushed it aside. Everything was going to be fine. Riley was going to talk to his parents and they were going to be fine. Still though, she'd feel much better if she knew that not only had Wendy been told about her relationship with Riley but maybe even given her blessing. Then she would know for certain and could stop worrying, then she could just focus on being happy. This entire summer had been her bouncing between two emotions – worry and happiness.

She smiled, thinking about Riley. Beginning a new relationship had been the last thing on her mind this summer. All she'd hoped was that she'd be able to survive it somehow. As it turned out, she'd had the most stress free summer and as an added bonus, she'd fallen in love.

She never thought that would happen again.

Kate found she couldn't sit still. She had all this nervous energy that she knew was the result of her desperate need to hear from Riley and know that everything had gone well with Wendy. Once that happened, she could go on with the rest of her day. Until then…well, she needed to *do* something and sitting at her computer wasn't going to cut it. Not by a long shot. She needed to do something that was actually constructive. The only thing that came to mind was something she put off continuously – cleaning her house. Hadley was sitting contentedly in front of the television so Kate opted to head upstairs and begin to work on what she knew was going to be something that resembled a locker room.

Most women she knew cleaned their home methodically – going from room to room ensuring each one was spotless before moving on to the next. Kate had never worked that way, instead always choosing to simply pick up clutter so that room gave the appearance of being organized and clean. Her house had never had the lemon-fresh scent that she'd often noticed when visiting other homes. She never seemed to find enough time to make her house smell like the inside of a Pledge can.

Part of her problem, she knew, was that the task always seemed so overwhelming. Cleaning a house from top to bottom? Surely she had better things to do. Besides, for the most part, it was only she and Hadley who were here so it wasn't as if anyone else would notice if there was a faint ring on the inside of her toilet or if there were little fuzzies of dust in the corners of her rooms. Kate was more than satisfied with the fact that her house gave the appearance of clean and organized and didn't need the satisfaction of knowing someone could eat off her floor without becoming ill. Still, she knew she needed to at least make an attempt to keep her home looking as though she spent time cleaning so she traipsed upstairs, fearing what she might find there.

Kate stood in the middle of Hadley's room, knowing that this was as good a place as any to start. She wasn't entirely sure why, of all the rooms, she would choose this one to start in since this room would be the one that most quickly resumed its current state of disarray. Luckily, Hadley's room was upstairs and rarely, if ever, seen by anyone other than her friends, who Kate was certain had similar rooms – at least until their mothers took control of the situation. Kate began by picking up stray items that were scattered across the floor and tossing them into the multi-colored bins that had been placed in every corner of the room. Once that was completed, she wandered into bathroom. Though this shower was rarely used since Hadley preferred to bathe in the tub in the master bedroom, the sink was used every night before Hadley went to bed. Kate peered in the sink, prepared to find the filmy white residue from several evening of tooth brushing. Had the disgusting white mess not been the result of her very own daughter, Kate knew she would have been unable to clean it. As it was, she had to scrub the sink without focusing on the fact that the mess was a mix of her daughter's saliva and toothpaste. She was just rinsing out the sink when she heard the low rumble of a car in her driveway. *Finally,* she thought, thinking Riley had arrived.

Riley drove to Kate's house wishing he had better news. While he was thankful his father was supportive of him, he dreaded telling Kate that his mother wasn't completely on board with Kate and Riley's relationship. But his mother's approval would come; he knew it would. It anyone could handle his mother, it was his father, he thought, grinning.

He pulled into her driveway and turned the engine off. Slowly, he made his way to the front door and knocked softly. She opened the door quickly, as if she knew it were him waiting there. She grinned at him, ever pleased to see him. The smile vanished quickly, however, when she saw the look of concern on his face.

"Riley? What's the matter?"

He stepped inside and pulled her into an embrace, inhaling the scent of her, a mix of her fragrant shampoo and the lotion he knew she applied daily.

She pried herself out of his arms and looked him in the eye. "Okay, you're scaring me. I take it telling your parents didn't go as well as you'd hoped?"

He sighed heavily and raked his hand through his hair. Kate once again felt that familiar feeling of emotion bubble up inside of her. She wondered how it was she could be worried and aroused at the same time. "Come on," she said, taking his hand.

She led him to the kitchen and sat down in across from him. "What happened?"

He shrugged halfheartedly. "My mom's not completely on board with this," he pointed to the two of them.

Kate felt herself deflate. "I knew it. I just knew it!" She cried.

"Now hold on," Riley said, taking her hand in his. "We just need to give her some time to get used to this."

She looked at him wryly. "Do you really think that's possible?"

He nodded. "But honestly? I don't really give a shit."

"Riley!" Kate gasped. "How can you say that?"

"How can I *not* say that? Look at it from my point of view. You tell me that my mother is giddy at the pool, telling you she's never seen me this way and then when I tell her it's you, she loses it? Come on. What happened to the 'I'm so happy for my son' speech she gave you? Why does it matter that it's you?"

"Because to her, I crossed some boundary. I dated her son. Maybe in her mind, you were off-limits."

Riley bristled. "Off limits? That's ridiculous. You make it sound like I'm her property or something." He shoved the chair back and stood up angrily. "She's acting like I'm still a little kid and it's enough!"

He began to pace the kitchen mumbling. Kate could only make out a few words...fed up, babied, hovering...but she knew exactly what he was saying. He was tired of being treated like he was a child, like he was four years old. Still though, the mother in her knew she had to at least support Wendy, even in the smallest of measures.

"Riley," she said standing up slowly. "I know it's hard for you to understand but to her, you'll always be her little boy. I think it's hard for any woman to think about their child growing up and not needing them anymore."

"See? That's the thing. I haven't done that. I've let her hover over me for twenty years. I've let her be involved – way involved – in every aspect of my life. How on earth can she think that me dating you means I don't need her anymore? Maybe I don't need her as much as I did when I was four, but...."

Kate stepped behind him and wrapped her arms around his waist. "I think it's different for mothers of boys. A girl tends to stay closer to her mother, even if she gets married and has kids. When a boy grows up, he tends to make a family with his wife and his mom...well, sometimes she gets a bit left out."

He sighed. "That sounds about right." He turned to face her. "But listen, I don't want you to worry about my mother. She'll come around. My dad said she just needs a little time."

She nodded her agreement. "I'm sure you're right."

"Of course I am," he grinned. "Now, where's Hadley?"

His smile was contagious and Kate smiled back at him. "She's in front of the TV. Where else would she be?"

He grabbed her hand. "Come on. Let's go sit with her."

Kate allowed herself to be led into the living room. She pushed her thoughts of Wendy from her mind, wanting to simply enjoy the time with Riley and Hadley. She had to believe that Bill would be able to talk some sense into Wendy. And until that happened, she just wasn't going to think about it. She had more important things to focus on she thought, as she looked at the two people seated beside her on the couch.

Chapter 27

Over the next week or so, Kate for the most part, managed to put Wendy out of her mind. Riley didn't seem at all phased by his mother's reaction and continued to spend as much time as possible with Kate and Hadley. But now, instead of heading to the public arena that was the community pool, they rented movies and spent quiet evenings at Kate's house, which suited Kate just fine.

In the middle of July, the weather took an uncomfortable turn, making the humidity even more unbearable than it usually was. Riley and Kate once again, opted to spend the afternoon watching a movie in the comfort of Kate's air-conditioned house. Though a time hadn't been established, Kate expected him to show up in the early afternoon – some time after he'd finished with swim practice. As noon approached and her anticipation heightened, it only made sense that when she heard the car in her driveway that she flung open the door before even peering out through the window.

The smile vanished from her face when she saw it was not Riley pulling into her driveway, but an unfamiliar blue Ford Focus. Getting out of the car was a somber looking woman holding a clipboard with some papers attached. She was wearing a button down white shirt, khaki pants and a pair of brown sandals. Kate momentarily thought she might be selling something or be one of those people who travels door to door trying to raise money for a mission trip. The humid air poured into the house and Kate felt a pang of sympathy for this woman who was outside wearing pants in this weather.

"Can I help you?" Kate asked, smiling pleasantly as the woman stepped onto the porch.

The woman's eye met hers, causing Kate's smile to vanish. There was nothing happy or even pleasant about this woman.

"Ms. Penner?"

"Yes?"

"My name is Karen Miller. I'm from the Department of Social Services." She held out a photo id which showed this woman was indeed who she said she was.

Kate felt a cold shiver of apprehension work its way up her spine, despite the heat that was still pouring in through the front door.

The woman continued as though she'd rehearsed the speech numerous times, which of course, she probably had. "I'm here to conduct an interview regarding the child currently in your care," she looked down at her clipboard. "A seven year old girl…Hadley?"

"Hadley? I…I don't understand. What do you want with my daughter?"

"Ma'am, we've had a report of neglect and abuse." The woman looked directly at Kate as she spoke. She didn't even blink. She glared at Kate as though daring her to deny the accusation. She looked at Kate as though she were already guilty.

"Neglect? Abuse?" She stammered.

"May I come in?"

"Of course," Kate replied, stepping aside. The woman stepped into the foyer and Kate closed the door behind her. "Come into the kitchen. Can I get you something to drink?"

"No, thank you." She peered into the kitchen and motioned to the table. "May I sit?"

Kate could only nod.

The woman sat down at the table and began to take out the papers that were held in the clipboard. She glanced up at Kate and then nodded to the chair beside her. "Why don't you sit so we can begin." It was more a directive than a friendly suggestion.

Kate slowly moved over to the table and sat down. "Ms. Miller is it?" The woman nodded. "I'm not sure I understand what this is about."

Ms. Miller sighed heavily as though running out of patience. "Ms. Penner, our department has received a complaint regarding the child in your care. There are some concerns that she isn't being cared for properly. I'm here to investigate those allegations."

"Hadley? Not being cared for? That's ridiculous! Who would make such an accusation?"

"Ms. Penner, I'm not at liberty to discuss the claim. I'm only here to determine whether or not the child is in any immediate danger and whether or not it's in her best interests to remain in this home."

Kate felt the blood drain from her face. "What do you mean,

'remain in the home?' Are you saying she could be taken away?"

"Why don't we just begin, all right?" The woman pulled out a pen and clicked, the sound caused Kate to flinch.

Kate could only nod. She knew if she were to open her mouth to answer, the only sounds that would come out would be the sounds of choking sobs.

"I've got several questions I need to ask both you and Hadley. Of course, I'll need to speak to Hadley alone. And I'll also need to inspect the home."

"Questions? Inspect the home?" Kate was beginning to think she'd lost her mind since all she was doing was repeating what this woman was saying. "Why do you need to inspect the home?"

Ms. Miller leveled her gaze at Kate. "I need to ensure that the home is safe and a good environment for the child in question."

The child in question. Her daughter no longer had a name, Kate thought.

"Mommy? Can I have some juice?" Hadley's head poked into the kitchen.

Oh, God, Kate thought, as she stood up. *I completely forgot she was in the living room.* "Sure, sweetheart. What would you like? A juice-box?"

Hadley nodded. Kate reached into the cabinet and pulled one out. She popped the straw into the tiny silver hole and handed the juice to her daughter.

Kate noticed that Ms. Miller had become much more alert since hearing Hadley's soft voice. She also noticed that her entire demeanor had changed. Instead of being stern and serious, she was now leaning forward and smiling at Hadley.

"You must be Hadley," she said. Seeing the nod, she continued. "My name is Karen. Would you like to sit with me for a minute?" Hadley looked at her mother for approval. Kate forced a smile to her face and nodded. Hadley walked over to the table while sipping her juice and plopped herself into the chair Kate had vacated only moments before.

"Are you a friend of my mom's? Hadley asked.

Karen smiled broadly. "Well, we only just met. But I'd like to be your friend. Would you like that?"

Hadley shrugged, still slurping her juice.

"So, Hadley, your mom and I were just talking and she told me you have a pretty cool room."

Any mention of Hadley's bubble-gum pink room would elicit a huge grin from her and today was no exception. Seeing the grin and viewing it as encouragement, Karen continued.

"I'd love to see it. Would you like to show it to me?"

Hadley nodded, jumped off the chair and reached for her mother's hand.

Karen reached her own hand out to Hadley. "I think your mom wants to stay here. She said she's got some cleaning to do." She giggled as though she were a teenage girl. "Looks like it's just you and me!"

Kate kept the smile plastered to her face, unwilling to show her daughter just how worried and stressed she was. When Hadley looked to her mother for approval, Kate nodded and encouraged her to take Karen's hand and ushered her toward the stairs. She watched as the two of them disappeared upstairs, Hadley practically skipping up the steps.

From where she stood in the kitchen, Kate could hear their footsteps as they made their way through Hadley's room and into the bathroom. She wondered what exactly this woman would be looking for. Would she judge Kate on how clean the house was? How many clothes were in Hadley's closet? The water pressure in the bathroom? What exactly was involved here? Kate had no idea. All she knew at the moment was there was a chance her daughter was going to be taken out of her home. She stumbled back to the kitchen table and collapsed into a chair.

Her world was falling apart around her and she knew she was powerless to stop it. What could she do besides answer all the questions this woman could throw at her and give her full reign to both Hadley and her home? And she had to do that, didn't she? If she hesitated at all, this woman would think there was something to hide, which of course, there wasn't. But still, her life and the life of her child's was dependant on the findings of this woman. Did Kate even have a say in the matter? She didn't think so. She knew with almost absolute certainty that she would have to abide by whatever this Ms. Miller decided.

She could have wept right then and there but she knew she had to keep it together for Hadley's sake.

She took several slow deep breaths in an attempt to calm herself.

It didn't work. This woman was upstairs alone with her daughter asking her God-knows-what and she was downstairs trying to figure out just how all this had happened.

Which was a very good question, now that she thought about it. How did this happen? She tried to recall if she'd ever done anything that would be viewed as questionable someone who didn't know her. Had she yelled at Hadley in the grocery store? Maybe spoken to her in some way that was overheard by someone as derogatory or belittling? She wracked her brain but couldn't recall anything of the kind. Well, someone had to see something that concerned them or else she wouldn't be in this mess. Not that it mattered; she needed to deal with the nightmare she'd been tossed into. She needed to clear this mess up and ensure that Hadley stayed right where she belonged—with her mother.

How would this all play out? What was the process involved? She had no idea. She'd never been through anything like this- didn't even know anyone who'd been through it. She had absolutely no idea what was going to happen to her and Hadley. Kate thought back to what the Social Services woman had said earlier....safe to remain in the home. Was that even possible? Did this woman have the authority to remove Hadley from their home? And where would she go? Paralyzing fear ripped through her at the thought of Hadley being in the care of someone else...someone she didn't know.

Kate felt a sob escape. She couldn't even bear to think about that now. All she could do was take this one step at a time. The thought of Hadley being removed from her home was a nightmare she didn't even want to consider.

It was a nightmare she wasn't sure she'd survive.

Hadley and Ms. Miller stayed upstairs for nearly an hour. Kate wondered what they were talking about but knew she couldn't go upstairs and check. The look Ms. Miller gave Kate was a clear indication that she wanted to be alone with Hadley...to perform her investigation. Kate shuddered. The word itself was enough to make Kate grow cold with fear, particularly when she was the focus of this so-called investigation.

Finally, Hadley and Ms. Miller came back downstairs. Ms. Miller thanked Hadley and gave her a quick hug. Hadley then bounded off toward the living room. Almost immediately, Ms. Miller's demeanor changed. Once again, she was the stern, unfriendly woman that had met her at the front door.

"Shall we sit?" She asked.

Kate nodded, swallowed hard, then once again sat down at the kitchen table with the woman who had the power to take her daughter away from her.

Once Ms. Miller was assured Hadley was out of earshot, the questions began.

How many hours do you work each week? Where does Hadley normally sleep? Is she ever left with a sitter? What are the names of her sitters? How may I contact them? What is a typical meal for Hadley? Where does she attend school? How many days did she miss last year? For what reasons? Can I verify those absences with her school? The questions went on seemingly endlessly, making Kate dizzy.

Ms. Miller made no response to any of Kate's answers; she only marked notations on her paperwork. Kate had no idea how she was performing and whether or not she was going to pass or fail. The stress of all of was giving her a migraine and making her nauseous. Finally, Ms. Miller finished with her barrage of questions, gathered her papers together and slid them neatly onto her clipboard.

"That's all I have for today," she said, standing up. "Someone from our office will be here in the next week or so to perform another site visit."

Kate nodded dumbly. "When will that be?"

"It will be a drop-in, Ms. Penner." Seeing the look of confusion on Kate's face, the woman continued. "Unannounced."

"Oh," Kate replied, finally understanding the process. Social Services would surprise her with a visit in order to 'catch' her doing something deemed inappropriate. She stood up and showed Ms. Miller to the door. As she pulled it opened, she wondered what the appropriate protocol was. Was she supposed to shake her hand? Tell her to have a good day? The questions she had were unnecessary since Ms. Miller slipped out the front door without so much as a backward glance.

The moment Kate closed the door, what little confidence she'd managed to muster evaporated. She slumped to the floor and let the tears fall.

Chapter 28

After sobbing silently on the floor for what seemed an eternity, Kate managed to gather herself together up off the floor and make her way into the bathroom where she splashed cold water on her face. She walked back into the kitchen and peered around the corner into the living room to check on Hadley. Instead of her daughter, there were several empty Tupperware containers Kate knew had been used for chips, goldfish, pretzels, and any other snack Hadley could find. She picked up the empty containers and placed them into the kitchen sink, then walked upstairs to find Hadley in her room, playing with an elaborate set up of Polly Pockets. She gave her a quick hug, then backed out of the room and headed downstairs, unsure of what she was going to do to occupy herself. She walked into the kitchen and plopped herself down into one of the chairs and looked around. Suddenly, everything looked different, less stable somehow. In an instant, like one year ago, her life had been shattered. This time, however, she would be forced to wait for the final blow; she would have to wait for someone else to make a decision. She felt completely helpless and terrified.

She looked at the clock on the microwave and was shocked to realize it was nearly four o'clock. Just as she began to wonder about Riley, she heard a car pull into her driveway, followed by the sound of door slam. Kate hoped this time it would be Riley and not another surprise guest. She glanced in the mirror before opening the door and while she could still make out the redness around her eyes, she hoped that Riley wouldn't be able to tell she'd been crying.

Of course, she was wrong and Riley noticed almost immediately.

He stepped into the foyer and gathered her into his arms. She collapsed the moment she felt his strength surround her.

"Kate?" He asked. "What is it? What's the matter?"

"Social Services has been here all afternoon!" She cried. "They could take Hadley away!"

"What? What are you talking about? Why would Social Services come here?" He half pulled/half dragged her into the kitchen where they sat down at the table. "Start from the beginning," he whispered, knowing Hadley was most likely within ear shot.

Kate wiped her eyes then began to tell Riley about Karen Miller showing up at the house. She told him about the interview with both she and Hadley and the follow up appointment. When she finished, she felt like she'd relived the entire horror all over again. "What am I going to do, Riley? They can't take her away from me, can they?"

Riley frowned. "I have no idea." He cringed the moment the words were out of his mouth but truth be told, he had no idea how this sort of thing worked. "Tell me what this woman said again? Someone filed a report? What does that even mean?"

She took a deep breath and then exhaled slowly. "Someone contacted Social Services and accused me of abusing Hadley! Why would someone do that? I'm a good mother!" She cried, tears filling her eyes once again.

"I know you are. Don't worry, Kate. We'll get through this."

"What am I going to do, Riley? What am I going to do if they take her? I can't lose her. I just can't!" Kate began to sob, her shoulders convulsing with each breath.

"Mommy?"

Kate's head shot up as she realized her daughter was standing beside her.

"Are you okay? Do you want to use my blanky?"

"Oh, honey," Kate sniffed. "Mommy's just a little sad, that's all. I'll be all right."

Hadley looked from her mother to Riley, fear etched into her features. Kate had always been someone who was honest with her child, answering her questions about anything and everything with the most basic of answers, regardless of the question. This, however, was one situation where Kate knew she couldn't be honest with her daughter and that broke her heart. Unfortunately, she also knew it was for the best. She didn't want Hadley to worry about what may or may not happen. For now, Kate knew she had to lie, or at the very least, avoid the truth. She cursed Karen Miller for putting her in this situation.

Kate leaned over and embraced her daughter, holding her tight. She pulled back after several moments and looked her daughter in the eye. "Now don't you worry about mommy, okay? Sometimes we grownups just get upset about grown up sorts of things. But I'll be fine." She tried to make her voice sound light and cheery but she failed miserably. Hadley seemed…well, not content with her mother's answer but somewhat placated with the answer she had been given, despite how vague it had been. Hadley stared at her mother as though assessing and then turned to Riley for confirmation. Seeing his nod, she looked back at her mother.

"You're going to be okay?"

Kate nodded. "I promise. Now, why don't you pick out a movie for us and I'll start making something for dinner."

"Can Riley stay?"

"Sure," she replied.

Hadley skipped into the living room in search of a movie for the three of them to watch. Riley's eyes remained on Kate, searching for signs of more stress.

Her eyes still trailing her daughter, she spoke. "I had to lie to my daughter. I hate that."

"I know you do. But I think you did the right thing." He took her hand in his own and held it tight.

"I'm so glad you're here, Riley."

He fixed his eyes on hers. I'll always be here for you. Whatever you need. You know that, right?"

She nodded.

"Come on," he said, tugging her up and into his arms. "Let's go spend some time with your daughter."

Kate smiled as she burrowed her face into Riley's chest. "That sounds wonderful."

Chapter 29

For the next several days, Kate was unable to focus on anything other than her own worry about the nightmare she found herself in the middle of. She barely left the house, choosing instead to quarantine herself and Hadley in her bedroom. She spent little to no time with Riley, which he tried his best to understand. It didn't help that Kate couldn't really explain it to either of them except to say that she felt as though she didn't deserve any pleasure at in her life until everything else was on track.

Oddly, she felt even worse than she had when her husband had died. When Todd had died, there had been no preparing for it. No anticipation of something ominous. She only had to deal with the loss after the event. Now, her days were consumed with 'what-if' scenarios. She'd even begun to ponder simply leaving everything behind and running away with Hadley. Of course, she knew without any means to support the two of them, it was only a fantasy. And then, of course, she'd be considered a criminal...a kidnapper, no less.

Thanks to the wealth of information available on the internet, she knew what would happen if the worst was to occur. Hadley would be removed from their home and placed with someone else – a foster family. Kate would have limited access, probably supervised visits, and this foster family would take care of Hadley. Kate wouldn't be there to kiss her in the morning when she woke or tuck her in at night. She wouldn't be able to monitor how much television she watched, or make sure she ate enough for breakfast, lunch and dinner. In essence, Kate would be completely shut off from Hadley's life and instead, be forced to hand over her daughter to complete strangers.

Kate couldn't even fathom a life without her daughter. If the worst were to happen, if Hadley were to be taken away from her, she doubted her ability to survive. No mother could survive losing her daughter...not like this.

Though she couldn't bring herself to tell Hadley what was going on, her daughter was very perceptive and knew something was amiss. Kate had to give Hadley credit: she never complained about missing swim practices or lying around in pajamas all day. She put up a good front, snuggling with her mother for hours at a time, picking out movies her mother enjoyed and being content with just the two of them to spend time alone in their house.

But even Hadley had her limits and after several days, she begged to go to the pool. Though Kate still had no desire to get out of bed, let alone leave the house, she agreed, knowing that Hadley needed some normalcy and needed to spend time with her friends.

They arrived at the pool in the early afternoon, which Kate was thankful for. Swim practice was over for the day and the pool had emptied out significantly. There were relatively few cars in the parking lot, some of which Kate recognized. One in particular made Kate grow cold with fear, knowing that a confrontation was probably unavoidable in such a small space, especially one that was surrounded by fencing.

Taking a deep breath, Kate walked slowly up the concrete walkway, trailing behind a giddy Hadley, who was running ahead of her while pulling her goggles over her eyes. Before Kate could even get into the fenced in area, she heard a splash and knew her daughter had jumped in the pool. She smiled, knowing this was exactly what Hadley needed.

Since she knew she wouldn't be able to handle any idle chit-chat, she walked over to a chair well away from the other families and quickly hunched down behind a magazine. Because she was buried behind her magazine, she didn't see Riley's approach and flinched when he sat down beside her.

"Hey," he said softly. A look of apology crossed his face when he realized he startled her.

"It's okay," she replied. "How are you?"

"How am I?" He looked shocked. "How are *you*?"

"Oh…I don't know…" Her voice broke off with a sob. "Okay, I'm a mess. I'm not handling this well at all."

"If it's any consolation, you look like you're doing all right."

Kate shook her head. "But I'm not. And what worries me is that if I'm like this-" she pulled down her sunglasses and motioned to her red, swollen eyes, "-after just the possibility of…Hadley… What am I going to be like if they actually take her? Riley," she whispered,

218

pain evident in her tone. "I won't survive if they take her."

He gripped her hands. "Listen to me. They are *not* going to take her. They're not going to find anything that would warrant them taking her. You are a *great* mother and they're going to see that."

A tear made its way down her cheek and she angrily brushed it away. She did *not* want to cry while at the pool with Hadley.

"Well, well, well. Isn't this a pretty little picture?"

The two of them looked up to find Wendy standing over them, hands on her hips. Kate heard Riley swear under his breath.

"Not now, mom. Kate's got a lot on her mind."

"I'll bet she does," she sneered.

"What is the matter with you? Why are you acting this way?" Riley went to stand up but Kate put her hand on his arm, stopping him.

"It's all right, Riley. I'm just going to head home."

Riley looked at her. "Kate," he whispered. "Don't let my mother get away with acting like this. She'd being ridiculous!"

Kate smiled gently at him. "It's all right. I'll go. But would you do something for me?"

"Of course," he replied, raising his eyebrows at the abrupt change of subject.

"Can you watch Hadley for a bit? Let her swim for a little while, then bring her home? She really wanted to spend some time at the pool."

He nodded. "Sure. How about I bring her home in an hour or so?"

She nodded, then stood up and began to gather her things. She fumbled through her bag and pulled out a towel and a bottle of sunscreen, which she handed silently to Riley. He took the towel and sunscreen, then gently touched her on the shoulder, knowing that there was nothing he could say to ease her anguish but at the same time, wanting to communicate to her that he would support her, no matter what. Without glancing at his mother, he turned and walked over to where Hadley's head would poke up out of the water every several seconds or so.

Out of the corner of her eye, Kate glanced at Wendy, who was standing beside them, arms crossed over her chest, watching their exchange. The expression she wore was one of disgust and disdain and in that instant, Kate knew that their friendship had been damaged, perhaps irrevocably. Kate heaved her large canvas bag over her shoulder and trudged wearily toward the gate and then down the sidewalk to her car.

"You make me sick."

It wasn't until she heard the words that were spat out of Wendy's mouth that Kate realized Wendy had followed her to her car. Her bag fell to the ground with a thump and she turned around to face the woman she once considered one of her closest friends.

Wearily, Kate looked up at her. "I beg your pardon?"

"You heard me," Wendy replied. "You make me sick. Cavorting with my son like that? I thought that behavior was beneath you. Clearly, I was wrong."

"Wendy, can we please do this some other time? I've got a lot on my plate right now-"

"Oh, I know all about what you've got on your plate," Wendy interrupted. She stepped closer to Kate and leaned forward. Despite the over ninety degree heat, Kate could feel Wendy's hot breath on her face when she spoke. "Believe me, I know *all* about it."

Kate sighed heavily, knowing Wendy wasn't about to let her leave without going a couple rounds. "Why don't you just say what you came to say."

Wendy leaned in even closer to Kate, leaning over her and glaring. There might have even been a hint of a smirk on her face. "How does it feel Kate? To know that you might lose your child? To know that you have no control over your child's life? That someone else might take your child away?"

"What..." Kate gasped. "How did you...?"

"Oh come on, Kate. Don't be such an idiot. Did you think I was going to let you get away with this?"

"Get away with WHAT? What are you TALKING ABOUT?"

"Taking my son away from me. Well, payback is a bitch," she spat.

It suddenly dawned on Kate exactly what Wendy was referring to. "Wendy," she whispered. "No...tell me you didn't..." Her voice broke on a sob.

Wendy stood in front of Kate and stared. After several moments, she looked away as though tired of the conversation. Then, as though to enrage Kate even further, she began to inspect her nails, turning her hands over and back to view them from several angels. "I'm certain I have no idea *what* you're talking about."

"How could you *do* something like that? Don't you understand what you've done? I could lose *my child!*"

She stopped inspecting her nails and glared at Kate. "Sucks, doesn't it?" She leaned forward once again, so close that Kate found herself leaning back uncomfortably. "You're getting a little dose of your own medicine. Learn from this, Kate. And keep your skirt down around your knees, where it belongs!"

Kate blinked several times, still trying to comprehend the venom that was spewing out of Wendy's mouth. She shook her head as though trying to comprehend what Wendy had just said. "Is that why you're doing this to me? Because of me and Riley? Wendy, I-"

"You stay away from MY SON! Or I'll do more than call Social Services. I will make it my mission in life to make sure that you experience the pain and anguish you have caused me."

Kate was frantically trying to figure out a way to fix the situation. Surely, there was someone at Social Services she could contact and explain the situation to. There had to be someone there who would listen to her. Feeling a moment of courage, she lifted her chin in a show of strength. "I won't let you get away with this. I'll call them myself and tell them you made a false accusation."

"Really?" Wendy hissed. "You think you're the first parent to try that? You actually think you might be the first parent to call and try to convince that bureaucracy that someone made a false claim because they were angry at you?"

Once again, Wendy leaned in towards Kate. She was so close that Kate could feel her hot breath on her cheeks. "No one will believe you. It will be my word against yours. And you have no proof."

"Yes, she does."

Both Kate and Wendy reared back and looked toward Riley, who was standing behind his mother. Kate was so engrossed in her exchange with Wendy, she hadn't even seen him approach.

Wendy immediately took the demeanor of a parent reprimanding a small child. "Riley, this doesn't concern you."

He took a step forward. "The hell it doesn't!" He stepped close to Kate, placed his arm around her waist and spoke softly to her. "Hadley's with Bethany. I just wanted to make sure you were all right."

Kate nodded, thankful Riley was so considerate, which just might save her from this entire nightmare. "How long were you standing there?"

"Long enough."

Riley fixed his gaze on his mother and began to speak. "I have never been so disgusted by you in all my life. What the hell were you thinking?"

"Riley!" Wendy admonished. "Don't you speak to me that way!"

He dropped his arm from around Kate's waist and stepped closer to his mother. In a slow, measured tone, he began to speak. "I think we're past that, don't you think? Now, it's your turn to listen to me. You are going to fix this. I don't know how. But you're going to do it. If you need to call every single person at Social Services, you're going to do just that."

"Riley-" Wendy interrupted, moving closer to her son.

"Stop!" He interrupted, holding up his hand. "I don't want to hear anything you have to say. I have put up with your involvement in everything I've ever done but this? This is too much. You've crossed *way* over the line!"

Wendy held Kate's gaze, anger seeping out. "You did this," she said, pointing at Kate. "He never acted this way until you came into the picture."

"Mom, just stop it!!! Don't you understand what you've done? She could lose her child! And all because you don't like the fact that we're dating?" He shook his head. "You need some serious help."

He turned toward Kate, his voice quickly resuming its normal tone. "Go home. I'll be there in a little bit. But don't worry, all right? We're going to fix this." He picked up her bag and placed it in the back of her car.

She nodded, then slowly got into the car and headed home. Riley watched her drive away, then turned toward his mother.

"You are going to fix this," he said angrily. "Today."

"Oh, Riley. Just stop it," she replied, waving her hand around dismissively. "You're being a little melodramatic, don't you think? Nothing's going to happen to Hadley. She's not going to be taken away...unless there's something going on in that house you're not telling me." She leaned forward, smirking.

"There is something seriously wrong with you."

"Riley!" She gasped.

"What is it, mother? Not used to having anyone speak to you this way? Not used to having anyone disagree with you?"

"I will not stand here and have you speak to me like this. I'm your mother, for goodness sakes." She turned away from her son, intending to walk back to the pool area.

"Then act like it," came the reply.

Wendy stopped dead in her tracks and slowly turned back around. "What did you say?"

"I said," Riley replied, "to act like it. Act like a grown up and fix this. You're the only one who can."

Wendy shook her head. "I'll do no such thing. Kate needs to see this to the end. Then she'll know how I feel." She thumped her chest for emphasis.

Riley's mouth opened and closed but no words came out. All he could do was look at her with pity and shake his head from side to side. "I never thought you were capable of anything like this. I thought you were better than this. Clearly, I was wrong."

Slowly, he began to walk away from her and head back toward the pool.

"She took you from me! She did this!" Wendy screamed at her son's retreating figure. He stopped, then turned around to face her.

"No mom. She didn't do this. You did." He stared at his mother, his eyes filled with sadness and pity for the woman who gave him life. "There is something seriously wrong with you if you think Kate is at fault here." He lifted up his hands in front of him in a display of mock surrender. "I'm done."

Wendy's mouth fell open as she watched her son walk away from her without even so much as glance back in her direction.

Donna Small

Chapter 30

Wendy felt vindicated…elated even. She looked deep inside of her for some feeling of remorse, but there was none. Never had she felt so exactly *right* in her behaviors. Now, and only now, would Kate know *exactly* how it felt to know that you were losing your child. And maybe, just maybe, Kate would think before she ever did anything like this again. Kate now knew that there were consequences for every action.

Well, almost every action.

Wendy had discovered, thanks to hours of research on the internet, that the great state of North Carolina was so invested in protecting their children that even those who knowingly made a false claim of child abuse were free from punishment. But of course, Wendy didn't *knowingly* make a false claim. Given Kate's behavior with Riley, God only knows what damage she might have done to her Hadley. Luckily, Wendy was there to step in and do her part to make sure that all was right within that home and that Hadley, bless her heart, was safe.

She still couldn't figure out Riley, though. Why was he still standing by that woman? Wasn't the stigma of Social Services showing up at your house enough of a deterrent for him? While she usually admired his loyalty, this was one circumstance where she just couldn't understand why he would have placed it with Kate. He should have been standing by his mother and not beside that woman who had played with his heart. Wendy normally considered Riley such an intelligent boy but that woman must have done some work on him in order to convince him they had a future together. Clearly, they did not. Riley would go back to school in a few weeks and forget all about this little fling with Katharine Penner. Then things would return to normal…well, not everything. That woman had ruined their friendship. She'd never be able to trust Kate again. It was just as well. Now that she knew the type of person she was. Wendy simply couldn't be friends with someone who would stoop so low as

224

to enter into a relationship with a man – no, child! – who was thirteen years her junior.

As Wendy walked back into the pool area, she glanced over at the digital clock above the lifeguard chair. She gasped as she realized she and the twins had been at the pool nearly all day. She decided it was time to gather the boys and head home. She gathered up her things and corralled the twins, which was a bit like herding cats. Finally, after some coercing that involved a promise of cheeseburgers for dinner with ice cream for dessert, she managed to get them both loaded into the van. As she slowly drove out of the pool area, she stole a look back at Riley who was still swimming with Hadley. She shook her head. That poor girl, she tsk-tsk'd. Having that sort of woman for a mother meant she didn't stand a chance. Such a shame, she thought. Hadley was always such a nice girl. Though, now that she thought about it, her phone call might be doing Hadley a favor. If she were to be placed in foster care, maybe the parents would be good, Christian folks and they could instill a good set of values in the child.

There might be hope for Hadley after all.

Wendy drove the short distance home. The twins bounded into the house, leaving a trail of towels and flip-flops as they went upstairs into their rooms.

"Boys! Your wet towels, please!" Hearing no response, she sighed then bent over to pick the towels up off the floor. "Don't worry guys. Mom will take care of everything," she said to the empty laundry room.

She peered down the hall into the master bedroom. The bed was made perfectly as it was each and every morning. Today however, it appeared much more inviting than it ever did. She slowly walked down the hall, pulled the comforter back and crawled in, exhaling her relief as she did so.

Wendy burrowed deeper under the covers and closed her eyes. She heard the muffled sounds of the twins from her sanctuary under the covers and knew they'd be entertained for at least an hour or so. Sleep came almost immediately.

She woke some time later to find Bill leaning against the bureau, arms crossed over his chest.

"What time is it?" She asked.

"Nearly seven," he replied. Wendy noticed his clipped tone and

Donna Small

knew he was upset with her. Rather than ask what was wrong, which she knew from experience was exactly what Bill wanted her to do, she chose the opposite and simply pretended she didn't hear the tension when he spoke. She rolled onto her back and sat up, leaning against the headboard. "You're just getting home? Everything all right?"

He raised an eyebrow. "Well, that depends."

"Depends on what?" Wendy raised an eyebrow.

"On what the *hell* you were thinking when you called Social Services!" Bill said through gritted teeth.

"Riley told you." It was a statement rather than a question.

"Of course he did. Wendy, what were you thinking?!" He got up and began to pace the room. "How could you do such a thing? And *why* would you do such a thing?"

"Why would I? God, Bill," she sneered. "You have absolutely no idea what I've been going through do you?"

"What the *hell* are you talking about? And how did this become about you? About what you're going through!? Kate is the one who's going through hell right now. And it's all because of you!"

"Oh, don't be so melodramatic," Wendy said, waving her hand around in front of her. "Kate will be fine. Hadley will stay with her mother and this will all be over for that woman soon. She's only getting a taste of what I've been going through."

Bill stopped in the middle of the bedroom and stared at his wife, mouth agape. "Wendy, I think you'd better start explaining yourself because I have absolutely no idea what you're talking about."

Wendy sighed heavily, more for dramatic purpose than out of weariness. When she spoke, she sounded like she was talking to a child rather than her husband of more than twenty years. "Kate is the one who pursued our son. She is the one who hunted him down, made him think she had feelings for him, made him have feelings for her! She took him away from us! Don't you see?! Riley was a sweet boy until that woman stepped into the picture. Now, god help up, he's probably not even a virgin anymore! All because of that woman! Well, I for one am not going to sit here and let her rip Riley from our lives. She's going to get a taste of her own medicine. And if she doesn't learn from this, I will call Social Services every so often just to keep her in line – give her a little reminder of what it feels like to have a child practically ripped out of your arms."

Bill stared at his wife as though she had just told him aliens had landed in their living room. Now that he thought about it, the whole alien thing might have been easier to believe. This? This was just nuts. He opened his mouth to speak but found he had no words. Instead he just stood there, staring at his wife and wondering when she'd lost her mind. "I…I don't even know what to say to you right now. Is that really what you think is happening here? That you're losing Riley?"

He rubbed his face with his hands like one does when they are in complete disbelief at what they've just heard. He resumed pacing and then began to mutter to himself. "Good god. This is all my fault. I should have done something sooner. I just never thought it would come to this."

"What? Come to what? What are you talking about, Bill?"

"Wen-, you're not losing him." He stopped pacing the bedroom and began to rake his hands through his hair, something he did when he was stressed. The movement reminded her so much of Riley, it made her chest ache. "You never were. But I'll tell you something, with all this bullshit you're pulling, you just might."

"What do you mean, 'bullshit'? I did what I had to-"

"Oh, SHUT THE HELL UP, WENDY!" She gasped at his outburst. She noticed that now his face was bright red with anger. Her eyes widened in surprise and she felt a tiny fissure of fear make its way up her spine.

He took a deep breath, trying to calm himself. After several moments, he spoke again and his voice, while calmer, still came out sounding like he was nearly out of patience. "Wendy, you called Social Services and filed a report about the abuse of a child knowing it was false! You accused a friend of yours of a very serious crime! I, for one, am not going to stand silently beside you while you attempt to ruin her life!"

"Well, she ruined mine," Wendy pouted.

He continued as though she hadn't even spoken. "You are going to fix this. Do you hear me?" Bill walked toward the bed, finger pointed at Wendy. His voice was measure, controlled, and it frightened Wendy, causing her to press against the headboard. "You are going to do whatever it takes…do you hear me Wendy? Whatever it takes to fix this. I don't care if you have to call, email, fax, or tweet every person at that organization! YOU WILL FIX THIS!"

227

The fear that had slid up her smile only moments before was now well gone. The emotion bubbling inside of her now was anger, and she was seething with it. She realized he was only concerned with that woman! There was no concern for his very own wife! The wife that had raised his three boys while he did nothing...NOTHING! to help her. He simply went about his business, wandering aimlessly through their house while she raised their children! Who was he to tell her what she should or shouldn't do! If he thought she was going to do anything to help that woman, he had another thing coming.

She tossed back the covers angrily and stood up. "How *dare* you!? How dare you stand her in our bedroom and support that woman? Do I mean nothing to you?! What about Riley? Doesn't he mean anything to you?! How can you *defend her?!*"

"Would you look at yourself?! Dammit, Wendy! You're a crazy person! You actually think Kate is taking your son away from you?!? Well, you are wrong. Dead wrong. The only person taking Riley away from you is *you.* "

"You think you know my son, do you? Well, let me-"

"Yes, I do."

Wendy looked up, startled and confused at having been interrupted with an answer to what was clearly meant to be a rhetorical question.

"You do what," she replied, through clenched teeth.

"I do know *our* son. And I know that this hovering you've done for twenty years has got to stop!"

Wendy gasped loudly, shocked at Bill's words. "How dare you say that to me! I don't hover! I'm a good mother!"

He looked at her, unsure of where to begin, then sighed heavily. "Of course you're a good mother. But you do hover, baby, coddle, or whatever the word is, and despite the fact that you don't want to hear it, you do all of it. And I should have stopped it years ago."

Mouth agape, Wendy backed up until she felt the side of the bed against the back of her legs. She placed her hand behind her to guide her down, then sat heavily on the bed. "I can't believe you would say that to me!"

"Look, it's not a judgment. It's an observation. An observation I should have done something about sooner. But for so long, Riley was all we had and I didn't want to get in the middle of you two. Then the twins came and I kept hoping you'd give him a little independence but you never did. Honestly? I don't think you're capable of it."

"I mean, we're close, but…I don't hover…"

"Yes, Wendy. You do," he said softly. "When Riley was younger, it wasn't as obvious but now? I can't believe he's put up with it this long."

"Put up with?" she snorted. "You're making me sound horrible."

Bill looked down at the floor, unsure of the appropriate response. "Think about it. You're involved in every aspect of his life. You check with his teachers about his homework, double check his duffel bag when he leaves for swim practice, text him at all hours of the day and night, trying to figure out where he is, what time he'll be home. Wendy, you even type his papers for him *after* you've checked them for errors! It's too much. All his life, you've hovered over him, treating him like he was incapable of making any sort of decision without you and I stood by and said nothing. Well, I'm not going to be silent anymore. Riley is a grown man. It's time to start treating him like one. And that means letting him date who he wants."

"What are you saying? I should just let him make mistake after mistake? What's that going to teach him?"

"It will teach him that mistakes are okay and that we learn from them. Wen, you're a good mother, but maybe it's time to stop all the mothering. He's all grown up."

"He still needs his mother." She huffed.

"Of course he still needs you but it's different now. He doesn't need you to cut his meat or inspect his friends. At some point, we've got to trust that we've raised him the best we can and have faith that he's going to make the right decisions."

Wendy pursed her lips together. "Well clearly, we're not there yet. Look at the string of horrible decisions he made when it came to Kate."

"Why is it so horrible if he dates her? Is it really such a bad thing? She's a friend of yours, so we already know her, we know what she's like, we know she's a great mother…and unfortunately, we know all too well that she's single."

She waved her hand around dismissively. "It's just sick. Her cavorting with Riley like that. How could she do this to me?"

"Why are you so hung up on the fact that it's Kate? Riley is free to date who he wants. Don't you agree with that?"

She shrugged noncommittally.

"If it were anyone else, would you have a problem with it?"

Wendy paused for a moment before answering. "Not if she treated him well."

"So you're saying Kate doesn't treat Riley well?"

"Look, I'm sure she treats him fine. But, it's *Kate*. Doesn't that seem somehow wrong to you?"

"No," Bill said, shaking his head. "It doesn't. And it shouldn't matter to you, either."

"I just want Riley to have the best. I want him to be happy."

"What makes you think he's not happy? Weren't you the one who said you'd never seen him so happy? Seems to me, the only thing making him unhappy is you."

"Me? I'm making him unhappy?" Wendy looked appropriately shocked.

Bill simply stared at his wife. "Do I really need to remind you the mess you made with Kate and Hadley?"

She looked appropriately guilty, then looked down and shook her head. "So you're saying we don't even get a say in all of this?"

"No, we don't. And after all the shit you've pulled, I can't say I'd blame him if he never spoke to us again."

"You can't be serious!" She looked horrified.

He shrugged. "I'm not saying he won't, but what you did....God!" He raked his hand through his hair again. "What the *hell* were you thinking?"

Wendy remained silent.

"Wendy, you've got to call Social Services and fix this."

Wendy wasn't quite ready to admit defeat or that she was wrong. She didn't respond to his statement nor did she give any indication she'd even heard him.

"Wendy...." He said sternly. "If you don't fix this, I will."

She felt the weight of him leave the bed and still her gaze remained focused on the floor. She heard the gentle click of the door and knew Bill had left the room. She knew in her head bill was right...but that meant she was wrong. And she wasn't ready to admit that just yet.

But what to do about this whole Kate thing? Was she really supposed to just sit by and let her date Riley? According to Bill, that's *exactly* what she was supposed to do. Wendy's head was spinning. All the things that Bill had said to her were just too much to take in during one afternoon. She hovered? Where had that come from? She thought for a minute about Riley. Slowly, memories came to her...Wendy sitting in Riley's class at the beginning of every school year...for hours at a time. She tried to recall another parent doing the same but none came to mind. At the time, she thought she was just easing Riley with his transition but maybe she hovered? Just a bit?

Riley asking to sleepover at a friend's house. Wendy always saying no. Was that hovering? Or was that her just being cautious? There were times when she didn't know the parents all that well...

Wendy contacting his teachers...*all* of his teachers. From kindergarten up until this past year. Initially, she thought she was doing a good thing by keeping tabs on her son...making sure he was behaving in class and getting his homework done. Maybe this was hovering as well?

Dammit. Maybe Bill had a point. But still. She loved her son. She wasn't just going to feed him to the wolves now, was she? Of course not. But maybe she could somehow...find a middle ground. Maybe she could learn to let go...just a little bit. It would be hard for her, of course, but she could try.

And maybe, just maybe, she could try to accept...well she felt certain she wasn't ready to accept just yet...maybe *resign* herself to the fact that Riley and Kate were dating.

She'd try. That was all she could promise at the moment.

Chapter 31

The first step was the easy part.

The second step? Well, that was like knowingly walking into a fire pit. She was going be burned. She just hoped she'd heal and the resulting scar tissue would be minimal.

The first step was the phone call to Social Services, which was only easy because it was over the phone. It was also difficult because it was over the phone. Apparently, everyone wants to talk to you when you file a report of child abuse. But retracting that same report? Not so much.

Wendy was shuffled around for what seemed like hours. Finally, she managed to get a hold of what she assumed was a supervisor who, when she initially came on the line sounded cheery and helpful. Once Wendy began to speak, however, the voice on the end of the line became cold and angry. Though there was no penalty for Wendy's actions, this woman strongly admonished Wendy for using the tax payers' money improperly. As she placed the phone down, Wendy felt certain the woman might have even recommended some form of therapy.

As frustrating as that call was, it was the second step - the visit to Kate's house - that caused real anxiety to build up inside of her. Coincidentally, it was the step that took her nearly a week to make. She got in her car and drove the all-too-familiar route. When she reached her destination, she sat in her car for several moments, trying to figure out exactly what it was she was going to say. After nearly fifteen minutes, she still had no idea.

"Oh, for Christ-sakes," she said, tossing the door open and stepping out of the car. "It'll come to me. At least it better."

She began to walk toward the front door and felt oddly like this was the longest walk of her life. Her own 'walk of shame.' But there was no avoiding it. This was going to be uncomfortable; eating crow always was. She reached the front door, took a deep breath and pressed the doorbell. From inside, she heard footsteps approach. She heard the click of the deadbolt and then the door swung open. Wendy knew the moment Kate registered who was actually standing on her front porch because the door began to close quickly. It would have slammed shut had it not been for Wendy's forethought to jam her foot in the way.

"Please," Wendy said, despite the searing pain shooting though her foot. "Just hear me out."

Kate released the pressure on Wendy's foot, opening the door another half inch or so.

"Ummm..." Wendy, visibly uncomfortable with the entire situation, kept her gaze low, unwilling to meet Kate's eyes, afraid of what she might see reflected back at her. "Can I come in?"

"No." Came the reply.

"Oh." She hadn't anticipated Kate's refusal, though in hindsight, she probably should have. If the roles were reversed, would she...Oh, hell, she didn't even want to go there. She was still working on that one.

"Look, I only came to apologize. I never...*never* should have made that call. It was horrible of me to do that."

"No, you shouldn't have made that call. *That call* nearly cost me my daughter."

"I want you to know that I've called them. Social Services that is. I told them that what I said was a lie. They're –"

"I know," Kate interrupted. "I got a letter."

"Oh, right. Good...good." Wendy busied herself with looking at the mat she stood on.

"Is that all?"

Wendy looked up at Kate for the first time since arriving. "I'm trying here. I really am."

"Try harder."

"It's just...I was just so...shocked to find out about you and Riley. I guess...I guess it just threw me for a loop. I wasn't prepared for it."

Kate opened the door another inch and glared at Wendy. "See that's the thing that I keep going over and over in my mind. You were so excited when you thought Riley was seeing someone. That day at the pool? You couldn't wait to meet this mystery girl. Then, you find out it's me and you're a raving lunatic. Care to explain *that?*"

Wendy took a deep breath, measuring her words before she spoke. "I don't know why I reacted the way I did. Maybe it was because of the age difference...maybe it was because you're my friend...or maybe it was because deep down, I knew what a wonderful person you are and I knew that if you were with Riley, I'd lose him forever. And I'm just not ready for that."

Kate stared at Wendy, mouth agape. "How can you even think that? You'd never lose him? What did you think I was going to do? Run away with him to Canada or something? Or is it you think so little of me that you honestly believed I would somehow keep him from seeing you? We were friends, Wendy! How could you think so little of me?"

"I don't know," Wendy whispered. "But I'm sorry. I'm truly, truly sorry."

"Are you done?"

"I think so." Wendy pulled her foot out from the door jam and shook it. She took a tentative step, placing some of her weight, then a bit more, onto the foot. Before she'd even stepped down the two steps onto the sidewalk, the door closed softly behind her.

Wendy sighed heavily. Her coming here today might not have fixed things but at least she'd made the effort. The ball was firmly in Kate's court now – not that she expected her to re-join the game... In any event, Wendy had done what she came to do.

Chapter 32

Kate had received a letter from Social Services clearing her of any wrongdoing. Immediately, relief washed over her. Riley, who was spending practically all of his time there, was there when she got the news. Suddenly, all the weight had been lifted from their shoulders.

Interestingly enough, Wendy's phone call, which had meant to drive the two of them apart, only made them closer. Kate knew she could rely on Riley and she also knew – before most women did – that the man she loved would support her even when the most significant other woman in his life was against her. That was the most convincing demonstration of his love she could have ever hoped for.

Despite Wendy's apology, Kate found it hard to simply forgive and forget. She knew she would have to at some point in time, especially since Kate was planning on a long future with Riley, and therefore, Wendy. But that was a while away.

The remaining four weeks of the summer flew by. Riley and Kate spent as much time together as they could, knowing that soon he would be heading back to school while Kate and Hadley remained some ninety miles away in Lancaster.

The heat of early August proved to be one of the hottest on record, forcing them to spend much time indoors, which suited them just fine. Most days, they would drive to the nearest RedBox and let Hadley choose a movie to watch. Some evenings, if the humidity allowed it, they would head out the pool for a swim.

Occasionally, Wendy would be there with the twins.

True to her word, she did make an effort to accept that Kate and Riley was a couple but it was obvious it was still a struggle for her.

As mid-August approached, Kate found herself dreading the day Riley would return to school. Though having a child that also needed to return to school, she knew from experience that the school year would pass quickly.

On the eve of Riley's departure, Kate and Riley spent their last night together. Bethany once again offered to keep Hadley for the evening, allowing Kate to spend her last night alone with the man who'd given her a second chance at love. They spent the evening wrapped in each other's arms, both of them barely sleeping for fear of missing one moment with each other. When dawn finally arrived, both of them had dark circles under their eyes from their restless night.

"We're a pair, aren't we," Kate said when she saw their reflections in the bathroom mirror.

"I'll sleep at school," he replied, pulling her close to him. "I can't wait for Thanksgiving."

The two of them had reluctantly agreed that this being Riley's senior year, it was important for him to remain at school and focus on his studies rather than come home each weekend. Kate repeatedly told herself that it was for the best and only for one year – well, nine months. Then, he'd be home forever. *This too shall pass* became her mantra.

Before long, it was time for Riley to head home, pack up his car and head back to school. While Kate would join him at Wendy and Bill's house for the final goodbye, both she and Riley knew their goodbye was now. Then, it was time for him to go.

Riley drove to his parent's house in order to finish packing his car. Kate followed shortly after, arriving at the house just as Riley was finishing up. He said his goodbye's to the twins, who ran inside, unaffected by Riley's impending departure and anxious to return to their video game. He embraced his mother, though only because his father insisted. Admittedly, things were not at all back to the status quo between Wendy and Riley but she knew they also had time to mend things.

Bill wrapped his arm around his wife's shoulder and led her into the house, leaving Riley and Kate alone for a few final moments. For that, Kate was immensely grateful. As they stood in the driveway, it hit them that it would be three months before they saw each other again. Slowly, Riley peeled himself away from Kate, then climbed into his car and backed out of the driveway, his eyes continuing to look back and find Kate's.

Long after he'd gone, Kate stood in the driveway, unsure of what to do and where to go. She felt as though a part of her was now gone.

But she didn't have the luxury of being able to wallow in self-pity. She had a child to take care of. And she had something she needed to do before she picked up her child…something she needed to be alone for.

Kate headed toward her car, climbed in, then headed home. She pulled into her driveway and grabbed the white plastic bag from under the seat. She once again felt a shiver of fear run through her as she realized how close Riley had come to seeing that bag. The last thing she wanted was for him to see *that*. Then there would be questions…questions she just wasn't sure either of them was ready to answer.

Slowly, she walked into the house. She laid the bag on the counter and slowly removed its contents. She stared at the little box for several minutes, as though it would give her the answer before she even did anything with it. She knew she was only prolonging the inevitable but there was something about the moment *before* that intrigued her. In the moment before you knew something definitively, there was still endless possibility. Once your question was answered, the realm of possibility became limited.

Kate slowly walked into her bedroom, carrying the tiny box. Stepping into her bathroom, she opened the box slowly, laying its contents on the countertop. She took the instructions out and threw them away immediately. It wasn't as though she needed them – every woman in the world knew what to do with this type of product.

She picked up the only other item that had come out of the box. She walked over toward the toilet, pulled down her pants and let the stream of urine flow over the cotton-like absorption pad. Carefully, she covered the tip with the cover and laid it on the shelf in front of her.

And waited.

Also from Indigo Sea Press
By Donna Small

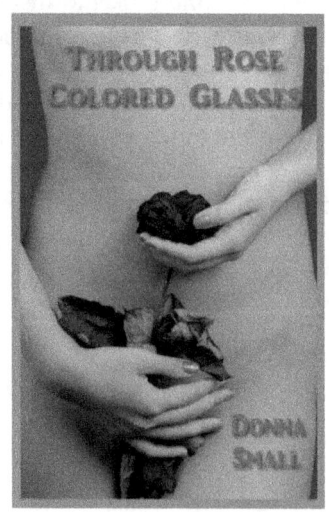

www.ingramcontent.com/pod-product-compliance
Lightning Source LLC
Chambersburg PA
CBHW060153180626
46813CB00007B/2728